TWISTED

Smile for the camera...

#1 Bestseller
Michaelbrent
COLLINGS

website: http://www.michaelbrentcollings.com
email: info@michaelbrentcollings.com

cover and interior art elements
© kriangkrai wangjai, Graphic design, Hyena Reality,
and Allure Graphic Design
used under license from Shutterstock.com
cover design by Michaelbrent Collings

For more information on Michaelbrent's books, including specials and sales; and for info about signings, appearances, and media,

check out his webpage,
Like his Facebook fanpage
or
Follow him on Twitter.

PRAISE FOR THE WORK OF
MICHAELBRENT COLLINGS

"[*Crime Seen*] will keep you guessing until the end.... 5/5. "
– *Horror Novel Reviews*

"It's rare to find an ending to a novel that is clever, thought-provoking and surprising, yet here Collings nails all three...." – *Ravenous Reads*

"*Crime Seen* by Michaelbrent Collings is one of those rare books that deserves more than five stars." – *Top of the Heap Reviews*

"I barely had time to buckle my mental seatbelt before the pedal hit the metal...." – *The Horror Fiction Review*

"Collings is so proficient at what he does, he crooks his finger to get you inside his world and before you know it, you are along for the ride. You don't even see it coming; he is that good." – *Only Five Star Book Reviews*

"Move over Stephen King... Clive Barker.... Michaelbrent Collings is taking over as the new king of the horror book genre." – *Media Mikes*

"A proficient and pedagogical author, Collings' works should be studied to see what makes his writing resonate with such vividness of detail...." – *Hellnotes*

"[H]auntingly reminiscent of M. Night Shyamalan or Alfred Hitchcock." – horrornews.net

DEDICATION

To...

Malina, who has read my stuff from the start and made me feel like I knew what I was doing (for good or for ill),

and to Laura, FTAAE.

Contents

ONE:
FIRST SUBJECT

Though it seems like an odd practice in modern times, it was viewed as normal, even praiseworthy, several hundred years ago. Thus, there were numerous people willing to give assistance as to the various idiosyncrasies involved in this specific subgroup of photography. Perhaps they did not attempt to address the minutiae, but most would discuss general details, and deem it perfectly normal to do so.

Others were more specific in their instruction, to the point of unhealthy fixation, as in this now-famous example:

> If the subjekt is styff, then it will be sympler. No
> stand will be nesesary, e'en tho' I rarelee use them.
> For in my hands the dead chyld sits easy, and my
> love holdz him fyrm.

- Silver, Charles M.
(afterword by Dr. Charlotte Bongiovi),
(2003) Berkeley, California,
Memento Mori, Notes of a Dead Man,
Western University Press, Inc.

WHISPERS

It was small, it was dirty. There was barely enough room for the boy to crawl, and there was no way at all that he could hope to stand.

That was right, he knew. Though young, though still a boy in the eyes of the world, he had seen enough in his life to know this: he was where he should be. He was on his knees, and that was the way Daddy wanted him. On hands and knees, crying and begging. Pantaloons tearing, vest and jacket fast becoming shreds of cloth.

And he was not the only thing that crawled down here. Many-legged creatures writhed over the boy's hands, into his clothes, through his hair. He could feel them touch his skin and bite his flesh. Spiders, perhaps the long centipedes that he had seen hidden under his home. The bites burned.

Blood dripped from the boy's nose and mouth. From a cut beside his blue, blue eyes. From too many places to count or contemplate. It splashed on his hands, rolled in thin rivulets to the earthy soil below his palms.

The boy crawled forward. Didn't know where he was going. Didn't care. Just hoped. Hoped he could crawl fast enough, far enough, to get away.

He whispered as he crawled. Words that no one could hear but him. Words that the earth sopped up as quickly and completely as his blood.

He wanted to fall. His sides hurt where the kicks had rained down. His face hurt where the fists had fallen.

Again, again, again. And then he somehow got away.

And he ran. Ran blindly, and found himself in this dark place.

This place where he crawled, and bled, and whispered.

Light seeped into the crawlspace from behind him. He hoped that didn't mean he could be followed. Hoped that didn't mean there was a hole large enough for a man. A man inflamed by desire, enraged by injury.

The boy whispered, crawled, bled.

Blood.

Tears.

Sweat.

The dirt drank it all in.

And then the whispers, nearly silent, turned to a scream as the wood above the boy's head collapsed. Splinters bit at his cheeks, more blood rained.

A hand punched into view. Bloody from slamming through the floor that was the ceiling off the boy's short-lived hideaway. The hand was one the boy knew well, from the thick black hairs on the knuckles to the well-bitten fingernails…

… to the stubs where two fingers had been lost in a mill accident, long ago.

The three remaining fingers grabbed the boy by his thick, blond hair. They yanked upward.

The boy screamed. His head hit the remains of the wood planking that topped the crawlspace. It didn't fit through the small hole that the fist had created.

It didn't matter. His head went through anyway.

The boy whispered. A few last words.

Then the three-fingered hand gave a final pull. The boy seemed to fall *up*, as though the earth had forgotten how to hold onto him. He tumbled through the wood, out of the crawlspace.

Into waiting arms.

The boy screamed again. A scream of terror that became pain, a scream of pain that became rage, a scream of rage that returned to pain once again....

And then, at last, the screams ended. No more whispers, no more shrieks.

But the blood still flowed, and the soil drank its fill.

TWO:
TAKING PLACES

This, of course, is one of the only – if not *the* only – example of this type of *memento mori*. But it is also one of the most fascinating, in that it melds obsessive concern with technical details with an equally frenzied need for what our primary subject terms "the artystry."

> No fewr than twelv lamps can be used and if possibl twente is bettr. The lite is of corse of critickal import, no less than the lines of the boys jacket, the fall of the girls skyrts.

> If theyr eyes are opin, the lamps kin be moved close, to giv a pleasing refleckshun on the darks of the eyes. If they are closed, then the lamps shuld be moved back, becuz to much lite will wite the linez of there buetifull faces and the colour in there cheekz will be lost fore'er.

> This MUST be avoided. The childrin are dead. But their soulz are alive. They are inosents with God, and sinse I sent them there I must also giv them propr funeral servis and memorials of artystry and luv.

> > - Silver, Charles M.
> > (afterword by Dr. Charlotte Bongiovi),
> > (2003) Berkeley, California,
> > *Memento Mori, Notes of a Dead Man,*
> > Western University Press, Inc.

THE BLOOD ON HIS HANDS

There are so many things they don't tell you about having a baby. Or if they do, it glances right off you, bullets bouncing off the impervious armor of inexperience.

And this makes sense. Indeed, it is a truth of human nature: we understand from within the sum of our experiences. One who has never been to war cannot truly understand the filth, the hunger, the fear, the excitement. One who has never truly loved another cannot comprehend the breathless anticipation that turns over time to a secure sense of belonging.

A person who has never had a baby cannot really understand what having a baby entails. Not just the *entirety*, but the small moments.

Blake Douglas thought that he would be prepared this time. It was, after all, his second spin on this particular merry-go-round. The first baby had come eight years before, and though it had been a while he could remember much of it with the clarity of a vision from God. Moments burned in his mind.

He remembered the sounds. The low beeps of heart monitors: one for Alyssa, one for the baby that kicked restlessly within her. The restrained *walla-walla-walla* of nurses and doctors coming in and going out. Once in a while they said something to him or Alyssa, but mostly they kept their own counsel, like priests and priestesses in a religion whose bloody altars had somehow survived to modern times.

Then the feel of Alyssa in his arms as she pushed. His right arm around her back, his left cradling one of her legs as she drew into a tight ball. The sweat that dripped down her forehead, down her neck, mingling with the sweat on his body. One more way he and she were then and always would be joined.

And the smell. That most of all. The antiseptic scent of the hospital. The heavy cologne of one of the doctors, so thick that Alyssa finally demanded he leave and only come back "after he had taken a bath and didn't smell like an ad for a European travel agency," which didn't make too much sense but was vivid enough that the doctor left and came back a half hour later smelling like soap instead of the latest Calvin Klein concoction.

The biggest smell was the baby himself. That was also the biggest surprise. Blake expected the crying, the blood, Alyssa's final sigh/scream of release as their new son's feet slipped free of her body. He expected the love that washed over him when he looked at the tiny body – though that feeling came much stronger than expected.

But he didn't expect the little thing in his arms to smell so *bad*. Acrid, a smell that tugged at his nostrils and pulled the corners of his lips into a frown.

"What is it?" said Alyssa. Her words slurred a bit – exhaustion, the halo of pain recently past, the drugs.

"Nothing," said Blake. But of course it *was* something. He pasted a smile on his face and concentrated on the love he was feeling and tried to ignore the realization that he was holding something that had just spent the last nine months swimming in a *very* confined space. A space that had to be mostly comprised of the baby's own bodily wastes at this point.

No wonder the kid smelled bad.

But it didn't matter. Smell could be washed away. Love couldn't.

And it all wrote itself across his mind. Memories that etched new furrows through his brain, formed new creases in his frontal lobe.

Creases that, he hoped, would cut down the other ones, the older ones. The ones that carried memories of his own childhood.

They didn't. The couldn't.

Just as the greatest future experiences can never be truly understood, so the worst past experiences can never be truly erased.

But because he'd been through the process before he thought this time, *this* time, he would be ready. Would understand. It was a little girl, but other than that, it was all going to be something familiar and easy.

And the beginning *was* the same. The low sounds, followed by much louder ones. The feel of his wife's skin as she pushed. The cries. The baby coming into his arms.

But she didn't smell.

I guess maybe little girls are *cleaner, after all.*

The thought was strangely disappointing. Maybe it was sexist of him, but he didn't like the idea of him and Mal being the two hulking, sweating, stinking creatures in the house while Alyssa and the new baby remained in pristine perfection. Because families worked and played together. They should get dirty together, too.

Then he realized he was being silly. Was ignoring

the obvious. Was avoiding his daughter's eyes.

Why would I do that?

He looked at her. Her eyes were closed, which was hardly unusual: many newborns didn't open their eyes for several minutes.

But as he looked, one eye cracked. Then the other. Narrow slits that couldn't see much. But they opened, and for some reason that mattered to him. Mattered a lot.

And the love came over him. Just like it had with Mal. Blake felt light, like he could do anything. And heavy, because he might well have to do everything.

Children: one more thing that made you into a man. And one more thing that made you realize your own childhood was long gone and would never come back again.

A good thing in my case.

He smiled at his baby. Then at Alyssa. She was waiting patiently. This was part of the deal: she got to carry the baby for nine months, he got the first few moments the baby came outside. Not that carrying a baby was all wine and roses, he knew that just from watching her.

But she told him how special it was, how sad it sometimes made her that he would never understand it. And told him early in her first pregnancy – Mal – that she wanted him to have this first moment. And he was glad.

Then his moment was over. He handed the baby to Alyssa. She was tired, her complexion was blotchy. She had put on makeup a few hours before labor started and she came in, but even Maybelline's top experts had yet to come up with labor-proof foundation or mascara.

Her hair was a wreck, too: stray strands of blond

hair streaking in every direction like the baby's spirit had ridden down on a lightning bolt and Alyssa had managed to get a hand on it before it dissipated.

Even her hospital gown was a mess. Unsnapped on top, sweat stains darkening the fabric, monitor wires trailing from arm and neck holes. She looked like a poorly-dressed cyborg.

And he didn't want to think about what was going on below. She had torn during the labor, and the doctor was now stitching up her flesh, his bloody gloves appearing from time to time in the brightness of the directed light above him.

She was, all in all, a vision of destruction.

And so, so beautiful.

If angels fell to earth, he supposed, they might get a bit dusty when they landed. But they would still glow. And the glow would always be what set them apart.

Alyssa took the baby. She smiled at the tiny girl, feeling feet, hands, cheeks. And Blake knew how soft the baby was, how unbelievably smooth and delicate. So fragile. But so much strength buried inside, waiting to grow.

Alyssa looked back at Blake. "What do you think?"

He nodded. "I think we were right." He looked back at the baby. Put a hand on her head, and suddenly remembered the times his father had touched *him* on the head. The memory was unwelcome, an intrusion that had no place here. He banished it as best he could, but it rested in the back of this moment like a thunderhead on the horizon during a lovers picnic.

"I think we were right," he said again. "She's

definitely a Ruth." He leaned down and kissed his baby girl's cheek. "Hello, Ruthie." Then he kissed his wife's cheek. "Hello, Mommy. For the second time."

She smiled wearily and began fumbling with the few snaps that still held up the shoulder of her hospital gown, drawing Ruthie into position for her first feeding.

Alyssa's hands shook so badly that Blake didn't know if she was going to be able to get the snaps undone, so he moved to help.

That was when he finally noticed he had blood on his hands.

Birthing was a bloody process. No surprise that some got on him. Still, it was a discomfiting sight. His daughter's blood on his hands, and staining his wife's gown.

Like father, like son.

THINGS BIG BROTHERS DO

Mal Douglas was only eight, but being only eight didn't mean he was stupid. He knew things. Knew there were certain rules a boy must live by.

Do *not* get into a game of "Mercy" with Tina Wipperfurth. She is double-jointed and will never lose.

Do treat girls nice, because they smell good and there is something strangely interesting about them and Daddy and Mommy both say to. Except Tina Wipperfurth, because she is basically a cheater.

Do *not* raise your hand every time in class, even if you know all the answers. Life gets weird if you do that.

Do work your hardest on tests.

Do *not* tell other people what grade you got. Life gets even weirder then.

And, above all: *do* love your family. Mommy and Daddy. And now a little sister named Ruthie.

When Mommy and Daddy told him there was going to be a new baby, he thought he was going to be irritated. And he was. He would have to share space, share toys, share Mommy and Daddy.

But the irritation lasted only a few seconds.

Then: excitement. He couldn't wait. Like Christmas and Easter and his birthday and every visit he'd ever had from the Tooth Fairy (eight, just like how old he was) all rolled up in one.

Later Mommy and Daddy clarified that it was going

to be a baby sister. He understood the reason for the time lag: Mommy showed him videos on the internet, and he knew that until then the baby was just a Blob or a Tadpole. But eventually the Tadpole grew girl or boy parts and blam! – baby brother or baby sister.

Again, when the Blob decided it would pee sitting down, he was irritated for a few seconds. "Baby sister" meant no cool brother to teach about *Star Wars*, about Fight War Attack Club (which he had recently invented), or about why cowboys would lose in a fight with ninjas.

Then, again: excitement. He would be big brother to a little sister. Sure, she would play with dolls, she would be interested in dresses. But he would get to watch over her, and protect her. Be an example and a mentor, like Yoda.

He decided to be the Best Big Brother of All Time.

And with that decision came love. He wondered if the love came first, or if it came *because* of that decision. He asked Mommy, but she didn't answer. She just got a strange look on her face. "You're an old soul," she said. Then she kissed him and gave him a cookie and twenty extra minutes of video game time.

He didn't know if that was an answer or not, so he thought about it during the video games, got no answer, and decided he would never really understand grown-ups because they were coo-coo-pants.

The thing he *did* understand, though: he was going to be a big brother. The best.

And now he was going to meet her. His little sister. Ruthie. This was probably the biggest moment of his life.

He had thought ahead: when Mommy yelled "It's time!" and Daddy started running around and Mr. Thayer came to take him to their house for the night, Mal grabbed not only his overnight bag, but an extra comb and some of Daddy's cologne he had... not stolen – he was going to give it back – but borrowed.

When he went into the hospital room he had slicked-back Sunday hair and smelled vaguely of Date Night. He hoped Ruthie would like it.

Daddy's arm was around his shoulder, pushing him gently through the door. Mal realized he was scared.

What if she's weird?

What if she doesn't like me?

What if she looks like Tina Wipperfurth?

"Come on, bud," whispered Daddy. "Let's go in."

Mal stepped through the doorway. He felt like he'd gone through a magic portal in one of his games. On one side was a stinky, bustly hospital with nurses who wore shirts covered in teddy bears and rainbows but who looked like they were about to kick someone.

On the other: peace.

There was a TV in the corner, playing softly. Mal didn't know what show was on. Something with a judge yelling at a man in a blue shirt.

There was a big window. The bedroom was on the first floor, and the window was pulled open a crack to show a screen. Some heavy curtains hung over most of the window, shading the room. They hung straight down, and the trees outside stood straight up, so Mal knew there was no breeze.

In fact, everything was motionless. Other than the judge on TV. And even he seemed to be stuck in Pointy

Finger Mode.

It was like the whole world was waiting. Stuck on "Pause," waiting for Mal to finally look at what he was supposed to look at.

Two beds. One was empty.

The other held his mommy. She was sleeping, with her blond hair curled over her forehead, her mouth open just a little bit. She looked really tired, but also kind of happy in a way she hadn't looked in a long time.

Mal looked down. The blanket at Mommy's chest moved. A pink face peeked out. It was wrinkly and so tiny it seemed fake. It could have been a doll, but then the baby yawned.

Ruthie yawned.

A tiny pink tongue poked out. Something bounced around in Mal's chest and in that moment he understood what he had only been playing at before. He understood, because it wasn't just a thing of tomorrow. It was a thing of *now*. It was real.

"I'm a big brother," he whispered. He didn't mean to say the words, but they had to be said. And he didn't mean to whisper them, but some words simply *had* to be whispered. The way you whispered your most important prayers at night, or your secretest secrets to a best friend....

Or the fact that you were now a teacher, an example, a protector.

A big brother.

He felt Daddy shake with low laughter beside him. "Pretty neat, huh?"

"What do I do?" Again the words came without

thought. He didn't want to seem dumb – not in front of *anyone*, but especially not in front of Daddy – but he wanted to do everything right. Everything.

He looked at Daddy. Daddy always seemed so big, so high-up. He was smiling down at Mal from that high-up place now. Still shaking a bit, a chuckle in his throat.

"You be a good example," said Daddy. "You take care of her. That's what big brothers – and daddies – do."

Mal nodded seriously. He turned his gaze back to Ruthie. "Can I touch her?"

Daddy nodded. "Just don't wake Mommy. She had a rough night."

Mal took the few steps to his new sister. They seemed to lengthen out, to become not three but three hundred. He didn't know if that was because God was telling him to stay away or just giving him time to enjoy the moment. He decided it would be the second one. Because the first one was stinky and he didn't like it.

Finally, after the one-second/forever walk, he was there.

The baby slept.

He reached for her. Wondering what he was going to do, where he would touch her. Cheeks? Nose? Should he push her nose and say, "Beep!"

No. Head. He would touch her –

The curtains fluttered. Almost flapped in a breeze so sudden and severe it was like a hurricane had erupted for a single second in the room.

Mal's hand hung in the air an inch from Ruthie's head. From the few hairs that held to her head and looked like spun gold.

The breeze died.

Mal looked back at his sister.

Her eyes were open. Mommy and Daddy had warned him that the baby wouldn't be able to look at him – or them – for days after being born. But right at this instant she sure *seemed* to be looking at him.

Mal smiled.

And Ruthie opened her mouth and *screamed*.

The sound was high. And it was loud! A screeching noise that cut its way through Mal's ears and bones and straight into his brain. His hands flew to his ears and he stepped back as Mommy opened her eyes.

When he stepped back he hit something behind him – maybe the tray with Mommy's food? Whatever it was, it sent him falling back. He would have fallen all the way down, but strong arms caught him.

Still shaking with laughter, Daddy lifted him back up. "Don't worry, bud," he said. "Babies cry. You'll get... used... to...."

Daddy's face changed and his voice fell off a cliff.

Ruthie wasn't just screaming. She was... was.... Mal looked for the right word.

Howling.

That was it. She sounded like a dog caught in some awful trap. The kind of thing not made just to capture it, but to *hurt* it, too.

The howls got louder and louder, higher and higher. Daddy looked at Mommy, and Mal looked as well.

Mommy was hitting a button on the rails of her bed.

Hitting it over and over with her thumb, then nearly punching it. Her look terrified Mal more than his new sister's screams. Because Ruthie was a new baby, and didn't know any better. Maybe she would get upset over little hurts.

But Mommy... Mommy was plenty old. She knew stuff. She knew what a bad sound was, and she looked scared.

A nurse came into the room. Not one of the teddy-bear-wearing-death-face ones, but a younger one. Pink shirt, and a face that looked like she didn't love the idea of punching rainbows.

She took one look at Ruthie, and did the scariest thing yet. She flipped back a clear plastic cover near the door. Under it was a red button.

Red buttons, Mal knew, are *never* good news.

The nurse hit the button. An alarm went off somewhere else in the hospital.

At the same time, the nurse leaned out the door and yelled, "I need some help in here!"

It seemed like less than a second later and the room was so full of doctors and nurses that there was barely space for Mal to breathe. They started saying hospital-y words. Things he didn't understand.

"Heart rate spiking...."

"Seizure...."

"Call the nickle-you..."

Then everyone ran out. And they were holding Ruthie.

Mommy was screaming. She was nearly howling,

too. "Where are you going? Where are you taking her? Where are you taking my baby?"

Big hands landed on Mal's back. Daddy shoved him toward Mommy. "Stay here," he said. "Take care of Mommy." Then, to Mommy, Daddy said, "I'll find out. I'll be back."

Daddy ran after the doctors and nurses and Ruthie.

Mal started to tremble. Because he thought he was going to be a very good big brother. But Daddy had just put him in charge of protecting Mommy. And that was a Daddy job.

I can't do that.

I'm not a Daddy.

I'm a big brother.

What if she dies?

What if I'm not a big brother anymore?

BIRTHPAINS

Alyssa Douglas was in pain.

Of course there were the obvious spots. The doctors gave her pain meds, they gave her ice packs, they gave her a little can of Dermoplast to spray on her stitches where her perineum had torn. But none of it really worked. It was the equivalent of putting a Band-Aid on the bits and pieces that fell back to earth after someone stepped on a land mine.

Her bones ached terribly. Her muscles shrieked at her whenever she moved the slightest little bit. Her face was a field of pain and she had no wish to see what she looked like in the mirror. Going to the bathroom felt like a fire-breathing dragon had taken up residence where the baby had recently been.

Her *hair* hurt.

Most of all, though, her heart ached.

It only took a few hours. Just a few *hours* between the time that they took Ruthie away and a doctor could be persuaded to take time off the ninth hole to come actually talk to them. A few hours, but in that time she felt like entire civilizations probably rose and fell.

Certainly *her* ability to be civilized was at an all-time low. When Blake came back and told her he hadn't been able to get anyone to tell him what was happening, she almost jumped out of the bed and clawed his eyes out.

She knew that was a combination of terror, exhaustion, and the incendiary bomb that had recently gone off in her internal hormone factory. But knowing it didn't change her urge to maim him for not knowing more.

He sat down and held her hand. She felt like kissing him for trying so hard, and then punching him for accomplishing so little.

They sent Mal back to Robyn and Greg's house. He was crying when "Mr. Thayer" came, and that almost broke her heart again. He didn't want to leave until Ruthie was "fixed and all better."

How did she and Blake explain to someone like Mal that some things might not *get* fixed or all better? Someone so young and, more important, so innocent and good?

So they didn't. They just told him they would come get him soon. Told him it would all be fine. Lie, lie, lie.

And then, at last, the doctor came.

She had decided that she was going to yell for the first ten minutes of the talk. But when Doctor Malalai showed up her urge to argue disappeared. Part of it was his face, which was so kindly, so sympathetic, that she couldn't really bring herself to be angry.

Mostly, though, it was just that she realized how crazy it would be to yell and scream and so delay the time to find out what was happening. What was wrong with their baby. With Ruthie.

He told them. Malalai had olive skin, thin wire glasses, a thin mustache that was impeccably shaped and groomed. His voice was as soft and kind as his features, with the subtlest trace of an accent. Probably Middle Eastern. As he spoke she was almost hypnotized by the sound of his voice, the subtle rolls of his *r*'s and lilt of his tone.

She was hiding from something ugly in the only beauty to be found.

Blake was speaking, she realized. Tears ran down his cheeks, into his mouth. They saturated his words, nearly drowned his voice. "So that's what we have to look forward to, what *she* has to look forward to? A life of transfusions, infections, strokes, organ failures, pain after pain after pain? And then after all that, she probably gets to die when she's in her forties?"

Alyssa didn't wait for Malalai's answer. He had already told them, and she couldn't bear to hear it again. Instead, she focused on something else he had said. Like a lawyer trying to spot a weakness in the other side's case, trying to tear it down and prove it wasn't true. "I don't understand," she said. She shook her head. "You said it was a genetic disease."

Malalai nodded. He seemed to approve of her noticing this fact. "It is."

"But we don't have –"

"No," he said. "So both you and your husband must carry the genetic trait, though not as a dominant gene. However, you were each able to provide a recessive gene to Ruthie, and together those resulted in her condition."

Alyssa felt like all the air had been vacuumed out of her lungs. She knew what Blake would say: it wasn't her fault, it was just the way things worked. But she didn't feel like that, and wouldn't believe him. *She* had given this to Ruthie. Without her –

(*without* me *without her mother the one who's supposed to give her everything and what's the first thing I give her?*)

– the condition couldn't have reared its head at all.

She glanced at Blake. His face was granite, a single thin line carved out for the mouth. And that made her feel doubly selfish.

What must he be feeling? Given his past, given what his father was... can he be feeling like this is anything other than his fault? Like he came from a tainted place, and passed on only evil himself?

She knew she was being selfish. Knew she should comfort Blake. He had to be feeling as bad as she was – maybe worse. But all she could feel was her own pain. All she could hear were the accusations she leveled at herself.

Pain did that. It took away your ability to notice anything but the animal. Dogs in traps snapped and bit even at the people trying to rescue them, and though the nature of the traps were different, human beings often acted just the same.

Blake spoke, and she could almost hear the weight of generations in his voice. "What now?" he said. "Is she going to.... I mean, will she...?"

He couldn't even finish the thought. A gurgle came from his throat, and for a moment his self-control lapsed. The granite fell from his face and the raw emotion beneath it was revealed.

Dr. Malalai leaned forward. Put a hand on Blake's shoulder. They were all in Alyssa's hospital room. She was still in her bed, and the hospital bassinet still lay empty beside her. A bare, cold reproach.

"No," said Dr. Malalai. "Usually this disease doesn't rear its head until after the first six months or so. This situation is highly unusual, and the fact is there's definite, immediate risk to Ruthie, so we'll take precautions. But we're going to remain optimistic."

Alyssa threw out almost everything but the word "precautions." "Precautions" was a word doctors used when the likelihood of impending awfulness was high.

The pain in her body was suddenly replaced by a numbing cold.

"What kind of precautions?" she said.

Dr. Malalai took his hand off Blake's shoulder. He pulled off his glasses and began cleaning them with his shirt. "Ruthie suffered a vaso-occlusive crisis – that's what caused her so much pain – and that may recur, I'm afraid."

"What does that mean? And what do we do about it?" asked Blake. Alyssa felt something fumbling around in her blankets and realized it was him, his hand looking for hers in the bed. They'd been married long enough that she suspected it was an automatic motion: muscle memory carrying them together in times of crisis.

"It means the cells, sticky and stiffened, have become stuck in the blood vessels. Like a stopped-up pipe in your kitchen or bathroom. That is what causes the tremendous pain that Ruthie experienced. As to what you do about it...." He stopped cleaning his glasses. He didn't return them to his face, but his fingers stopped their circular motions, his body froze from the neck down. "Mostly you watch. Keep her hydrated. If she screams like that again, bring her to the ER immediately. Keep her from getting too cold and be on the lookout for fevers. Infection is a huge danger for her."

Blake asked the big question. Alyssa was glad, because she didn't know if she would have been able to. "Can we cure it?"

Malalai put his glasses back on, and Alyssa sensed it had nothing to do with his vision. He was trying to hide what was on his face, the look in his eyes. "No," he said once his glasses were in place. "But we'll give you the information you need to keep watch and properly respond. Even without a cure, medical science has come up with some excellent aids and controls. We're going to refer you to several specialists who will likely put Ruthie on a medication regimen to help with the disorder. And before you leave we'll give you some information packets, and even some clothing that changes color if her core temperature rises or drops too much."

Malalai grinned widely. But the grin barely turned up at all at the ends – nearly a straight line that seemed less to brighten his face than to slash it violently in half.

"So that's it?" said Alyssa. The anger that had fallen away from her before now climbed back into her heart. "We get some pamphlets, a referral, and a temperature-sensitive onesie?"

Blake's hand finally found and clenched over hers. He probably meant to comfort her, to calm her. But his palm was awash in sweat. His own rage and terror and pain could not hide, not from her.

Malalai just stared at them, that violent cut of a grin fixed on his face. Not saying anything, and the silence itself saying everything there was to say.

Alyssa's anger fell away again.

She felt pain once more. Not the pain of the birth. Not the pain in bones and joints and muscles. Not the pain of a womb newly empty, not the pain of her perineal tear.

Ruthie had screamed so loudly, had been in so much

agony. And that agony had instantly become Alyssa's. Holding the baby, she had also held her own heart, her own soul.

The baby was hers to hold. Hers to keep. Hers to protect.

She had already begun to fail.

And the failure, more than anything, was what caused Alyssa's pain.

FIRST STEPS

They brought the baby home.

The home itself was newish and niceish. Two stories, five bedrooms, two-and-a-half baths. The first floor had a kitchen/dining area, a living room, one bedroom, and the half-bathroom. The second floor had the other four bedrooms, two bathrooms, and a closet that hid the washer and dryer hook-ups.

It was the kind of place that a growing family could not only settle down in, but could continue to settle in*to* over the years.

Many homes are designed with "curb appeal" as the first and last goal. These are the kind designed to *sell*. The kind where the builder/developer puts in just enough work to get out with the maximum profit after spending the minimum money. These are the houses that look lovely, but inexplicably fall apart three months after the "no hassle, wall-to-wall" warranty period ends.

This house, on the other hand, had been built with something else in mind. Profit, yes – whoever built it likely didn't do so with the goal of *losing* money. But this building also had the feel of a place that intended to stick around. To grow old with its owners, see them into the ground, and then allow a new family to settle down in and settle in*to*.

The feeling of a place that perhaps had been built on the shoulders of other buildings. Older buildings. Buildings and homes long gone but never quite forgotten.

This house was a place that seemed built with a

solid roof, and that roof seemed to be built on sturdy walls, and those walls gave the impression of resting on a sure foundation.

Blake didn't notice any of that. He just got out of the car and helped Alyssa out of the backseat. She leaned against the side of the junker sedan. She grimaced. Still in pain, body and heart.

Mal got out the other side. He went to his mother. He put her arm over his shoulders and she smiled and thanked him as though the gesture meant actual support. And perhaps it did, though it was of a mental or emotional nature, certainly not a physical one.

Blake looked at Alyssa. He mouthed, "Okay?" and she nodded.

He got Ruthie from her car seat in the center of the backseat. It was the newest model, with a five-star rating on Amazon, Consumer Reports, and Parents.com. It was far too expensive, but Alyssa demanded it and Blake gave in with no fight. How much was a child worth to them?

Ruthie was asleep, and slept on as he picked her up. A pink fleece blanket lay lightly across her, and he balanced both infant and blanket over his folded arms, the movements flying across the years that separated this baby from the baby that Mal had been, once-upon-a-time, so long ago, so very recently.

Blake carried her to the door while Mal "helped" Alyssa. This was what they had agreed on.

When they married, Blake carried his new wife over the threshold of their home – a tiny apartment in a part of town that was so questionable he got nervous when she went to get the mail.

When Mal was born, he asked Alyssa if it would be all right if he carried the boy across the threshold, as he had done with her. She consented. He carried the swaddled baby across the dividing line between the outside world, so frightening, so terrible, so dreary, and the place that would be their boy's home: a townhouse that was across the street from a Nissan dealership, a place where the baby woke up every hour or two because the salesmen honked the horn of every car they sold.

And now Blake would carry his new daughter across the threshold of *this* house. He would carry his new, sickly child through the doorway, into a place that the family wished could provide her safety, but knew never would.

He carried her into the house that seemed secure.

That seemed solid.

That seemed *safe*.

He disappeared into the house.

Mal brought his mother up the walk. Alyssa walked so slowly it seemed the new baby might enjoy her first birthday before mother and brother made it inside to see it. And that made Alyssa sad, because what if Ruthie never made it that far?

Mal just focused on his mother. His mommy. He understood she was hurting, though the scope of her hurt was beyond his understanding.

They, too, walked into the house.

All of them were smiling as they stepped onto the porch.

All of them, for some unknown reason, stopped smiling as they stepped inside.

The house did not comfort.

There was no safety here. Not for Ruthie.

And, though none of them said anything, all of them felt – for just an instant – that there was no safety here for *any* of them.

Not in this house that only *seemed* safe.

A MOTHER'S HANDS

Blake was waiting for Alyssa in the grand foyer of the house.

Of course, it was nothing of the kind – the space was about ten feet by five feet, with a large door leading to the living room on the right, the stairs straight ahead, and a hall beside them that led down to Mal's room and the kitchen. It was barely an "entryway," let alone a "grand foyer."

But when they had bought the house, Blake went through the place, renaming everything. The living room became the "sitting parlor," the kitchen became the "serving area," their room "the servant's quarters," and several other names Alyssa didn't remember. All of them had been one-off jokes – little bits of Blake-humor that faded as fast as they appeared.

For some reason, though, "grand foyer" stuck. The entrance was always called that, or G.F. for short.

Blake was looking around the G.F., holding Ruthie. She was still sleeping, which was a blessing. Alyssa was terrified that the little girl would wake up and need feeding. Alyssa's milk hadn't fully come in yet, and if her experience with Mal was any indicator she was going to let down slowly each time. Which meant a cranky, crying baby.

Only when Ruthie cried, it could mean the precursor to something quite different and more serious than just an empty belly. And Alyssa didn't know if she was going to be able to handle that tension for months or a year or more, depending on how long her milk held out and Ruthie kept breastfeeding.

"What now?" asked Blake.

Alyssa knew he wasn't really asking the obvious. His question was deeper, going to the care of Ruthie, of Mal, of her –

(*and the bills and the business failing and the bank account, don't forget all that*)

– and all the other responsibilities she knew he struggled under right now.

"Let's put her in the crib and see how she does," she said.

Blake looked at her sharply, as though he'd suddenly forgotten she – and Mal, who was still parked under her arm – even existed.

He smiled sheepishly. "Yeah, that'd be a good idea, huh."

Alyssa looked at Mal. "Honey, would you get my bag out of the back of the car?"

"Do you need anything after that?"

"Yes. You are under orders to watch at least a half hour of cartoons. Or else."

Mal threw her a solemn salute, then grinned his slightly buck-toothed grin before spinning on his heel (and almost careening into the wall). He went through the front door. He was singing the theme song to *Phineas and Ferb* as he left.

Blake took Mal's spot under her arm. He moved so slowly and tenderly it made her want to cry. She knew that was partly the hormones that were trying to decide whether to cling for dear life or flee out of her big toe in a single chunk.

But it was also that Blake was straight-up, truly sweet.

And damn cute.

"Can you make it up to the room? Or do you need me to carry you?"

She chuckled. Even that hurt. "How you going to do that, Romeo? Just throw me over one shoulder and Ruthie over the other?"

He looked so genuinely wounded by the suggestion she laughed – and winced – again.

"No. You carry her, and I carry you. A twofer."

She shook her head. "I'll take my chances walking."

Each step hurt. Halfway up the stairs she was berating herself for trying this. But then she asked herself what she was going to do – stay upstairs, stay downstairs? Stay confined to one spot in the house while her family proceeded with life?

No. Undoubtedly the doctors would say to do exactly that, but doctors always told you what to do without any kind of perception of how it might impact real life. And her real life was this: she was a mother. She was a wife. She had to move. She had to be a part of what was going on.

She would survive.

And in the middle of those thoughts, she realized she had stepped over the top stair.

"Made it," said Blake. "You okay? You want to rest?"

She almost laughed – a courtesy laugh, to be sure – until she saw the worry in his eyes. He wasn't joking, he was truly concerned about her ability to hobble the last few feet to Ruthie's room.

The worry made her feel like they might make it through all this. He seemed to have forgotten the situation with Ruthie, the bills that were still waiting for them, the problems with the business. He was looking at her like she was the only thing that mattered.

And if he could look at her like that, if she could muster up the same kind of looks for *him*, well… they could get through anything.

"Let's keep going," she said.

The last few feet hurt less. They stood at the open door to Ruthie's room in only a few moments. "You need me?" he said.

She shook her head. Blake disappeared down the hall, though she had no doubt he was listening for any sudden noises that might signify she had keeled over and needed to be rescued. He was nearby.

But out of sight. Because just as they had agreed he would carry the baby through the front door, so they had also agreed this would be *her* experience. Her moment alone with the baby.

She carried Ruthie into the baby's room. It was dark. They had put blackout curtains over the window, so even in the middle of the afternoon it would be like walking into a mineshaft were it not for the nightlight beside the door. The light was shaped like a cheerful Strawberry Shortcake, seemingly caught in mid-jump, a happy bit of brightness they thought would be perfect for their little girl's room.

The light was pink. Almost red.

Alyssa took her baby to the crib. A mobile hung from the backboard: red and black and mirrored surfaces – colors that the experts agreed were among the first infants could recognize, among the most stimulating for them. Alyssa touched a button on the side and the mobile began to spin, the toys at the ends of the arms bouncing up and down as it did.

The mobile made a quiet noise as it turned, the sound of a never-ending wave: *whrrrrr*.

Ruthie cooed.

Alyssa put her daughter down. The baby lay on her back, sucking hard at the green pacifier she had gotten at the hospital.

She was wearing a pink onesie. The hospital had given that to them, too.

Alyssa put her hand gently on the baby's stomach. Ruthie gasped, but didn't wake. Alyssa almost cursed at herself. She didn't want to wake the baby, and knew she shouldn't be doing this. But a sudden terror grabbed her, shook her, wouldn't let her go.

She left her hand on her daughter's stomach.

Then, finally, withdrew it.

Her handprint stayed behind, a darker red on the pink fabric. Relief flowed through her: the onesie was working. It would give them an early warning of Ruthie's temperature changed suddenly, going too low (the onesie would shift to blue) or too high (a red shift).

She leaned down, but stopped herself from kissing the baby. *This* she would resist. She'd tempted fate enough for one day, and it was a truism that you should let sleeping dogs and babies lie.

"Stay healthy, Ruthie," she whispered. Her voice was so low that she herself could barely hear it, but Ruthie began sucking harder, faster.

The baby moved slightly, and the onesie shifted. Alyssa's handprint shifted as well, altered by several folds that appeared in the fabric.

A chill rippled down the nape of her neck, through her spine, to her buttocks.

The handprint now looked like a skull.

Then Ruthie moved again, and the onesie pulled tight, the folds disappeared. The handprint was just a handprint again.

And then it faded away.

But the skull remained in Alyssa's mind. She felt like she had just seen something important.

Something terrible.

She hobbled out of Ruthie's room.

But left the door open.

As soon as she left the room, she could tell something was wrong. The faint noise of Mal's cartoons wafted up the stairs like comfort food. Sometimes the noise bothered her – too raucous, too crazed. But other times it was a reminder that this was home, that this was normal life, that this was the motherhood she had hoped and prayed for her whole life.

Now, neither of those feelings was present. The sounds were crazy as ever, as familiar as ever. But she felt neither irritated nor comforted. They slid off her. Dismissed.

She turned toward the back of the hall. Her room.

She moved slowly, hobbled by injury. And her slow movements made whatever was bothering her seem even worse. Seem more critical.

The skull.

No. Not that. That wasn't real.

She moved to her room. And knew.

Blake was there. He had a drafting table set up where he did work from time to time. But he wasn't working now. At least, not on anything from the business.

Instead, he had a mass of envelopes spread over the slanted surface. The usual colors: red and white. The usual words: "Final Notice," "Urgent" "Open Immediately."

Alyssa limped over to him and to her ears she made more noise than a Clydesdale in clogs dancing on a teak floor. But he still jumped when she put her hands on his shoulders. He always got jittery when he was stressed, and that made him worry about what he might do if he got *too* jittery (or who he might do it to), and that made him more stressed, which made him more jittery, and on and on and on.

The vicious circle of self-feedback: one of nature's cruelest jokes.

She put her hands on his shoulders, wrapping them around his neck, holding him tight. He touched her hands. It made her shiver.

One of the envelopes on the table was marked "ST. FRANCIS HOSPITAL OBGEN." That almost made her laugh.

"Boy, they didn't waste any time," she said, pointing

to it.

"They never do. Doctors may be slow when it comes to talking to you, but they sure know how to get a bill out." He sighed. "And the deductible is going to kill us." He pounded a fist against the table, and the envelopes and letters all took a single leap sideways.

"It'll be okay," said Alyssa. She massaged his neck.

"Will it? Between the business, the house, this...." He gestured at the envelopes, the bills. Then the hand went up to rub his eyes. An exhausted gesture that made him seem strangely old. "We shouldn't have moved here. It was too much."

Alyssa turned him toward her, the office chair squeaking slightly as it spun around. She sat on his lap. Tried to keep her face impassive, but a grimace ricocheted through her features. Just a second – half – but Blake noticed.

"I'm sorry," he said. "I shouldn't be carrying on when –"

"It's okay," she said. She kissed him. The kiss was warm. Always warm with him. "It'll be okay." Then she felt something in the kiss. Over a decade of marriage and she finally felt like she knew when her husband was feeling something he wasn't showing. Not *what* he was feeling, but at least that he was feeling *something*. "What's really bothering you?" she said.

He hesitated. Looked away. He looked like a kid who'd been caught reading under the covers when he was supposed to be asleep. "I yelled at Mal today. Really hollered at him."

Alyssa stared at him. She knew what he was saying.

What he was *really* saying. And she hated it. Hated that he still worried about it, that it was still an issue. Most of all she hated the man who had done this. Had made Blake feel this way.

"You're not your father," she finally said.

He still didn't look at her. "One-third of abused children grow up to be just as bad as their parents," he said. And, as always when he said it, he sounded half ashamed and half... what?

Hopeful.

The thought sickened her.

"But two-thirds *don't*," she answered. "And most of the ones who do are abused – *tortured* – over a long period of time. They aren't just born monsters, they learn to be that way. You've never abused Mal or me at all, and I'm sure you'll be just as great with Ruthie." She leaned against him, resting her chin on his head. "Every parent yells at their kids sometimes. Even the good ones. Like you."

She kissed him again.

And this time, though the kiss was real, though she felt the same love for him as always, she nearly pulled away in shock.

Because the kiss was, for the first time ever, not warm. It was cool. Nearly cold.

And she thought of the skull she had seen on Ruthie's onesie.

She shivered as she had a moment before. Shivered, though for a very different reason.

THE BLACK HOLE UNDER THE BED

These are the things Mal loved about his room:

It was big, without being so big that cleaning it was a huge gigantic ridiculous pain in the bottom.

It had a lot of his favorite toys, but not all of them, which meant he always had something to look forward to on Christmas and his birthday.

His bed was awesome because it had three different sets of sheets: Superman, Batman, and blue (which was his favorite color).

There were posters on his walls, which were all Superman and Batman. None were just blue, because that would be silly, but the Superman one had a lot of blue *in* it.

And, most of all: it was *his*. His best friend, Oscar Easterwood, had eight kids in his family, and he shared a room with two brothers, which was *nuts*. They all had to share the same closet, no one knew whose toys were really whose, and forget about keeping your toothbrush out of some other kid's mouth.

But Mal had his own place, his own space. He thought that was cool. So did Oscar, who always wanted to spend the night at Mal's place when they did sleepovers.

Usually Mal fell right to sleep, even if there was a super-bright moon shining through his window. He just dropped the shades and whammo! Sleepy-time darksville.

Tonight, though, he lay in bed a long time. Mommy

and Daddy kissed him good night, Mommy sang to him. She didn't usually do that because she knew he was Becoming a Big Boy, but he was glad she did tonight. Being with the Thayer family for over a week freaked him out, as did all the stuff they told him about Ruthie.

He thought about what he could do. Maybe he could do like Phineas and Ferb and invent some kind of Cureinator that would fix her. He'd have to think about that. It might be worth it. Ruthie was really cute.

He heard a cry. He hadn't known that babies' cries were made of diamonds and dirty ice, but that was what it seemed like. Ruthie's screams cut right through his ears and into his brain, and made *him* want to scream, too. Maybe that was to balance out the cuteness.

He'd have to think about that, too.

Something went *thud-thud-thud-thud* above him. The solid sounds of someone running through the second floor hall. Probably Daddy, since Mommy still wasn't moving super-fast.

A second later he heard a door slam against a wall – definitely Daddy, he was always opening doors too hard – and then loud *shhhh* sounds.

Mal gave up trying to sleep.

He slid out of his bed (Batman sheets!), and sat on the floor beside it.

The room was what Mommy called "a mess" and what Daddy called "a disaster." Mal called it "perfect," because he could reach a toy no matter where he was.

Right here, for instance, just sitting next to his bed, there were three Transformers, two chapter books, his Beyblade stuff, and two Hot Wheels.

He picked up one of the Hot Wheels – a van whose doors opened and shut for real! – and fiddled with it while he thought about the Cureinator idea. He'd definitely have to go to school to be an engineer and inventor. Maybe doctor school, too.

A sudden scream from above!

Mal jerked, his hands flapping out like he was trying to fly away. He blushed at the reaction – very Not Cool – but at the same time worried for Ruthie. What if this was one of The Attacks that Mommy and Daddy had warned him about? What if they were going to rush back to the hospital?

What if Ruthie died?

He didn't want to think about that.

Ruthie stopped screaming. Her voice just *ended* like she'd run into a brick wall or fallen from the jungle gym at school and got knocked out or something.

Another thing he didn't want to think about.

Where'd my Hot Wheels go?

Yeah, that was a better thing. He could think about that and not feel like crying.

It must have flipped out of his hands when she screamed. He looked around the room, but even with all the stuff on the floor, he quickly saw it wasn't there.

That left....

He turned around.

The space below the bed always seemed darker than it should be. Like there was a black hole under there that sucked up all the light that went in. Daddy told him about black holes last year and it was the only thing that made sense: a black hole was the only thing that could make the light just *stop* like that.

Daddy said no way. Said that a black hole would eat the whole house.

Mal had his doubts. He thought it likely a black hole was down there, and it wasn't waiting to eat the whole house. Just him.

But his Hot Wheels was down there. And it was the van with the cool for real opening doors.

He reached under the bed.

His arm disappeared right away. Like it was cut off. Or like he'd never had one to begin with. Like his memories of using that arm and that hand weren't memories at all, but just dreams. Wishes.

He waved his hand back and forth under the bed. Didn't feel anything. Tried to convince himself that meant the van wasn't there after all.

But he knew he couldn't reach all the way back. His arms weren't that long. Maybe the van was farther than he could reach. So if he wanted to find it – and if he wanted to be brave, like Daddy – he had to look more. And go farther in.

He wiggled under the bed. And now his head was in the darkness. His upper body was on the edge of the black hole.

He looked ahead and saw nothing. Nothing. Nothing. Noth –

There!

It was like the darkness was a cloud that parted: suddenly Mal could see something. Could see the bright yellow of the van.

It was on its side, resting on the floor. It looked like it had been cut in half...?

Mal frowned. He reached for the van. Couldn't... quite....

He pushed forward. Almost completely under the bed now.

Above him, the *thud-thud-thud-thud* happened again. The other direction this time, and slower. Daddy going back to bed.

Mal felt alone. Would Daddy hear him if *he* screamed?

His fingers touched the van. And he understood why the toy looked like it was cut in half. It had fallen into a crack in the wood floor. One of the boards had split, or maybe two of them had moved apart. Either way, when Mal yanked the van out he saw a dark shadow where the van had been. A hole.

He couldn't see how deep it was. Couldn't see if it was only as deep as half a Hot Wheel or if it went straight through the earth.

Mal writhed backward. He expected something to grab him. To stop him.

He had, after all, found the black hole. And Daddy had been very clear that black holes do not allow anything to escape from them. Anything at all. Not even a little boy just looking for his Hot Wheel.

He crawled out from under the bed. From the strange darkness thrown by the black hole into the normal darkness of his room.

Only no, it wasn't "normal" anymore, was it? The darkness under the bed seemed to have reached out a bit. Like a dark ooze, it surrounded the bed.

Mal jumped onto the bed, leaping over that darkness. Drew up his legs, pulled the covers up until they rested right below his nose.

He decided to stay up all night.

Because Daddy had told him about black holes. But he had never said that they seemed to *look* at you.

Or that, if you looked carefully, you could almost see things moving inside them.

Above him, Ruthie started to cry again.

MOTION UNMOVED

Silence.

It is late in the house, in this place the Douglas family calls home. Late, and all are abed, all are asleep.

Nothing moves.

Not in the kitchen, with its food from a dinner that went uneaten, prepared with care but overshadowed by exhaustion....

Not in the living room, with its boxes of baby paraphernalia scattered about, its playpen and monitor and pink clothes....

Not in Alyssa and Blake's room, hushed save the low hiss of a baby monitor that whispers a*ll is well, all is well*....

And not in the baby's room itself, the room where little Ruthie sleeps soundly, bathed in red light, the many-armed mobile above her head casting spider shadows across her face and chest....

Nothing moves.

And then... something *does*.

The mobile.

Not much. Hardly at all. And it doesn't move in the circular fashion for which it was designed. The spider-arms, red and black and shiny, do not move round and round. Instead they move up and down, like the rim of a plate that has been balanced on a ball.

Or like a hand unseen has tapped on the toys on one

side.

Up, down, up, down.

Then the mobile slows. Stops.

There is no movement. No sound.

Only the hiss of a monitor in one room.

All is well, all is well….

Motionless silence.

And then both are broken again. The silence shattered slightly, and unmovement transformed to action.

There is a dark spot, deep within the house. The lowest point in the house, under the bed of a boy who, like all the others in this place, sleeps quiet and deep.

The dark spot has been opened. Things once confined are now at liberty. Are now loosed.

The dark spot was a crack, but now it widens. It becomes a fissure. A hole that leads to nowhere but a greater and heavier darkness than that which saturates the rest of the house.

Small legs appear at the edge of the fissure. Two. Then four, then six. And then they are legion. Insectile legs, jagged and long and clawed.

The sound that comes with them scratches and scrapes. It is sound that speaks of things writhing, things crawling, things creeping. It mimics the noise of the monitor, but it bears a different message. Not, *All is well, all is well*. No, something else. Something as dark as the fissure from which it comes.

Something is coming, something is coming, something…

… is here.

SCREAMS

Blake was sitting up before he was fully awake, his body reacting to the sounds before his mind had a chance to fully process them. Though in the next instant they pounded their way at least partway through the clouds that enveloped his sleep.

Screams.

He reached out to turn down the monitor, figuring he'd get Ruthie and bring her to Alyssa for feeding.

Alyssa grunted in pain as she sat up as well, the same reactions taking over in her as those that compelled Blake to shoot up in a state of near-sleep.

"I'll get her," she said.

"You rest. If she needs feeding I'll bring her...."

He stopped talking. Looked at the monitor. He realized that it hadn't even dawned on him that the sounds might be *the* sounds. The dreaded sounds that would send them back to the emergency room –

(*and how will I pay for that*)

– or worse. He had just automatically assumed these were normal feeding noises. The screams of a hungry baby.

And in the next moment he realized that didn't matter. Because it was neither hungry baby nor baby in pain. It was something else entirely.

Alyssa blinked. Her eyes widened. She looked at him for the half-second he remained in bed, and then he was throwing the blanket and sheet aside and leaping to his feet.

The monitor was hissing. Nothing more: just the white noise of empty air, the wave-sound of an unused radio band. And the LEDs on the monitor were not dancing the mad dance that always accompanied the baby's screams. They were silent, dark.

The sound he had heard wasn't Ruthie. Screams, yes. But not Ruthie.

Mal.

Blake was on his feet as the thought pounded the last clinging mists of sleep-cloud away, then he jumped over the corner of their bed as he tried to get to the door in as straight a line as he could. Alyssa got in his way, moving far too slow. He almost punched her as the panic of the moment transformed her from wife and lover to mere obstacle, just a thing that had gotten between him and a child in trouble.

He didn't hit her. Not quite.

He ran around her instead. Passed by her so close that he felt her hair, stirred up by the air of his passing.

Then he was in the hall.

The screams were louder here. Louder still when he hit the stairs, taking them two at a time, then grabbing the newel post and slingshotting around so that when he let go he seemed to be running down the hall at twice the speed as before.

The kitchen door loomed ahead of him.

But before that: Mal's room. The screams.

Blake grabbed the doorknob. A knob he had turned, a door he had opened more times than he could count. It had never given him any trouble. Never stuck. It was never locked... it didn't *have* a lock.

Now the knob refused to turn. He pulled, pushed, yanked. Nothing.

He backed up and kicked the door. Again. Again. Again, againagainagain*again*.

Mal's screams bled together, turning into one single shriek, a sound that rose and fell but never quite ended. Blake kicked –

(*againagainagainagain*)

– and his son shrieked and then the door shrieked, too, shrieked the tortured scream of wood falling to pieces under the repeated pounding of his bare feet.

Screams, splinters, shrieks. All of it blending, blurring, bleeding together.

Now Blake was screaming, too. Screaming his son's name, screaming for God and Jesus, screaming for Alyssa.

The door screamed one last time, then finally gave way.

What was left of the door flew inward and hit the wall of Mal's room. Blake heard the inside knob break through the drywall and anchor itself there.

Mal: screaming. Shrieking. Never stopping for anything. Not even breath.

How is he doing that? How can he –?

Then Blake saw. And knew.

And shrieked as well. Screamed and screamed and did not stop to take a breath.

Mal finally seemed to notice his father's presence. His screams changed from a wordless siren-call to, "Save me, save me, save me, Daddy, save –"

His boy's pleas stopped Blake's own hysteria. At least enough to answer, "I'm coming! Don't move!"

But he didn't move, either. He didn't move to save his boy, he didn't move out of the hall, he didn't take a single step into the room.

That would be... unthinkable.

Because the room had disappeared.

Or at least it had become a thing unseen. Still *there*, but cloaked in a living, writhing carpet that covered every surface. A tapestry whose warp and weft were legs and chitin, antennae and mandibles.

Centipedes.

Each one was six to eight inches long. Red heads, bright yellow legs that seemed to glow in the dark room. They covered Mal's walls, ceiling. The huge window that dominated one wall of his room was a writhing memory. The small desk in one corner of his room, his toy box were only discernible as large lumps under the slithering masses of insects.

The floor was invisible. Just the things, creeping over each other, attacking each other, *eating* each other as they slithered madly from place to place.

And Mal was still screaming. Still screaming from the one place that had not been coated by the monsters. Yet.

His bed. Mal's Batman sheets hung a few centimeters off a slithering floor, throwing a static Batarang that would help no one in this situation.

The legs of the bed *did* touch the floor. And the

things were climbing them. Feeling their way upward.

Blake looked for a way around. A way across as Mal continued shrieking.

"Save me! Save me, Daddy!"

Nothing. No way to cross, to reach his boy. Just the centipedes. The bugs. The *things.*

"Save me!"

One of them dropped from the ceiling onto Mal's bed. Batman now had a writhing monster curling along his cowl, one that the comic book writers had never envisioned.

"Save me!"

Another centipede fell. This one only inches from Mal.

Blake moved.

There was no way to miss the centipedes. No way to avoid them. So he stepped over them. Across them.

On them.

The snaking bodies crushed below his feet, he could feel them whipping around as he smashed them. Pops sounded through the room as their exoskeletons burst under his weight, and the tickle of hundreds of legs on the sides and backs of his feet made vomit rise in his throat.

Then the burning came. The tickle disappeared, replaced by what felt like pins pricking the arches of his feet. The pricking moved to the balls and heels of his feet. Then the pricking became hot coals. Not like he was walking on them, but like someone had surgically inserted them into his feet and legs.

He almost screamed. It was only Mal that stopped

him. Only Mal's own screams, and the knowledge that seeing his Daddy shrieking in pain might be the final straw that broke his sanity.

Blake bit back his screams. Bit down the pain. Stepped forward on feet that felt like they had seared off at the ankles. On what must be mere stumps.

He stumbled, righted himself. Fell.

Mal caught him. Still screaming. "Save me, save me!"

Blake would have laughed. Because it was the boy who had saved *him* in that moment. The boy who had provided an anchor that kept him from careening bodily into the carpet of centipedes.

He swept Mal into his arms. A flood of the insects fell from the ceiling as he pulled his boy off the bed, and now Batman and Robin and all the Caped Crusader's friends and foes were covered by centipedes. There was no more bed, just as there was no floor, no ceiling, no walls. No nothing. Just the bugs.

Blake turned. His ears were ringing, panic driving blood through his temples in such quantities that the sound of it in his ears was all he could make out. No more screaming, no more popping. Just blood. Just fear.

"Close your eyes! Close your eyes, bud!" he screamed. Thought he screamed. He couldn't be sure. All he heard was the blood-sound. Hopefully Mal heard the encouragement. Hopefully Mal felt like his Daddy was there to save him.

Blake ran. Three large steps on ever-burning stumps, legs that had been amputated by the bites of tiny monsters and now were being cauterized over and over and over again.

And then they were out of the room.

POSTPARTUM PAIN

Alyssa didn't know which was worse: the sounds she heard Ruthie making in the hospital, or the sounds her son was making right now in the safety of their home.

And neither was within a mile of the pain *she* felt as she hobbled down the stairs after her husband, following him and the trail of screams that Mal was leaving, like sonic breadcrumbs to some unspeakable place in the dark forest their house had suddenly become.

She was halfway down the stairs when Blake began screaming as well. Halfway down, and try as she might she couldn't push her body to go any faster. The pains left behind by the birth were too great. The only reason she wasn't doubled over on the side of the steps was that Mal – her baby, her other baby, her *only* baby boy – was in some kind of terrible pain, terrible trouble.

So she moved as fast as she could. A fast hobble that would have made any centenarian jealous. Shooting for the kind of speed that would win a footrace with a ninety-year-old. Feeling herself failing.

She made it off the steps. Rounded into the hall. The empty hall.

Partway down.

She saw that the door to Mal's room was open. Screams coming from inside. Her heart stopped.

What's happening? What can I do?

The answer came instantly. Not the answer she wanted. It was an answer that felt like it pulled out everything the birth had left intact, and burned it to ash.

Nothing. You can't do anything. Useless.

The doorway exploded.

Her heart nearly exploded with it. Mal. Mal, held in his father's arms.

Blake nearly threw their son to the floor. "Run!" he screamed at Mal. "Get to the living room!"

Mal didn't move, struck motionless and dumb by whatever had happened in the room. Blake's face turned to something frightening. A thing unkown, very much a stranger. For a moment she wondered if she was seeing a shadow of the man Blake lived in terror of, the man Blake both feared and feared *becoming*.

"*RUN!*" he shouted.

Mal did. He spun and sprinted down the hall, tearing past Alyssa on his way. She reached for him, wanting to hold him, to assure herself that he was all right. But he ducked under her hands. She didn't know if he was running because he was afraid of what had happened in the room, or because he was afraid of Blake. Neither was a good alternative.

Blake locked eyes with her. "Get some towels!" he yelled.

"What?" Confusion ripped through her, created small earthquakes in her brain that made her thoughts go jittery. What could he need towels for? "What do you –?"

"Just get them!"

She turned a quick circle, momentarily unsure whether to get the towels from the kitchen or from the linen closet upstairs. She realized in the next instant what a stupid question that was. Turned back to the kitchen.

Stopped.

Blake was gone again.

HAMMER FIST

Blake threw Mal down. Screamed something at him. It barely registered what the words were. What his tone of voice might be, or its effect on an already-frightened child.

Who he might be becoming.

All that registered: the centipedes. The tens, hundreds of thousands of them. And, more important, the several dozen or so that had ventured over the invisible dividing line between Mal's room and the hall.

He had to get the door closed.

They were coming out.

Blake reached for the door. It had originally opened outward, but he had re-hung it when he realized that anyone opening it would have a good chance at killing anyone passing by in the narrow hall on the way to the kitchen.

He regretted that choice now. Now, with the door seemingly miles away, the knob on the other side embedded deep in the drywall of Mal's room.

Blake reached for the doorknob. He heard Alyssa moving behind him. Hoped – prayed, *begged* – that she was doing what he told her to. Her footsteps were uneven, ragged. The awkward dance of a woman torn.

And for a moment he hated her. Hated Ruthie. Because Ruthie was the reason Alyssa couldn't move faster. And if Alyssa didn't move fast enough, the things were going to get out.

He couldn't let that happen.

(*why not? why not just… let it…?*)

The words stopped him. Not long, but long enough that another segmented thing slithered by him, into the hall.

The voice seemed like it was coming from far away. So far away the speaker might be on the other side of the world, the other side of Time itself.

Or just in Hell.

The voice sounded like Blake's father.

(*just let go….*)

Blake gritted his teeth. Not just against what he had to do – again – but against the words. So light, almost playful.

(***C'mere, kid. Daddy's gonna play a game.***)

This time the words were different. Memory. Before they had seemed farther, but more present. More… *now.*

(***Don't you run from me, you little bastard! Little shit!***)

Blake closed his eyes. He ran forward, grabbing blindly for Mal's door, the doorknob. Feeling once more the slithering/grabbing/biting/*popping* of a thousand insects under his feet.

(*don't do it, son, don't*

run from me, you'll regret it, you

can't escape this, won't escape

what you are!)

And then he had the knob under his hand. But couldn't move.

(*don't, please, don't you know*

I never meant to hurt you, never meant to hurt

those others, to hurt

your mother.)

The voices drove through him. He felt the hand on his face. The belt on his back. The ping-pong paddle landing on his thighs, his groin.

He couldn't move.

A scream sounded behind him. Not the sound of a man long-dead and long-burning in places somehow both ablaze and dark as truest Death. It was Alyssa. She must have returned with the towels. Must have looked in. Must have seen.

"What's that? What's *THAT*?"

He hated her before. He loved her now. Because her scream seemed to battle the voices – the same-different-same-different voices – that had come so close to driving him to his knees.

Blake's hand tightened around the knob. He yanked it back. Crackling as the other side detached from the drywall. More crackling as he took a last step through the centipedes.

The door swung shut. Sweeping along the floor, sweeping dozens, maybe hundreds of the insects into the hall. But leaving a thousand thousand times that trapped in the room.

Where did they all come from?

Doesn't matter. Stop more from getting out. Deal with the closest problem first.

Blake grabbed towels from his motionless wife.

Started stuffing them under the door. But the centipedes seemed to be made of rubber, twisting and turning through the smallest cracks in the cloth.

Alyssa ran away.

He felt another spear-jab of anger. An unsettling moment of wishing he could have locked her in the room.

Then it passed. He hoped she had gone to Mal. Was taking comfort in their son, letting him take comfort in her.

Then she was back. Something cold dripped on his back. The temperature and the surprise combined to create a white-hot trail down his spine. He spun around, still in a crouch, centipedes pushing through the towels wadded at the base of Mal's door.

Alyssa was holding more towels. These were sopping wet. She moved him away.

"These'll work better," she said. She began pushing the sodden cloths under the door. And sure enough, each spot blocked with a wet towel proved impenetrable to the centipedes. Soon there were no gaps.

But Blake knew the job wasn't done. His feet ached. Burned. The things had been venomous, and there were easily a hundred of them in the hall, squiggling and crawling on the floor, the walls.

He wrapped one of the dry towels around his hand.

Began hobbling after them. Each step pain, each footfall agony.

They had cracked, popped when he stepped on them.

They did the same as he brought his towel-covered fist on them. One at a time, time after time.

Pop....

Pop....

Pop....

Alyssa gestured. He nodded. No words needed to be said. They both knew that there was a boy who needed tending. Two jobs. One was hers. One was his.

Pop....

Pop....

Pop....

Each sound a tiny explosion in his skull, a blast that he prayed would destroy whatever part of his mind had conjured up the voice so long-gone, so nearly forgotten.

And what about the other voice, Blake?.

He ignored that. Yes, it had sounded almost like two voices in his mind. But that was memory for you: a strange thing that gave halos to so many dead, and transformed imps to demons and demons into Lucifer himself.

No, just one voice. Just Dad. Just a sad old man who died knowing how pitiful he was. How weak.

He smashed the bugs. Working down the hall, toward his family. Away from Mal's room.

Away from his past.

Pop....

Pop....

Pop....

SINGING SOUNDS

The house is no longer silent.

After so long mute, so long asleep, it has at last been given its tongue. It has spoken, and it will not be quieted again.

The hall on the first floor sits empty. But not silent, not still.

Many bodies lay in the passageway. The first fingers, eyes, tongues of the house and its owner. Its *real* owner.

Now the bodies are nothing. Just crushed carapaces, feelers mashed into wood planking, legs that were once quick and strong now mangled into single, undefined masses whose only value is grotesquerie.

Centipedes are vicious, eating anything small enough – including each other. Many are venomous, and their poison comes not from mouth but from modified feet/hands behind their heads.

They are nocturnal.

All this and more makes them fitting messengers for the house's owner. It makes them appropriate servants, slaves, to the darkness that begat them.

One of the insects in the hall is not dead. Its rear portion smashed, but its head whips back and forth. Not in pain, for it lacks the nociceptors, the spine, the brain to feel such. But it *does* feel stimulus. And it does not understand why it cannot move.

Then, suddenly, the creature's few undamaged segments straighten. They stretch upright.

And then the insect tears in two. As though a sadistic boy in a playground had found it and pulled it limb from limb.

The head and upper segments fall on the floor. It thrashes once, then is motionless, as is all else in the hall.

But that is not to say silence reigns. Sound fills the space. A rasping, writhing, creaking.

The door in the middle of the hall leads to the boy's room. Wet towels have been driven deep in the centimeter between the floor and the base of the door. Dull silver duct tape wraps around the sides and top of the door, binding door to jamb. There are no breaks in the seals.

But the noise still steals through.

The chittering. The rasping.

A million feet sliding over wood and cloth and plaster and plastic. What was once a place where a child slept and read and played is now a place where the mindless beasts have dominion.

Those beasts can be heard throughout the empty hall.

And, soon, they will move beyond the room, and their sound will hold sway through all the house.

The doorknob suddenly twists. Just a quarter-turn. The kind of thing someone might do to check if the lock is engaged. A child, getting ready to creep out of his room unnoticed. Or a sneak-thief, readying himself to creep *in* and steal all that he can find.

Even life.

The house is awake. The house's true owner is present once more.

And he will not be contained.

THREE: UNFAMILIAR DEVELOPMENTS

One may ask (with all sincerity) why a prestigious educational institution would devote time and money to the study of this "barbaric" remnant of the past. The answer is that the question itself is strictly inapposite. The adjudged "barbarism" is a construct of present-day relativism. We cannot view the past through the lens of present morality, for one constant of civilization is the inevitable change of what the masses may term "eternal righteousness." In truth, there is no such thing. There is only what we are used to.

Once again, our primary subject provides an able statement applicable to the matter (and note that even his spelling changes, entry to entry: another perfect metaphor for the ebb and flow of human nature):

> Mye room is betr then other rooms for the pykchers. But any room wil do. The onlee thing I need is my camera, sum lite, a chair for sitting, and THE CHYLD.

- Silver, Charles M.
(afterword by Dr. Charlotte Bongiovi),
(2003) Berkeley, California,
Memento Mori, Notes of a Dead Man,
Western University Press, Inc.

NOW I LAY ME DOWN TO SLEEP

Ruthie slept in a corner of the living room, dead-center in the portable playpen, her mobile clipped to one side like they were just on a trip to a friend's house and not hiding from invaders in their own home. Alyssa kept glancing at her, almost as though to assure herself that her baby hadn't disappeared.

Or been carried off by a legion of bugs.

She shivered. Terror and revulsion kept fighting for control of her system, and she truly didn't know which was worse.

Blake hissed suddenly. His feet were propped on an ottoman. It was a second-hand thing that they bought at a Salvation Army store when they were first married, and it had followed them through their time together. House to house, year by year. An ugly bit of furniture, but it had the beauty of a thing that meant Beginnings.

And it wasn't as ugly as Blake's feet. They were red, swollen. What looked like hundreds of tiny red spots dotted the bottoms and sides, seeping blood and yellow fluid.

She dabbed at another spot, using some of the cotton and hydrogen peroxide she had grabbed from their bathroom when she hurried upstairs to get Ruthie. The trip had been near-agony, but she wasn't about to leave her baby alone, and she wasn't about to let Blake suffer longer than he had to or perhaps get an infection. Not after what he had done.

So... cotton balls, hydrogen peroxide. Ruthie and a playpen.

Mal wanted to come, but she told him to stay with Blake. To help his father, to comfort him.

Mostly, she didn't want him leaving the living room. Because she was fairly certain that if he saw any more of those horrid bugs, those centipedes from Hell, he'd go immediately comatose. The kid was tough, but she could tell he was at the end of his rope.

That was why, when Blake hissed again, she looked over at Mal to make sure he was okay.

He wasn't, of course. His eyes were wide but unfocused. His face white as a summer cloud, dots of sweat on his forehead that mirrored the dots of blood on his father's feet.

She almost asked, "You okay, Mal?" but bit it back at the last second. It was the kind of question that wouldn't help. He'd answer in the positive, and then she would have done nothing but draw attention to his state of mind. That vicious circle of self-feedback again.

Instead she looked at Blake. Rolled her eyes toward Mal and dabbed his feet again. She said, "Easy. The 'net said you wouldn't die," in the kind of tone reserved for crybabies in a ballgame.

Blake got it. He spotted Mal's face, figured out his state of mind, and glued a smile over the pain. "Then it *must* be true," he said. "I read about a guy who gave birth to a three-headed monkey who is an expert at video games, and I'm pretty sure I saw the thing at Best Buy last week, playing three console games at once."

He glanced at Mal. So did Alyssa. The little guy still had that faraway stare on his face. Like he was looking for something on the horizon. Somewhere distant that he could run to and be safe.

"It's okay, bud," said Blake. "They're stuck in there."

And in one of those acts of cruelty that only an uncaring universe can bring off with such perfect timing, right then they heard it. The noise. The *things*.

Scratch, scratch, scratch.

She could practically see them in her mind. Their snake-bodies writhing over each other, profaning the sacred space of a little boy's room, sullying his toys, his clothes, his bed.

"Safe," repeated Blake. Then under his breath he added, "For now."

Alyssa thought he meant it to be heard only by him. Either that or meant it as a joke. Either way, he failed. The words sounded deadly serious, and they wrapped the room in a sense of doom.

"Not in front of Mal," she whispered. She nearly bit off each word, anger at Blake's sudden selfishness gritting her teeth, clenching her jaw.

She put more hydrogen peroxide on Blake's foot, and this time she failed to dab it. She *jabbed* it at him.

He hissed again. "Sorry," he snapped. "I guess I get irritable when my feet feel like I stuck them in a damn furnace!"

Another cruel universe-joke: the *things* fell silent. Like Blake's anger hushed them. A lullaby for the wicked.

Mal stepped back. Away from his father. From his

daddy.

Blake's face changed instantly. He knew he had gone too far, and *Alyssa* knew he was thinking what he always thought when he yelled or lost his temper or did anything else that any normal parent did at least a thousand times a day.

He was worried about *his* father.

She ached to hold him and tell him it was all right; that if anyone had earned the right to be short-tempered, it was him.

But she couldn't. Just like she hadn't been able to a few moments ago. Because that would be admitting the seriousness of the problem in front of a terrified little boy.

Welcome to Parenting 101, in which we will learn how to constantly feel like one person in the family is getting emotionally screwed for the benefit of another.

Blake got up. He grunted slightly as he put his weight on his feet, but other than that there was no sign of his pain. He smiled and walked toward Mal. Slowly. A smile on his face.

"Sorry I got mad, bud. Just tired. Hurty feet." He shrugged.

Mal nodded. Still wearing that long stare. But it focused a bit when Blake put a hand on his shoulder. "Why don't you lay down, bud?" He gestured at the couch.

Mal shook his head.

"You're safe," said Blake. "We'll be right here. All of us." He looked at Alyssa with his eyebrows reaching for his hairline in an exaggerated question. She nodded. "See? We'll all be right here."

Mal remained motionless for a long time. He looked like a statue. Alyssa wanted to run to him, but held back. She was pretty sure he was still teetering on the brink of some precipice. Too much stimulus – good or bad – could push him over the edge.

Parenting 101, Lesson Two: in which we learn that being a mommy sometimes means standing back and letting Daddy do the comforting. Even though that will make you feel like your heart is being shoved in the garbage disposal.

And it was the right choice. Mal went slowly to the couch. Sank down. Blake limped to him and covered him with an afghan as Mal curled into a tiny ball. So small-seeming. So frail.

"No worries, Mal. Sleep," said Blake. "I'm here." He kissed their boy.

"What about my toys?" asked Mal.

Blake's back was to her, but Alyssa could sense his grin. "Don't you worry about that. I'm sure G.I. Joe will kill a few of those things for us."

Mal smiled. He closed his eyes. They popped open again almost instantly, as though to make sure Daddy was still there.

They closed. This time didn't open.

The noise sounded.

Rasping.

Creaking.

Alyssa looked at Mal. His eyes stayed closed. He must already be asleep.

But she knew she wouldn't sleep. Not tonight.

Maybe not ever again.

DECISIONS, DECISIONS

They waited long enough to make sure Mal was asleep.

No, not just asleep, but *out*.

There was a difference, one that Blake had learned a lot slower than Alyssa. But he had caught on eventually.

Asleep: eyes closed, even breathing. Able to pop up instantly, run out, and interrupt whatever happened to be going on.

Out: eyes closed, even breathing. Not likely to get up for the next six to ten hours. Able to sleep through screaming, loud movies, and thermonuclear attacks.

Blake had learned the definition of "asleep" when he put Mal down one night. He sang extra songs, gave kisses, and waited for the boy to get nice and motionless before sneaking silently out to meet Alyssa in their room.

Alyssa was wearing very little. And soon nothing at all.

Another definition of *asleep*: putting your three-year-old down, feeling your wife's hands all over you, wondering where the third hand (on your ankle, thank goodness!) had come from. Looking down to see a pair of blue eyes peeping over the top of the mattress and hearing a tiny voice saying, "Daddy, what are you doing to Mommy?"

After that, *out* was critical. So was a well-locked door.

Tonight, Blake was on "Mal Watch," Alyssa took "Ruthie Duty." They didn't have to speak about the division, they just took positions instinctively. After just over a decade of marriage – good marriage – you just *knew*.

Alyssa was at his shoulder in seconds. "She's down for a while."

She whispered so quietly he could barely hear her, but somehow Mal seemed to sense the words. He sighed and shifted under the afghan.

Blake tensed. Felt Alyssa do the same.

Then Mal snored. The most telling sign of "out"-ness.

Blake nodded, and Alyssa walked stiffly to the kitchen door. He hobbled through behind her.

Quite the pair we are.

They left the door open, not just so they could see the kids, but so Mal would easily see them if they awoke. He'd never forgive them if he came to and couldn't find the family that had promised their presence.

Once in the kitchen, Blake nodded to Alyssa. She nodded back, again understanding his unspoken question: *Mind if I sit down?* Some might have thought it an unnecessary question, but it was important to him. Being raised by a monster had given him the need to turn himself into what he saw as the thing most distant: a gentleman. And gentlemen didn't sit while their recently-pregnant wives stood. Not without a by-your-leave.

She nodded: *Of course.*

He went to the table and slumped into a chair. The kitchen was a kitchen/dining room, which he knew some people thought was terribly gauche. He liked it, though. Liked seeing where the food he ate had been made. Liked being able to leap up and just grab something forgotten. It struck him as cozy. The essence of family.

He also liked it – he had to admit – when Alyssa went to the refrigerator and bent over to get something. Like now.

He didn't know if that made him a tactless pig or not. On the one hand, he knew plenty of men who seemed almost proud of the fact that they barely paid attention to their wives' bodies. They preferred porn.

Blake was proud of the fact that after a decade Alyssa still drove him crazy physically. But he felt like a bit of a cad thinking that way right after she'd had a baby, even though he knew he would never act on the impulse until she signaled she was ready.

Finally he shrugged his mental shoulders and decided there were more important things to think about.

Like the python-sized bugs infesting our house.

Alyssa stood up holding two beers. Let the fridge door fall shut behind her. "Beer?" she said.

"If ever there was a night...," he replied, and held out his hand.

She opened them both. Handed him one. Blake's right eyebrow cocked.

"I thought they were both for me. You're nursing."

Alyssa shook her head. She looked very tired. Blake felt a pang of guilt. Wondered for the millionth time if she wouldn't have been better off without him.

"Dr. Blake said I could have a half once in a while. Tonight definitely qualifies as 'in a while.'"

She took a swig, looking both relieved at the drink

and a little defiant. The beer was a sign of how distressed she was: she was ultra-careful about what she ate and drank while nursing. Blake had never even seen her drink a caffeinated soda when she was nursing Mal.

The sound crept in through the other door: the door that led not to the living room but the hall.

Scratch-scratch, scratch-scritch....

Alyssa moved to the hall door. Nearly slammed it shut. She spun and leaned against it, her arms across her chest. Not like she was relaxing, but more as though she was getting ready to brace against the door and keep something out.

She was still holding the beer. Some of the liquid spilled on the t-shirt she was wearing in bed before the nightmare began. She didn't notice.

"We have to leave," she said.

Blake felt hypnotized by the sound of the things beyond the door – doors. The sound of darkness, of creeping things. Perhaps of a long-rotted hand, reaching for him once more.

Gradually her words sank in. He shrank back. As though he could dodge what she had already said.

"How? We can barely afford the mortgage here, the bank account is tapped. How are we going to afford a motel for however long it takes us to fix this –?"

"*Us?*" Alyssa shook her head. More beer spilled. "This is not a job for *us*. This is nothing we can handle."

Blake felt his face twist. Twist and twist into a tighter and tighter knot. They couldn't. They didn't have the money. He couldn't afford to miss the work.

And she was right.

"Our insurance is never going to cover –" He began, but didn't expect to finish. Just a last straw at which to grasp.

And she cut it off. Not with razor-sharp logic, but with the much sharper statement that was, really, all they had left. A statement of faith.

"We'll find a way."

She smiled.

He could tell she didn't believe it.

Neither did he.

Behind her, behind the doors, the many legs crawled, the darkness rippled, the dead man reached out in his mind.

ON THE RUN

Bugs.

Mal kept waking up to them. Crawling on his feet and his hands and his legs. That wasn't the worst, though. It wasn't even the tickle-feeling of them on his face, or the fact that every time he woke up he had to pull at his waistband and make sure nothing had crawled into his underwear and was curled around his you-know-what.

That's what he woke up *to*.

But the thing that actually woke him *up* was Daddy.

In his dreams Daddy was chasing him. Running after him, following him with this angry face and saying things that were Very Bad Words.

Daddy kept catching him. No matter how fast Mal ran, Daddy always caught him. He reached out, and grabbed him, and it hurt. Oh it hurt so bad, so bad. It felt like he was getting his arm pinched right off and he looked and he started to cry because it wasn't Daddy's hand it was someone else's, and that hand only had three fingers that grabbed tighter and tighter and pinched harder and harder until his arm got bloody.

And when Mal looked up to ask Daddy what he was doing, he never could. Because when he looked up, Daddy's face was gone. Not like it was different, or maybe like a different person was there the same way a different hand was on Daddy's wrist. Daddy's face was totally *gone*. Just a hole where Daddy's face should be, and he could see right through it into his brain.

But there was no brain to see. There were bugs. Bugs, and behind it... something scarier than the bugs, scarier than Daddy, scarier even than that three-fingered hand that belonged to someone else.

Scarier than all of it.

Mal thought he saw another face. A face inside Daddy's head. A *thing* inside, gray and dead and looking out.

That woke him up. Daddy chased him, Daddy caught him. A dead thing saw him.

And he woke up to the feeling of bugs on his body, crawling all over him, even in his underwear.

He didn't sleep well.

But when it was morning (finally!) Mommy said they were leaving and she got him out of the house before he even had breakfast. He asked what they were going to eat, but only because he thought he was supposed to ask. He really didn't care. He didn't think he could eat with that weird noise in the hall.

He walked past the hall, once. He had to pee.

There was a man, standing by the door to Mal's room. The man's back was to Mal, and for a crazy second he wondered if the man was the person with the three fingers, come right out of his dream to kill him or maybe drown him in bugs.

Or, worst of all, shove him in that hole in Daddy's face and make him meet whatever monster lived there.

But the man turned around and it was just a guy. A man with a big tummy and gray whiskers and almost no hair on his head. He had a little sign sewed onto his shirt that said, "TOMMY."

Tommy waved at Mal, but he looked like he was thinking about something else. Something bad.

Mal knew what. He knew that this man had looked. Looked in the room.

Mal went to pee. He had to poop, kinda, but he wasn't about to sit down on the toilet. What if the bugs crawled out of it and up his bottom? If that happened he would die. No one, not even Mommy or Daddy, could save him from that.

When he got done, Mommy was waiting outside the bathroom with a little bag and a change of clothes. She looked away while he put the new clothes on, then took him to the living room. Ruthie was there, and Mommy asked him to hold his bag, the diaper bag, and another little backpack while she picked up Ruthie and the folded up playpen.

"What're we doing?" he asked.

"We're going for a trip, honey."

He almost shouted for joy. But he didn't. He didn't even smile. Not in this place. Not now. Maybe not ever again.

They went outside. There was a van in front of the house, a brown one. It said, "PEST IN PEACE" on the side next to a drawing of dead bee with a super-big stinger and Xs for eyes. Mal smiled – safe to do now they were outside the house – at the joke. Mommy had been teaching him puns and things like that. He liked the joke on the van.

Daddy was standing in front of the house with Tommy the fat man, and they argued while Mommy and Ruthie and Mal went to the car in the driveway.

"Three days?" shouted Daddy. "You said one, maybe

two!"

Tommy got a hard look on his face. "That was before I saw the room."

Mommy swung the back door open and put Ruthie in her car seat. Mal wondered where they were going. He also wondered if he would have a chance to make Ruthie's onesie change color. He thought that was awesomely cool to breathe on her chest and watch it change, but it made Mommy mad so he only did it when she wasn't looking and wouldn't worry.

Daddy sounded worried now. "Can't you... I don't know... cut a corner or two?"

Mal glanced over and saw the older man's face get tough for a second. "Look, Mr. Douglas, I've got my own problems, you know? I got three guys out with fevers, I got a computer that hates me. Hell, someone even stole one of our tents a few weeks ago." Then he took a breath. His hand went over his face a few times, like he was wiping his mad away. When he stopped he looked less angry, but more tired. "I've already cut it to the bare minimum for you. We're going to saturate your house with phosphine" (that was a word Mal filed away to ask Mommy about) "so do you want to come home to everyone puking and explosive gas pooled on your floors?"

"Dammit!"

All Mal's muscles got jerky for a second when Daddy screamed. He felt like he was in the dream.

"Is Daddy mad?" he whispered to Mommy. When he looked at her she was staring at Daddy like she was worried about that, too.

But she smiled and shook her head. "No, honey.

He's just worried and scared. He'll be fine." She hugged him. Then she clicked the last clicker on Ruthie's seatbelts and said, "Why don't you hop in the other side?"

He did. Ruthie was in the middle, and when Mommy went to her side to get in he puffed on her. That spot on her onesie turned red.

Mommy and Daddy said Ruthie wouldn't smile for a while, or that if she looked like she was smiling it would really just be her farting.

Well, she must be farting a lot, *because that looks like a smile to me!*

He put his finger in her little hand. She had a super-strong grip. He smiled at her. And for sure *he* wasn't farting. It was a real smile. She was a cool sister.

Her grip got tighter. Like a little monkey holding onto a tree.

Or like Daddy and his three fingers holding you until you bleed.

Mal's smile went away.

He wondered if they were leaving the monsters behind, or just taking them to a new place with them.

Daddy got in the car.

ADVENTURERS AWAY

Alyssa was on her cell phone, and so glad they had decided to keep it.

A few years ago it had been a non-question. It was part of life, the same as their cars, their house, their internet connection.

Business was great. Lots of clients coming to Blake. A new house.

Then business dried up. One of the cars turned into a money pit and ended up as a piece of modern art at some junkyard.

The other one was repo'd.

Now they had a junker, given to them by a friend who was about to move and who decided they needed it more than his sixteen-year-old.

They were barely hanging onto the house.

And just last month they had been talking about cancelling their remaining cell subscription. The only thing that kept it from happening was Blake. He insisted he wanted her to have a cell, at least while the baby was young. He wasn't worried about himself, but he wanted something for her in case "anything happened."

And it looked like they were well on their way to a heaping plateful of "anything."

"Okay," she said. "Thank you. Thank you so much." She hung up. Looked at Blake. He didn't even glance at her, which was a bad sign. When they were dating and then first married he had almost crashed a few times, looking at her too often and too long. And even after so many years he always looked at her. Let her know that he was listening, that she mattered.

He only avoided her gaze when he was incredibly angry at her, or so shaken by something that he could only concentrate on one thing at a time.

She didn't want to talk, but knew she couldn't just let him drive forever. Life would continue moving forward, whether they wanted it to or not.

"The owners of the house said it was okay. They'll let us extend our stay, no problem."

Blake nodded, an up-and-down of his chin that was barely more than a controlled twitch. He still didn't look at her.

"How much?" he said.

"Forty a day."

"How'd you find this place?"

"My sister used them once."

"Heather stayed there?"

"No. She didn't use this particular house, she used the service I used last night. It's a website that puts up empty houses for people to stay in short-term. Like vacations and things. Cheaper than a motel."

Another barely-there nod. "Yeah." Still not happy, and Alyssa couldn't blame him. But she also couldn't tell if he was simply angry at the situation, or also at her.

"Blake...."

He still didn't look. And she chickened out. What was she going to do either way? If it was the situation that was upsetting him she could hardly go over it with Mal in the back. If it was her... she didn't think she'd respond well to that. Blake wasn't the only one at the end of his rope.

She looked away from him. Twisted toward the backseat. Her body still ached, especially everything within a foot of her pelvis. For a few moments in the middle of everything she hadn't felt much pain – the blessed effects of adrenaline. And then this morning the pain had been consumed by a desire to get away from the infestation that had attacked their home.

But now it was all back. With a vengeance.

Still, she forced herself around. Looking behind her.

Mal had his mouth on Ruthie's outfit. Blowing hard, trying to make a patch of red appear on the pink onesie with the heat of his breath.

He spotted her turning and sat up quickly, putting on a smile that he no doubt thought was sincere and innocent. It was neither. It screamed, "CAUGHT!"

But it was also hilarious. The first moment of normalcy in almost twelve hours.

Usually Alyssa would have chewed him out for what he'd just done. Ruthie's onesie wasn't a toy, it was a failsafe to make sure her core temperature never rose or fell beyond acceptable levels. And normally Mal would have heard that, delivered verbatim in a stern speech.

Now, though, Alyssa giggled. Mal's "Oh crap" smile was replaced by one with a bit more sincerity. He smiled, too.

"Ready for an adventure?" she said.

He nodded. Gave a thumbs up.

Alyssa blew him a kiss then faced front again.

Blake still didn't look at her.

"You hear that, Ruthie?" whispered Mal behind her. "We're going to have an adventure!"

Alyssa smiled.

And then remembered that adventures all-too-often ended not in treasure, not in glory, but rather in the death of men and women who would never be found, and whose bones would rot, unburied and unhallowed into eternity.

"An adventure!" Mal whispered once more. And Ruthie pooped loudly and Mal giggled and Alyssa felt her skin grow cold.

DOORWAY UNCOVER'D

The first man comes, the first man goes.

Then more come. And like the first, they look in, then jump away.

Next they begin "preparations." First they make the door as it is now: strips of heavy tape around all the edges, binding door to frame even more solidly than before.

In front of it hangs a sheet of thick industrial plastic. Colorless but opaque, only the vaguest outline of the door can be seen through it. A smear to mark the doorknob.

The *sound* still comes through unmolested. The noise of an army, a horde. A host, in so many senses of the word.

The hall begins to darken. It is not dusk, no storm clouds have come. But outside, a different kind of plastic lowers over the entirety of the house. This plastic is neither colorless nor opaque. It is, instead, bright. Almost merry. The color of a circus or carnival.

Or a warning. Something so garish it cannot be mistaken for anything but what it is.

The plastic lowers, and as it falls it covers window after window. The inside of the house dims.

And when the hall is dark – not completely dark, but dark *enough* – something happens.

The sound is silenced. The unseen horde that jitters across the many surfaces of a boy's room suddenly ceases all movement.

The transition from noise to stillness would be

maddening if there were any to hear-then-not-hear it. Insanity can be found in the knife edge of certain changes. This is one of them.

Silence. The instant stretches. Becomes a moment.

The hallway darkens still further.

Outside, the colorful plastic drops.

And inside, behind the colorless plastic... movement. Not the horde. A single thing.

The doorknob. The smear behind the plastic shifts slightly.

There is a click. Then tearing that sounds like muscle ripping from bone as the door pulls away from the frame.

The door opens. Still just a vague blur beyond a sheet of polyethylene whose only purposes – to reassure the workers that everything within can be confined, that this is just one more job to be done – are now proven to be lies.

The doorway frames darkness. Not just absence of light, but of *right*. Something *wrong* stands behind the sheet. Evil, yes. But also something that should not be. Something that rubs at the fabric of reality, rubs it raw and eventually scrapes it away to nothing.

The plastic sheet over the door flaps to the side.

And the thing steps forth.

VOLUNTARY MADNESS

Blake pulled up to the rental house, but didn't look at it. Not yet.

They had gotten lost twice on the way, relying on an old Thomas guide and a Google Maps printout. Life without GPS had once been the norm, but life post-GPS – too *expensive* GPS – was surprisingly difficult.

One more bit of rug yanked out from under us. One more thing we allow ourselves to need, just in time to have it taken away.

Blake looked at Alyssa. Suddenly wondered if she would leave, too. She was, without a doubt, his greatest and most valuable possession, the one thing he had given himself to without reservation – and he knew it was safe to do that. Safe to give himself to her, because she had given herself to him. They owned each other, they belonged to each other. That was what "being one" in a marriage really meant.

That was why it hurt so badly when they fought: it wasn't because he felt bad about the *fight*, or because he was angry about losing the argument. It hurt because on those rare occasions when they screamed, on those even rarer occasions when one of them walked away – just took the keys and drove around the block to cool off – it wasn't an argument with another person, it was a division with the *himself* he had chosen to become. A strange kind of schizophrenia that was only available to married couples who were truly and deeply in love.

Maybe that was all love was. Maybe it was a headlong flight *into* insanity. A voluntary committal to an institution where madness was the norm, where lunacy was the real thing that bound two people "'til death do us part."

Still, he preferred madness with Alyssa to sanity with anyone else. It wasn't even a question. He preferred *anything* with her to *anything* with someone else.

So when he looked at her as they pulled up to the curb and suddenly felt – knew – he was going to lose her.... It wasn't a loss of someone else. It was a loss of himself. It was a spiral into death, because how could he exist with half of himself – literally his better half – cut off and secreted away?

"We're here," said Alyssa. She wasn't talking to him, really. But he pretended she was, and was glad that she spoke. Her voice was a rope that kept him from falling too deep into the bleak thoughts that sometimes dragged at him. That threatened him with memory and past and a hint of future that must be.

(*C'mere! Daddy's gonna play a game.*)

He glanced at Mal in the rearview mirror. The kid was asleep.

(***Don't you run from me, you little bastard! Little shit!***)

He closed his own eyes, then opened them and – finally – looked at the house.

"How was *this* cheaper than a motel?" he said.

Alyssa giggled. She sounded like a child, and he loved her for that. One of too many things to count. "Don't look a gift horse...," she began.

He rolled his eyes. "Come on," he said. Trying to sound businesslike, serious. But still gawking at the place they were going to call home for the next three days.

The rental house was a two-story affair. Gabled, with eaves that hung over a porch that surrounded the whole place like a white skirt flared out by a whirling dancer.

The windows – at least at this time of morning – reflected the outside light. Not transparent, but almost white. Eyes once clear but now clouded by cataracts, dimmed by time.

Roses climbed several trellises, irises surrounded the patio. Charming.

At least during the day.

Alyssa went for Ruthie while Blake went to get Mal. Rousing his son was harder than he thought it would be. And when Mal finally opened his eyes he pushed into the seat, scrambling to get away from Blake. Only the seatbelt kept him from leaping away; perhaps leaping completely out of the car.

Then his eyes settled from the full moon of panic to the waxing crescent of gradual waking. He rubbed them. "Where...?"

"We're here, bud," said Blake. In an appropriately deep voice he added, "The adventure begins!"

Mal smiled. Then he was out of the car and up a bluestone path after his mother, who was already halfway to the house.

Blake caught them –

(*Caught* up to *them, Blake. Big difference.*)

(**Don't you run from me, you little bastard! Little shit!**)

– just as Alyssa found the keys where they were hidden under the pot of what looked like a bonsai tree.

She put the key in the door. It slid home with that subtle grind of an old, well-used thing.

The door swung open with a slight squeak. Hinges cared for, but ready for maintenance.

The family walked in.

MINUTES AND MUSIC

Alyssa had to keep from gasping. It was hard. Then she decided it wouldn't hurt anything and did it.

The inner décor matched the outside: old, well-kept, classy.

To the right of the entry – which, unlike in their own home, actually *was* large enough to be termed a foyer – was the dining room. A beautiful table, big enough to seat twelve, sat in the middle. Dark wood, cherry or oak. Behind it was a matching buffet side table with silver tea setting. The silver was slightly tarnished. Purposefully so, she guessed, since it didn't seem trashy or unkempt. It just added to the overall sense of classy antiquity.

A crystal chandelier hung over all of it, catching the sun and breaking it into rainbow shards that it then cast all over the room.

To the left of the entry was a living room. Or perhaps in a place like this it was actually a parlor. Someplace people sat and talked and "entertained."

Baby grand piano. Black, with gold lettering, gold hinges, gold accents on the wheels. Gilded chairs dating to an age that somehow managed to be at once more genteel and more violent.

Several tables. On them sat matching lamps. The lamps were clearly expensive, but these Alyssa did not care for. They sported red glass shades, and the glass seemed to snatch the light in the room, then return it bathed in blood.

And directly in front of the door and the family:

stairs. Sweeping, a grand semi-circle of a craftsmanship generally lost in the houses of today. Back home Alyssa knew exactly which of the treads would creak on her staircase, which would sigh and groan as she passed over them as though exhausted by the work they did.

These, though… she could tell by looking at them that they would bear their burdens in solemn silence for a long time. Maybe forever.

Over it all was a sound. *Tick-tock, tick-tock, tick-tock.*

A grandfather clock stood next to the stairs. Well over two meters tall, it was elegant and at the same time somehow forbidding. The face looked like ivory, dark numbers scrolled at the traditional points, except for at the midnight position. There, a moon dial showed a picture of a moon with a painted face.

The face reminded Alyssa of something. Someone. She didn't know which, and honestly didn't care to. It –

(*scared her terrified her run Alyssa get out get out!*)

– made her feel uncomfortable. She looked away.

Tick-tock, tick-tock, tick-tock.

The sound of a life counting down.

What made you think that, Lyss?

She glanced at Ruthie. Asleep in her arms. Unworried about anything. Though soon she'd want to feed. They all would.

Beside the clock, atop a table that was almost hidden behind it, was a small wood box. A metal wheel with tiny pin-like extrusions could barely be seen over the top of it. Alyssa didn't recognize it at first, then realized it was a music box. Not one of the cheap things that kids got for birthdays, with a plastic ballerina and a hidden compartment for childhood "treasures." This was a deluxe antique, something people used to dance to when no orchestra was available.

For some reason, the music box made her even more uncomfortable than the clock

Mal was rubbernecking, eyes going from room to room to stairs. "Cool," he said.

"Remember, it's not ours," said Alyssa. She didn't even think about it. Just automatic entry into "Mommy Mode." "So be careful what you touch, okay?"

"But you can have whichever room you want," said Blake.

Mal started to run, then stopped so fast it was just a lurch. "Can't I sleep with you guys?"

Blake nodded and knelt next to Mal. "If you want to."

Mal nodded, too, and Alyssa could see what her little boy was thinking. She wanted to shout to him, to scream, "Just sleep in our room, stay with us! Now isn't the time to be a big boy!"

But she knew Mal. Knew that saying such a thing would just end up making him feel bad later. Like he had failed in some class he was taking, some course of which only he knew.

"I'll find my own room," he finally said. "It's what you'd do, right, Dad?"

Blake smiled. The smile was forced, and Alyssa knew he wanted Mal with them as much as she did.

And in this installment of Parenting 101, we will learn

how to let the child do things that absolutely kill you, *because they will be good for* him. *Remember:* "*parenting*" *is just another way of spelling* "*gradual suicide*"!

Blake tousled Mal's hair. "I'll get the luggage." He took a few steps to the door, then turned. "You think you're strong enough to lift some of it, bud?"

Mal made a muscle. "Check this out!"

Blake felt it. Nodded. "Let's go."

They went out.

Alyssa stayed.

Tick-tock, tick-tock.

The sound of life counting down. Falling away.

The sound of minutes lost, and never to be found again.

Tick-tock.

APPLE TO SONG

The new place was definitely cool. It had lots of old stuff, a neat-o piano, and the living room looked like it belonged in a castle or some house where if you opened the right door you'd fall right into a magical land where you were the hero and guaranteed to vanquish the bad guys.

"Vanquish" was also cool. Mal had learned the word the week before Ruthie came, and when he used it, it made *him* cool, too.

Lots of coolness. Plenty to go around.

But at the same time, there was also a little bit of not-cool. A little bit of dark, a little bit of danger.

The clock was creepy. The noise it made could be heard everywhere through the house, and Mal wondered what kind of people needed to know what time it was so badly that they put in a clock that reminded them of every passing second.

Also, he definitely got a bad feeling from the box thingy behind the clock. Mommy said it was a music box, and told him people used to dance to it. She offered to see if it worked.

He told her no. Reminded her that this wasn't their house. She said he was "a great kid" and "an example," and he didn't tell her it had nothing to do with being good.

He just didn't want her to touch it.

Just like he wouldn't want her to touch a rattlesnake, or a bottle of acid, or a nuclear bomb. Some things were bad. You didn't touch bad things.

But the rest of the house was pretty cool. And the fact that it had televisions and working bathrooms made it even cooler. For a second when he saw the oldness of it he was worried he'd be running to one of those wood buildings with a moon carved on the door every time he had to poop. Worse, he was worried he'd have to sit around listening to the radio or reading twenty-four/seven.

But apparently the owners of the place appreciated old stuff *and* wanted the good parts of new stuff, too. There were a couple flat screens, a few computers tucked away in some corners here and there, and the bathrooms all looked like they had new-type toilets that flushed.

Mommy led him into the back of the house, into the kitchen. She looked pretty impressed with the place, too.

"You like it?" she said.

"Yeah!"

The kitchen was the same as the rest of the house. Old, but cool. The walls were a happy orange color. A white table that looked like it Old MacDonald probably ate breakfast at it sat in the middle of the room. Pots and pans hung from a bunch of hooks over a stove that stood on actual metal legs carved like the feet of a lion or a tiger. A coat rack full of cozy coats hung on the wall near the door to the hall.

The clock-sound bounced around in here, *tick-tock, tick-tock*. It made Mal's stomach drop a little, made his privates feel like they were sucking up inside him. It was not a nice feeling.

"Check this out!"

Mommy was pointing at the fridge. It was a gross green color that Mal guessed was probably popular a hundred years ago. But on it someone had taped a big piece of paper that said, "Help Yourself!"

Mommy looked at him. "Shall we?"

He nodded and hustled over to her. She swung the door open.

Inside, every shelf seemed completely full – even the little ones on the door. Milk, lunch meats, bread, fruit. All of it laid out neatly (much more neatly than in *their* house), fresh-looking, yummy.

"Hungry?" asked Mommy.

Mal realized he hadn't eaten in what seemed like hours. Maybe days. Maybe *years*. Maybe if he took his clothes off there'd be just a skeleton underneath.

He nodded and grabbed an apple. It was one of the green kind, which were his favorite because they were sour and they didn't get mushy like a lot of the reds.

He lifted it to his mouth. About to take a bite….

And dropped it as a jarring sound, like a hundred house keys clanging together in a trash bag, bashed its way into the kitchen.

Mal looked at Mommy in near-terror, then realized the metal sound had turned into something weirdly like music.

The music box.

Mommy was frowning. "Blake?" she shouted.

Daddy was unpacking upstairs. It must be him. He must have come down and turned on the music.

So why doesn't he answer?

Mal bent down to pick up the apple. He didn't think about it, it was just what you *did* when you dropped an apple. Especially a green one, because of the ten-second rule. It was still good.

But Mommy grabbed his arm and pulled him with her and his fingers brushed the apple but he didn't grab it.

She pulled him out of the room.

Mal frowned.

Had there been shoes below the coats when they came in?

Maybe. He didn't remember seeing any, but he hadn't really been looking.

Were they here?

For a second he thought not. Thought they were new, and had just appeared out of nowhere. Then he realized that was weird and stupid.

There musta been here. 'Cause they're sure here now!

Besides, these sure looked they'd belong here. They were old, like a lot of the stuff in the house. Only to be honest, these seemed even older than most of the house's decorations. Like over a hundred *years* old. Dusty and brown. They were small, too. Like a kid – maybe someone his age – would have worn them once.

Then Mal was past coats and shoes and into the hall.

Following the music.

COATS AND SHOES

The boy and the woman rush from the room. The shoes do not rush. The shoes are motionless.

But only for a moment.

Then they shuffle to the side. A quick step-step, as though the owner unseen is trying to decide whether or not to follow mother and child.

Mother and child do not see the movement, for they are already gone.

They do not see the movement, just as they do not see the stockings that now appear, misting into reality above the brown shoes. Gray, tight in the shape of small legs. Tattered in places, with stains from long ago, and holes that reveal nothing beneath, because there is nothing beneath the stockings, nothing to hold them in that shape. Only cold, cold air.

A small hand emerges from behind the coats.

This hand is about the same size as that of the boy who just left with his mother, but this hand is ash gray. And the coats to either side of it grow cold, nearly brittle.

The fingers stretch forward, as though the hand is climbing out of the coats. Like it is pulling itself free from their grasp, or perhaps even yanking itself out of the wall behind.

Or maybe it is *not* pulling away from something. The fingers angle, crooked like talons, and now they appear to be reaching *for* something.

100

Or someone.

MINUTES AND MUSIC

Alyssa ran into the hall, then slowed so fast Mal bumped into her from behind.

What am I running for?

At first gripped by a strange and sudden panic, an overpowering need to see the music box, to watch it and see its movement, now she was gripped by an equally sudden sense of danger. Mal seemed to feel it, too. He was pulling on her. Silent, but his body language was screaming, "Let's go. Let's go back!"

Only Ruthie, deep in one of the twenty or so hours a day that new babies sleep, was not disturbed. She just breathed deep in Alyssa's right arm. As though lulled by the music that plinked out of the music box, somewhere out of sight down the hall.

"Blake?" she called. And it wasn't "Blake, why did you turn on the music box and freak me out?" but rather "Blake, is that you?"

Stupid. Who else would it be?

But she called again. And this time made it explicit.

"Blake? That you honey?"

She realized suddenly that the clock was still ticking and tocking. And that the swing of the pendulum was in exact time with the music floating down the hall.

What were the chances of that?

Perhaps stranger still, Blake hadn't called back. Yet she was still heading down the hall. Her feet seemed like they belonged to someone else. Someone who possessed an overabundance of curiosity, but a dearth of common sense.

Maybe he's playing a joke.

Maybe he's so close to the music box he can't hear me.

Maybe —

(MAYBE YOU'RE GOING TO DIE)

Her feet stuttered, and with that she realized she had even been *stepping* in time with the music, her movements trapped by the plinking notes and the *tick-tock*. Prisoner to a strange countdown.

She stumbled the rest of the way into the entry of the old house.

She couldn't stop herself. Gravity held her — both the actual force, and a gravity of a different sort. A sort that demanded she know. That demanded she see Blake, standing in the entry. That demanded she know —

(*where the voice in my head came from*)

— what was going on.

Nothing. Nothing's going on. What could *be going —?*

The music shut off as she nearly fell into the entry space. Like her presence triggered some off switch she wasn't able to see.

There was only the clock. *Tick-tock, tick-tock, tick-tock.*

Nothing else.

No *one* else.

Alyssa began a slow circle, turning to look at the living room, the dining room. Hoping to see Blake in one or the other, grinning a stupid grin, ready to stab a finger at her and say, "Haha!" or something equally creative.

No one.

She faced the kitchen again....

CRASH!

She and Mal both jumped at the sudden noise, the slamming of wood on wood. Ruthie woke up and started wailing.

"Sorry! Sorry!" shouted Blake.

Alyssa spun around again.

Blake had opened the front door. Hanging onto a few last pieces of their luggage, including Ruthie's folded playpen.

"Door was stuck," he said. "Had to almost kick it open."

Mal went to help his father.

Alyssa looked back at the clock. *Tick-tock.*

At the music box.

Suddenly she wanted Mal out of here. Out of this room, this house.

"No," she said. She had to yell to be heard over Ruthie's scream. He turned to her and she slapped a quick smile over her confusion, her – what, fear? "I've got this, Mal. You go clean up your mess in the kitchen."

Mal ran off.

His footsteps kept time with the ticking of the clock.

HOLY PLACES

Mal ran back to the kitchen, and he was super-glad to do it, too.

He didn't like being alone. He hadn't liked being alone since he woke up to an avalanche of creepy-crawlies all over his room. Not even to go to the bathroom – he almost asked Mommy to come in with him the first time he peed after *that* happened. Then he realized he might have to do more than pee, and there went that idea. He was not about to have anyone – even his mommy – watch him doing *that*.

Still, even more than being alone, he disliked the idea of being out there with that clock and that music box thing.

How did it start playing?

For a terrible second Mal imagined one of the centipedes hitching a ride in his luggage, sneaking in the house, and turning on the music box with one of its two mijillionty-billion legs.

Nope. Daddy hadn't brought in the luggage yet.

Then how *had* it turned on?

And…

… and where was the apple?

He looked around the floor.

I dropped it right here.

At least, I thought I did.

No, I did. For suresies.

Didn't I?

The floor was tile, black and white checkers like an old fashioned ice cream shop. A green apple should have been easy to spot.

But he didn't see one. Not where he thought he dropped it, not near the fridge.

He turned to look under the coats.

Maybe it rolled off by the —

There were no shoes.

Hadn't there been shoes?

No, there must not have been any. Because there were none now, and Mommy had been with him, and Daddy had been out front. So unless Ruthie was a ninja baby who stole shoes, he must have imagined the shoes being there.

They were too old, anyway. They were pilgrim shoes, the kind with buckles and all made of leather. Too old even for this place. So he *must* have imagined them.

Like I imagined the apple, maybe?

No, Mommy saw it, too.

So he maybe imagined the shoes. Or just saw wrong – he'd been in a hurry, after all. But that didn't explain the apple.

He looked around again. Even got on his hands and knees, then on his tummy and looked around the floor from what he called his snake-view camera angle. He found stuff all the time that way. Mom laughed and said, "It's all about point of view!" whenever he did. Mal didn't understand that, but he laughed, too. Laughing with Mommy or Daddy was better than video games.

Snake-view didn't help this time. It was just tiles and chair legs and table legs and nothing else until the black under the oven, and that was too low for an apple to get underneath.

He stood up. Left the kitchen.

He didn't want to be there, either.

What if the bugs came in and took the apple?

Turning on a music box would sure work up an appetite.

He walked faster. Didn't look back.

Mommy and Daddy must have figured out whatever was up with the music box, because Daddy was heading down the hall toward the kitchen. Mal almost crashed into him.

"Hey, bud!" Daddy said. "Want to find your room?"

Mal nodded. Going upstairs meant going away from the entry and the kitchen. That sounded awesomely good right now.

They went upstairs. The stairs themselves were cool. Hard wood that felt solider than iron. No squeaks at all. Mal thought these stairs would probably be around when people had turned into dinosaurs and then turned extinct. He told Daddy that and Daddy laughed.

Mommy had already picked out a room for Ruthie and was setting up the playpen.

Mal picked a room beside Ruthie's. Daddy came in and put his bag on the bed.

"You good here?"

"What?"

"You need my help?" asked Daddy. "I should see if Mommy needs me."

"No, it's okay," said Mal. He still didn't want to be alone. But part of being grown up – part of being a *man* – was doing what needed doing, whether you wanted to or not.

Daddy kissed the top of his head. Then he hugged him and left.

The bedroom wasn't as cool as his was. Or as cool as his *used* to be. Before it was covered in centipedes.

He wondered if those bugs pooped. Even if the men from PEST IN PEACE killed all them, would he come back to find bug poo everywhere?

"Yuck," he said. Then he looked around to make sure no one heard him. Mommy and Daddy had enough to worry about without thinking he hated his new room.

Even though he kind of did.

It looked like a gramma room. Everything was flowers and tiny toys. Only the toys weren't the cool kind, with jet fighters and little guns. They were the kind Mommy called "nick-nacks." All glass and brittle and "Don't touch that, it'll break!"

Even the bed looked like a flower store had barfed on it. The blankets had so many daises and roses and other flowers printed on them he could almost smell them blooming.

But they looked thick and warm, so that was nice. And they looked good for hiding under in case monsters or killer bugs came, so that was nice too.

There was a big cross on the wall right across from the bed. It was made of wood, but was so shiny it almost looked like plastic. Mal could tell it was expensive. Even more so than the nick-nacks.

There weren't any crosses on the walls of his house. Mommy didn't like them, and staring at this one he could see why. He knew about Jesus, but he had never pictured him quite like the man on the cross. Body twisted in pain, mouth open like he was on the verge of screaming. Blood carved so perfect it seemed about to run right over the brown face.

Mal wanted to look away, but he couldn't.

He stared at the scream. At the man in pain.

And he felt like something was dropping from under him. Like the world had gotten a little less real.

A voice came into his head. He didn't know if it was from Jesus. He doubted it. Because he didn't think Jesus used words like the ones that came in his head.

Don't run from me, little bastard.

Little shit.

LITTLE ONES

The room that Alyssa chose for Ruthie was a craft or sewing room. Alyssa chose it because it was something that said "home." And home meant safety.

She wondered if she would feel at home when they went back to the house where they lived. If it was even possible to feel safe after seeing Blake's feet, all red and bloody; seeing him smash those insects to nothing.

Seeing the anger on his face.

It wasn't just a sense of violation. Violation was something outside that forced its way in. This was something that had been there, with them, *inside* them, all this time.

And she'd never seen the smallest trace of it. Never suspected.

So she picked a room for Ruthie that was like the one she remembered from her childhood. A room where her mother spent so many hours sewing torn pants and dresses, making Halloween costumes and outfits for school plays.

This room was much tidier than her mother's sewing room had been. Her mother's had been piles of cloth, loose spools of thread, two different sewing machines, several hampers with clean clothes that she was always in the process of folding – one of the never-ending chores that went along with family life.

This room was just a small table with a single sewing machine that looked like it had been pulled out of the box yesterday. Another table with perfectly piled cloths, a carousel-style desk organizer with various sewing notions and supplies. A single rolling chair that obviously served double-duty for both tables.

On the wall there was a frame. Too dark in the room to see what it held, exactly. That was another reason Alyssa chose this place to put up the playpen: it was dark.

Mal had been a terrible sleeper from day one. At times it seemed he was less baby than tiny government assassin, sent to kill her and Blake through systematic sleep deprivation.

Ruthie, so far, was the opposite: the biggest problem was getting her to wake up long enough to feed. At first that worried Alyssa, but a few talks with the on-call nurses at the hospital had reassured her.

More or less.

The one thing Ruthie needed to sleep, though, was a dark place. So when Alyssa saw the thick curtains in the sewing room, it was a no-brainer.

Alyssa lay the baby in the playpen. She draped a light blanket over her. Touched her head. Ruthie, like Mal had before her, enjoyed the hairline of a very old man. Wispy strands that clung in patches around her ears, to the back of her skull. Alyssa didn't understand how that could result in such an awesome level of cuteness, but it did. Sometimes she didn't just want to kiss her daughter. She wanted to bite her, to hug her so tightly she worried the baby's tiny bones would crack.

Violence and love. She wondered if they were tied together for everyone. The way sometimes after she and Blake made love she would find scratches on her back. The

111

way high school kids found hickeys – glorified bruises – on necks (and other places) after serious makeout sessions.

She turned to the frame on the wall. Curious. Also worried. What if it was some creepy thing? She wasn't worried about it being a picture of a pedophile or something beheading endangered pandas. But....

But you never knew.

It was an embroidered picture. Cross-stitching so intricate she could barely make out where one threaded "x" ended and the next took up. It was the image of a vaguely Santa-ish man praying, so detailed she could almost see the veins on his old hands, could almost hear his murmured prayers.

It was far from creepy. It was beautiful. A Saint, perhaps. Perhaps simply an image of righteousness.

Either way, it was an appropriate watchman for her Innocent.

She put the baby monitor on the table with the sewing machine. Plugged it in, fumbling as she always did for the outlet. She could deal with social media, with the newest updates to her computer operating systems.

The ability to successfully navigate the small prong and large prong on a plug into the appropriate outlet receptacles continued to elude her.

She finally managed to do it, and only winced ten dozen or so times as pain ran through the center of her body. Another ten dozen times as she straightened up.

She barely felt like throwing up at all. So she was definitely healing.

She left Ruthie's room. Walked a few paces and saw Mal in a room that looked like something decorated by a deranged grandmother with a flower fetish.

He was staring at an intricate cross on the wall. It gave her the heebies, and maybe half a case of the jeebies to boot.

"You okay?" she said.

Mal didn't respond for half a second. Not a long lag, but long enough that a different kind of feeling rippled through Alyssa's center. A feeling that something was off. Wrong.

Then Mal nodded. He didn't look away from the cross.

She almost went into the room.

Almost.

A sound arrested her movement before it began.

It was a dull thud, coming from a bit further down the hall. The sound of something solid hitting something solid. Not metal-on-metal. More like wood-on-wood, though that wasn't it, either.

She looked over, her body following the sound without conscious thought. She didn't feel bad about it, didn't feel bad about looking away from her son's sudden obsession with religious symbology. People are hardwired to look to the unknown, because sometimes that is the only thing that stops them from going mad. Even if knowing means only that you comprehend the manner of your demise, that is better to most people than the greater pains of ignorance. The infinite terror of our imagination allowed to ravage the dark halls of our mind.

Thud.

The sound repeated.

This time Alyssa pinpointed it. There was a small accent table next to the wall, about ten feet away. All dark wood and beautiful hardware.

The door to the front compartment had opened. Just a crack, but she worried suddenly that it would open further, that whatever was inside would spill out. That it would be fragile, of inestimable value.

And that it would break.

That's just what we need. Being on the hook for replacing the Holy Grail or whatever they have stashed in there.

She moved to the table and tried to push the door closed. Gingerly at first, then more firmly. The door wouldn't stay closed, and she could feel something behind it. Whatever had caused the thuds had wedged behind the door, forcing it partially open. Maybe something had fallen off a shelf inside the table, then fallen against the door.

Waiting to fall the rest of the way out and break.

Still, she kept pushing. Not wanting to open someone else's private things. Not wanting to intrude.

And, at last, giving up and intruding. But she looked up and down the length of the hall as she did so, as though worried that Blake or Mal or even Ruthie might come out and see her.

The door was barely open when a book fell out. She caught it, and it almost dragged her hands the rest of the way to the floor. Heavy. Wider than it was tall, and she could see that the individual pages were strangely thick, each one warped and yellowed.

The cover was blank. Just a black expanse of leather.

She opened the accent table's door the rest of the way. Nothing else was inside, just a short shelf (as she had expected).

She lifted the book to return it to its place.

Then stopped.

Another battle. Privacy locked with curiosity in a fight to the death.

There was no fooling herself this time. She couldn't rationalize what she wanted to do. It wasn't about saving someone's property, wasn't about saving herself and the family from possible liability.

She just wanted to see. To know.

Human beings are wired like that. The need to know.

She lifted the book. Put it on the shelf. Closed the door.

Then opened the door and took out the book and opened the cover.

Her hand went over her mouth. She turned the pages. She stifled a gasp that she knew would turn into a moan that she knew would become a scream.

She didn't stop turning the pages. People have to know.

The book was a photo album.

She had heard of pictures like these, but had never seen one. And she had certainly never seen – and never heard of – a grouping of them like this.

Page after page. Leaf after leaf.

They were memorial portraits. Old photos – she guessed they were from the late nineteenth century, maybe before – that featured the newly dead.

Some of the subjects lolled to the side. Others sat

strangely upright, braced by an unseen harness or perhaps nailed to wooden frames. Their faces had also been posed: rictus grins and staring eyes. Cheeks that, even in sepia tones that had darkened with passing years, Alyssa could tell had been rouged.

All of the pictures featured children.

They all sat or lay or reclined on a high-backed chair. Alyssa felt something under her fingers and realized she was tracing one of the photos. It was a little girl, maybe two or three, in a long lace dress. She lay to the side, propped on one of the chair's arms. Eyes closed and hands under her cheeks as though she were asleep.

But something about her position. About the angle her body was in. She was not asleep. She couldn't be.

Alyssa ran her fingers around the girl, following the outline of the chair. It was strange, and strangely distinctive. The legs were filigreed, intricately carved in reliefs that could be made out even in the pictures.

The legs ended suddenly as a black cloth took over. The cloth draped over the top of the chair in a strange, lumpy shape: disturbing in its own right.

Alyssa felt as though she was in a trance, and with that realization came the ability to pull herself out of it. She jerked back to herself, and her fingers jerked away from the photograph of the dead girl.

She slammed the book shut. Pushed it back toward the table.

And something fell out of the book.

It was an envelope. Just as old and yellow as the pages in the book. Unmarked, the flap unsealed and hanging loose.

She put the book down. Opened the envelope, nearly hypnotized.

Inside was a single sheet of paper. It felt strange under her fingers. Nothing like the paper she knew, so crisp and flat. This was parchment paper. Thicker, somehow managing to feel both tougher and more fragile. Yellow with age.

The paper had was folded around something. A square sheet of something that was made of something different than the parchment, though she had no idea what. Like the parchment, the square was age-yellowed, curling up slightly at the edges. It said "Matthew, Jr." in faded cursive scroll.

Alyssa flipped the square over. And knew as she did how stupid she had been to do so, but now unable to stop herself.

It was another picture. A boy. Long, blond hair and what she suspected would have been intensely blue eyes. Dirty pantaloons, and a vest and jacket that looked like they had been put through a shredder.

He was sitting on the cloth-covered chair.

His throat had been slit. Blood running freely over his white collar.

Alyssa cried out, then clapped a hand over her mouth. She looked at Mal's room, expecting him to come out, to look for her and ask what was wrong.

He didn't.

Alyssa looked down and realized she had dropped the envelope and parchment paper.

And, like the picture of the dead boy, the paper had writing on the back of it.

Not a name, though. This time it was just a single word, in bold letters.

RUN

BEDROOM GAMES

The bedroom was as beautiful as the rest of the house, and somehow that just managed to piss Blake off even more.

Part of his anger came from the situation. The insect invasion that couldn't have come at a worse time. The fact that they had to live with fear every minute of every day because of Ruthie – whether she ever manifested any problems or not. The last project he was working on –

(*and after that nothing after that what then nothing that's what*)

– when a year ago he was juggling two dozen.

And, he knew, part of it was just the fact that Alyssa had found this place.

He had never thought of himself as a chauvinist. And maybe he wasn't. He didn't know. He'd have to think about it. Regardless, all he *did* know was that he felt like he was failing at his basic responsibilities.

Provide money for the family: fail.

Keep them in a nice house: on the verge of failing.

Keep them fed: who knew. A couple more months like this and beans and Spam would be a luxury.

And now, when an emergency hit, he wasn't the one to save the day. Sure, he'd arranged for the exterminators. But if it had been up to him they'd be staying at a motel, smaller and less comfortable for a higher price.

Alyssa found this place.

119

He knew he should be happy. He knew he should be proud to be married to a smart, resourceful woman.

And he was. He truly was.

But he also hated himself more than a little. And hating himself meant he hated her a bit, too. Because you can't hate yourself without hating the rest of the world.

He tossed his and Alyssa's bags on the bed – king size, solid, beautiful like everything else in this damn place – and then unrolled some architectural plans he'd brought with him on the card table he had already set up. He doubted he'd get much work done here. But he had to try.

He had to try. Maybe this last job would lead to one more. One more, then another.

Stupid thing to hope for, but it was all he had.

The laptop went up next. The owners of the place had left a card next to the bed with the WiFi security code written on it, so he was tapped into the internet seconds after the laptop turned on.

Of course they had a faster connection than the one he was providing for Alyssa and the kids.

He sighed, then tried to think what Alyssa would say. "Cheer up. Count your blessings and enjoy what you have while you have it."

She was right. And that was one of the reasons – one of the *many, infinite* reasons – why he loved her.

He smiled a bit.

Alyssa came in. He turned the smile up, directed it at her.

And the smile fell off his face when he saw the look on hers. She looked like she had just sat in on a war crimes tribunal. Or, worse, like Mal had finally realized that he wasn't the greatest child in the history of the world and had actually done something wrong.

"What is it?" he said.

Alyssa dropped something on the bed. She wiped her hands when it fell on the sheets, like what she held was covered in slime.

It was a book. Old-looking, leather cover and binding. Some kind of letter or envelope stuck out from between its pages.

Alyssa didn't speak. She opened her mouth, then closed it. Repeated the motion a few times. Blake moved toward her, his arms outstretched.

She jerked her head back and forth in a quick "no." Pointed at the book.

He felt curiosity and concern mix, a strange brew he couldn't remember experiencing at these levels before.

He opened the book. Turned a page. Then another. Not because he wanted to see, but because he couldn't believe it.

Children. *Dead* children.

He slammed the book shut. The sound was a thunderclap in the confines of the room. He felt it in his bones.

Or maybe that was just revulsion and fear. A new mix that had replaced the curiosity and concern.

"Has Mal seen –?" he began.

"No way," Alyssa said, so vehemently she almost shouted.

Blake stared at the thing on the bed. It lay there like

a cocoon, bearing an unimaginable evil waiting to be born. Only this evil could be born and reborn, over and over and over, every time anyone cracked open the cover. "We should hide this from Mal," he finally said.

"We should *burn* it."

He looked at it again. Low, dark.

Evil.

He nodded. Picked up the book. It felt slick and slimy under his palms, and he understood now why Alyssa had wiped her hands after dropping it on the bed.

"What are you doing?" she asked.

He put the book in his suitcase, rearranging his clothing so the book lay at the bottom. "I'm hiding it. I'll get rid of it as soon as I can."

Alyssa looked suddenly uneasy. She stared at the mound of clothing that hid the book. "Maybe we shouldn't."

"What the hell –?"

"It belongs to the house."

And, just like that, Blake felt like he could do something for the family again. Felt like he wasn't just failing and failing. He could provide something needed, in this moment.

He could provide a decision, and reassurance that it was *right*.

"I don't care who it belongs to," he said. "It's disgusting. It's *wrong*." He held out his arms again, and this time Alyssa didn't refuse his embrace. "They probably won't even notice it's gone, and if they do we'll deal with it."

His wife looked at him. Maybe he imagined it, but he thought he saw something there that he hadn't seen in a while. He thought he saw her admiring him. Appreciating him.

Needing him.

"Thank you," she said.

He winked. "Baby down?"

She nodded. Looked around. "Do you think she'd be better off in here?"

And Blake decided again. He reassured again. He felt like a man again. "She's fine where she is. I mean if you really disagree, let's talk about it. But I think we're on the verge of collapse as it is. We need our space and our sleep."

He paused. Then grinned. The grin pulled his face tight, and it wasn't a stretched-thin kind of tightness. It was the pleasant pull of a *good* moment. Of happiness and confidence.

"Or at least," he said, "we need our sleep *or* a lack of interruptions if we decide not to sleep."

Alyssa laughed. A tired laugh, but she sounded happy, too. Happy like she hadn't really sounded since they got the news about Ruthie. And Blake wondered how much of that had been his fault. How much of her worry was the fault of his fears, his bitching and moaning, his terror that he too freely shared.

No more. I'll do better.

"Quite the Don Juan," Alyssa said.

"What can I say? Giant bugs eating me from the ground up always make me horny."

She kissed him. Softly. Not passionately. Lovingly.

123

That was enough.

"It hasn't been long enough," she said. "Since Ruthie came."

Blake hugged her. Firmly, but without crushing her. "Babe, it's our second kid. I know the drill. I'll joke, but I'm not pressing. You just let me know when you're ready." Then he sighed melodramatically. "And if I simply explode from pent-up sexual frustration before then... well, you know where the life insurance policy is."

Alyssa giggled. "So romantic."

She kissed him. And this time it was more than simple softness. Heat crept in between them.

Then a bucket of water: a loud knock at the front door. Followed almost instantly by another, and then the doorbell ringing.

Alyssa made a sound that was a weird composite of moan and laugh. Blake knew exactly what she was feeling. He groaned, settling for a simpler version of the noise because he wasn't sure his throat could manage what hers was doing.

"Sorry," he said. "The office said they might courier over some papers." He headed for the door, then said. "At least it wasn't the kids."

Alyssa laughed again. He loved that sound.

He tossed out one last sally. "I think we might be cursed, honey."

And his wife stopped laughing. Stopped so fast he looked back to make sure she hadn't fallen down dead right there in the bedroom.

THIRD STEPS

Mal saw something moving outside his window and his whole body got tight, like it was deciding whether to yank itself into a ball and roll away or jump right out of the universe. Because his room – his borrowed room – was on the second floor. What would he see moving? Other than ghosts, or vampires, or maybe centipedes that were flapping their little legs so fast they had learned to fly?

It wasn't any of those things.

Baby. Stupid baby. How are you going to be an example to Ruthie? How are you going to protect her if you wet your pants at everything?

It was no evil monster. It wasn't even anything outside his window. Not *right* outside his window, anyhow.

He had seen the flash of a bike out of the corner of his eye. Driving up and skidding to a stop at the curb in front of the house. Maybe he'd seen the rider running up to the porch, too. He wasn't sure. If he had, he couldn't see the rider now.

He looked at the bike. He had seen the type before, always belonging to guys who brought stuff to his daddy. The bike looked cheap, just a bare frame that seemed like it had been made out of a wire hangar. But Mommy and Daddy had both told him at different times that these bikes weren't just fast.

These bikes *flew*.

They had no brakes. A lot of them didn't even have

pedals. The riders took off everything that didn't move them forward, and all that was left was a bike that looked junky but could outrun the family car.

A knock on the front door startled him. Only for a second.

Get over *it, Mal. Be a man.*

He kept staring at the bike. Wondering what it would be like to ride that fast. To move so quickly that he got hired to deliver important papers.

It'd be cool.

Another knock, and this time he didn't jump at all. Well, barely. Then the doorbell rang.

He was totally cool as ice.

Feet pounded by in the hall. He heard Daddy yell, "Coming, coming!"

A second later, there were more thuds, also running.

He figured it must be Mommy. She didn't yell.

A second later, he heard a third set of thuds. *Thud-THUD. Thud-THUD.*

The sound of someone limping.

Mommy.

The little hairs all over his body stood up so high and hard he felt like they might pull right off. Just rip away, pull his skin with them, and leave him nothing but bones and blood and inside gunk.

Daddy.

Mommy.

And who had run by between them?

SPECIAL DELIVERIES

Blake took the treads two at a time. "Coming, coming!" he said, and said it again every third step he took. "Coming, coming!" As though it was a counter-password that would be required to receive whatever the courier might have for him.

It wasn't that. Just a simple case of sexual frustration. He had meant what he said to Alyssa: he was content to wait. That was fine.

But the kissing had been nice. More than nice. And to have someone show up at the perfect time to buzz-kill a rare moment of "nice"... that was frustrating. He felt like he had to do something about it. So he could either –

(*beat the kids beat the wife kill them all*)

– start screaming or laughing hysterically or both, or he could find some more appropriate way to vent. Apparently his vent was to say "Coming, coming," over and over and over.

And just as he hopped off the stairs he realized how else that word could be taken. And he honestly couldn't tell if it was simple coincidence or the kind of thing that would make Freud giggle in his grave.

"Almost there!" he shouted. Because it was a different phrase. And then he realized that wasn't much better, so he just shut up.

He opened the door.

He had expected a courier, and that was what he got. The office often used them rather than rely on the post office, especially if they had to send documents that needed to be somewhere in under a day, or if they were particularly fragile. And even though this was his last job, even though the business was hemorrhaging money every day, Blake was giving everything he had to this last job. Because maybe if he did, something would come of it.

That was the hope.

Hope. Stupid hope.

Blake looked the courier up and down. He thought he knew most of the folks at Runners, Inc., the service his office used. But this guy was unknown to him.

No, not a guy. He was a kid. The *R.I.* cap was pulled down low over his forehead, but not far enough to completely cover the acne on his face. Nor did it do much to restrain the nimbus of red hair that seemed caught in a perpetual nova around the edge of the hat.

The kid, though he couldn't have been older than nineteen, already had a wealth of faded tattoos. That wasn't unusual for couriers, who tended to be the type of people who reveled in being "edgy." Which was a word that, as far as Blake could tell, meant "working hard at being unemployable after thirty-five."

Unlike every other courier he'd ever seen, though, this kid's tattoos weren't Maori tats or skulls or barbed wire, angels or devils or moons or stars.

His were hearts. Teddy bears. A few My Little Ponies. And they all had the word "Mom" written somewhere on them. "Moms Rule," "Love Ya Momma," "Mom Be Three" (which Blake didn't understand), and "Moms are TOTES Awesome."

It was enough that he was glad the kid had his gaze

glued to an electronic tablet. If it hadn't been he would have seen Blake gaping at him – openly and rudely.

The kid yanked a shipping tube from his pack. "I've got a parcel for Blake Douglas?" he said, the last words lilting up into a question. His voice was as young and unfinished as the rest of him. High, breaking slightly in the middle of the sentence.

"That's me."

The kid handed over the tube, still not looking up. He pulled a stylus off his belt, where it hung from a Velcro attachment. Used it to check something off on his tablet. "All right," he said. "Many thanks."

"Want a water or anything before you go?" said Blake.

"Sure," said the kid. He shoved his tablet in his pack. "That'd be...." He finally actually looked up, his body releasing him from the confines of automatic movement.

His acne was red, almost blazing. And more so as the rest of his face seemed to drain of all its color.

"No," he said. "No, thanks." He was looking past Blake.

"Sure?" said Blake. He had an urge to look behind him, like in a monster movie where the baddie is about to get the jump on the hero. But he was scared to look away from the kid – he looked like he was going to pass out. "You look like you could use –"

"No!" the kid practically shouted. Then he turned and walked away without another word. He broke into a run halfway to the bike that waited at the curb.

Blake finally turned, his nape prickling and sweat dripping down the small of his back. What if there *was* something behind him?

There wasn't. Just the hall, the open doorway to the kitchen.

And Alyssa, standing on the stairs, leaning on the banister. "What was *that* about?" she said.

Blake turned back. Looked out the door.

The kid was still there. Sitting on his bike, staring at him.

"Beats me."

Blake realized the kid wasn't looking at him. The angle of his face was wrong. No, he was looking at something else.

At the house.

Again, the base of Blake's skull tickled. Again, he turned.

Again, other than Alyssa there was nothing. He was alone with his wife.

He turned back.

The courier was gone.

Blake closed the door.

OUTRUNNING THE DEAD

"Ralph? You're name is *Ralph*? That ain't the name of a messenger. A posenger, maybe. Maybe even a fakenger. But not, never, no-how, a *messenger*."

That was the beginning and end of the interview questions Ralph Hickey got from Ali when he walked into Runners, Inc., and asked for a job.

He knew there was no way in Hell he was getting a job – or even a second interview question. Not with his red hair, his weird tattoos, his lack of body piercings or general toughness-vibe that seemed to be required for all bike messengers.

But he needed the job.

More important, he *wanted* it.

So when Ali stood and told Ralph to get out of his office – adding a flurry of inaccurate racial slurs and three instructions that were so biologically impossible that Ralph decided he really liked this guy – he whipped around, dodged under Ali's stringy arms, and stole his would-be boss's lunch.

The lunch itself was nothing big. A tuna sandwich with a small bag of Fritos. But it sat in a genuine vintage Buck Rogers lunch box, with Gil Gerard at his manliest and Erin Gray looking super-hot even with her head half-covered by the dorky space helmet.

Ali saw the lunchbox disappearing through his office door. He roared.

Everyone   onsite   at   Runners,   Inc.,   came

(appropriately) running.

And the chase was on.

Half an hour later, Ralph called Ali from a public phone at the train station across the city. Reports from the other couriers were already coming in: they had failed to keep up with the kid, the nobody. Not *lost* him. He hadn't turned, hadn't twisted. He'd just ridden hard and fast, and no one could keep pace.

Ali was apoplectic. He demanded the return of his lunchbox. He demanded a full apology. He demanded that Ralph start work at R.I. immediately.

He also demanded that Ralph never tell any of the other messengers his name. "You're just The Runner from now on, kid," said Ali.

That lasted until Ralph's first run, when he walked into R.I. and someone started screaming that there was "hot work all over the desk" – meaning a red-hot item that needed to be delivered yesterday.

He ran to the desk, scooped the package into his bag, and said, "Tell 'em to rest easy. Ralph Hickey is on the job."

Ali nearly had an embolism, an aneurysm, and terminal diarrhea all at once.

But Ralph got the package where it needed to go. And no one questioned that he got it there faster than anyone else could have.

Ralph was Ralph after that. He had a place at R.I. A job that he loved. A boss who tolerated him.

More than he'd ever enjoyed before.

Enough.

And the best part: the more he rode, the faster he drove, the harder he pushed, the fewer dead he saw.

Even driving in cars, he could never be sure of looking over and seeing an empty seat. The time he saw a guy in the back seat, calmly looking out the side window and fingering the hatchet buried in his throat, that was the last time Ralph ever drove a car.

The hatchet had gone in so deep that the dead guy's head hung by a string. It wobbled around constantly, making the world's most horrific bobblehead. And it happened on his first – and only – date with Elizabeth Deetz. She got out pretty quick at the first red light after he screamed.

He'd only worked on getting that damn date for all of high school. But it only took one scream to scare her away.

The dead guy stayed in the car, which was not very classy, in Ralph's opinion.

The dead rarely bothered him much. Even the occasional unwanted passengers generally didn't do much… just rode along. One of them told him they were simply "catching a ride." Ralphie didn't know if that meant they wanted to actually *get* somewhere, or if they were just bored and wanted to do something. He thought it was the second one. Because he knew that the dead didn't need cars to get around.

But there was no room for a ghost to go all Douglas Adams on the back of a bicycle. No room for hitchhikers, no room for tagalongs, no room for no one but Ralph Hickey, deliverer extraordinaire.

The dead were just occasional blurs as he rode.

A body lying in the road next to a red smear that trailed into a nothing that was not quite normal, and whom none of the passers-by seemed to notice.

A woman standing stark naked in the middle of the sidewalk, firing a shotgun at random pedestrians. None of them falling.

A man in a nice suit who fell down in a pile of French fries, lay there choking, then went still. Then got up and did it again like he was rehearsing a performance.

On and on. But just blurs as long as Ralph pedaled his hardest.

That was why he was so fast. Because though most of the dead didn't bother him, and some were actually friendly, a few of them surprised him – i.e., The Headless Cockblocker.

And a few were... *bad*.

Ralph didn't understand many of the rules. If there *were* any. But he knew that some of the things he glimpsed over the years had nothing but ill will for the people and the world around them. He didn't want to talk to them, didn't want them "catching a ride," didn't even want to *see* them.

He especially didn't want to see a particular one of them. One he had left unfortunately buried under a million tons of water, and whom he hoped would never come to him.

But he feared she would. Feared it every day.

So he rode. Rode hard, rode fast, rode as much as he could.

He only stopped for deliveries. To check off the finished job on his tablet so HQ would know it was done.

And he kept his head down when he was doing it.

But he let his guard down delivering the tube to the Douglas guy. He sounded so nice, and it was a hot day, and Ralph had forgotten his water bottle back at HQ.

He looked up.

A man, standing in front of him. Holding the package.

A woman, standing on the stairs. She looked crappy. Pretty, in a wholesome way, but crappy nonetheless. Like she'd been through a meat grinder.

Neither of them saw the third person in the house.

Ralph had to keep from screaming. He liked his job at R.I., and acting like a kook would get you fired.

But he hauled ass outta there.

Got to his bike. Ready to ride.

Wondering why he was so scared. He'd seen the dead his whole life. Ever since his mom died. He had his suspicions about that. But just suspicions.

One thing that wasn't a suspicion: the dead never looked at him. They talked to him occasionally, but always while looking away. Never a direct stare. Never even a glance in his direction. Like *they* were the scared ones. Like *he* was the monster under *their* beds.

The one in this house, though…. That was why he ran.

And when he got outside, that was when he made the next mistake.

He looked up again.

He looked at the second floor this time.

There was a boy at the second floor. Ralph almost

peed himself, thinking it might be *him*... the one he had seen.

But no. It was just a normal kid. Cute one. Crazed hair, the kind of smile that made you think of Calvin and Hobbes cartoons.

The kid waved.

Ralph waved back.

Then froze.

Because behind the boy... *he* appeared.

The other boy.

The dead boy.

The boy who had shown up behind the man, just below the woman where she stood on the stairs.

He was dressed all Olde Tyme. Gray shoes. A tweed-ish outfit that was shredded and bloody. White face.

A slit throat.

And now as before, the dead boy stared right at Ralph.

No expression. Just staring.

Ralph looked away. Fast.

He got on his bike. Road away, wobbling.

"I don't want to see. I don't want to see."

Ralph Hickey rode. Fast. Faster. Fastest.

He tried not to look up.

He tried not to think of what the dead boy wanted with this family. With little "Calvin."

He failed at both.

He saw the dead all the way back to HQ. None of them looked at him. Not like the dead boy had.

But they knew he was here. Knew he was near.

And, he felt, they all hated him.

He rode even faster. And wondered if he would outrun them, or if his heart would burst and he would find himself *among* them.

SCREAMS AND DARK

Mommy said once that there was good and bad hiding in everything. She said that right after one of Mal's Transformers pinched the heck out of his thumb while he was turning it from robot to dinosaur. He guessed that meant that good and bad were all mixed up together.

That was for sure the way it was at bedtime.

Mommy always put him to bed. Always. Sometimes Daddy was there, standing in the doorway with arms folded and looking at him like Mal was the best thing – even better than Transformers. But even when he was there, he let Mommy do the actual work of tucking him in.

Mal loved that feeling. Her hands shoving deep under him, pushing the blankets down until he was a wiggle-worm made of blankets and little kid.

Then she would sing a song. Then she would kiss him.

Tonight she had already tucked him in. The blankets were extra-tight. So tight he could barely move. Usually that was the best feeling *ever*. But this time he knew that he would wriggle out of the covers as soon as Mommy left. It felt like he was in a soft prison. He couldn't move, and he felt that was a bad idea.

Gotta be able to move.

To run.

Those thoughts scared him. He told his brain to shut up. It didn't work.

Gotta be ready to run.

To run.

Run.

Run run run....

Mommy didn't sing the song. She seemed like she was somewhere else. Maybe she was worried about Ruthie. She was worried about that a lot. Mal understood. He was worried about her, too. She was his sister, and he had to protect her. That meant he worried, too.

And if that meant that he didn't get his song, that was fine. At least once in a while.

Mommy bent down and kissed him. The light from the window fell all over her face. It was bright outside, with so many streetlights that normally he would have worried about being able to sleep. Here, in a new place –

(*in* this *place*)

– he knew he would leave the shade up. That the lights were the only thing that made it so he could possibly get to sleep without having Mommy sit in the room with him all night.

She kissed him again. Her lips were cool and just the right amount of wet. Some people didn't know how to kiss and it either felt like sandpaper or a snail crawling on your face. Mommy did it perfect every time.

"You've been great," she said. A whisper, just for him. "Thanks for all your help today."

He smiled and whispered back, "You've been good, too."

She smiled, a smile as quiet and secret as her whisper had been. She walked to the doorway of the bedroom. Her hand went to the door. "Open?" she said.

Mal nodded.

Mommy left.

He waited until he heard her dress go *swish swish swish* down the hall. Then the door of the bedroom she and Daddy were using closed.

He wiggled out of the covers. Not all the way. He just got himself un-trapped. He pushed one leg out from under the blankets, too, because it felt really hot all of a sudden.

He pushed out the leg that was close to the wall. If he had flipped the covers off the other one, that would mean his ankle would have been only about a foot away from the dark place under the bed. And Mal was brave, but he wasn't a coo-coo bird.

He lay there for a second. Then he flipped around completely so he could see the cross on the wall.

Jesus was still screaming. But Mal wanted to see the image. It wasn't happy, but it helped him feel better. Like there was still a normal world, where Mrs. De Marco taught school and there weren't giant bugs under beds.

He felt better. The only problem now was that the open door let in the sound of that big clock downstairs. *Tick-tock, tick-tock.*

So loud.

His heart started beating in time.

Tick-

(lub-)

-tock,

(-dub,)

tick-

(lub-)

-tock.

(-dub.)

His eyes kept closing, too. He pulled them open each time. Didn't want to sleep. Well… he *did*. But every time he closed his eyes, he worried about what might crawl out from under the bed.

Just check, dopey.

No way. You check.

His thoughts were getting stupid. Getting tired.

Tick-

(lub-)

-tock.

(-dub.)

And then he realized that the clock sound was gone.

He blinked, his eyes fluttering open and closed like moth wings banging against a window.

What was going on?

Did I fall asleep?

He looked over. Realized why the clock was quiet.

The door was shut.

Did Mommy close it? Did I fall asleep and she closed it?

No. No way. There was no way Mommy would have done something like that. When she left the door open, it stayed open.

He turned again, looking for comfort.

Jesus was still screaming. Only now he was screaming at the floor. The cross had swung upside-down.

A cold feeling ran up and down Mal's back. A claw dipped in ice tickled him, then the tickles turned to stabs as he heard noise. Not the clock. Not the creepy *tick-tock*. But something that made him *wish* for it.

It was a scraping. A scratching.

He looked around. Looking for the sound. For where it came from.

(*Get out.*)

He didn't know if the thought was his or not. It sounded like something he should be saying, but at the same time... it wasn't his voice.

The scratch/scrape got louder.

It was coming from below his bed.

And now Mal *was* thinking it. For sure it was his mind thinking it: Get out, he thought. Get out, Mal, get *OUT*.

But he couldn't. Because if he jumped off the bed... that meant he could be grabbed by whatever was under it.

So he had to see. Had to find out if he should leave, or even could leave.

He leaned over. His fists turned into tight balls with hunks of blanket at the center of each one. He felt like a mountain climber looking over the side of a volcano.

Farther.

Farther....

The scratching got louder.

The dark below his bed was blacker than anything he'd ever seen.

He thought about pulling himself up. And didn't know if he *could*. His body was already halfway over the edge. His fists barely holding him up.

He learned about gravity in school, and thought it was a cool idea. But right now he hated it. Because he felt it pulling/dragging/*yanking* him down.

He looked deeper under the bed.

The sound turned into a chitter. Suddenly so, so familiar.

The sound of legs, of mouths clicking.

He leaned farther. Nothing else *to* do.

The chitters fell together, like snowflakes packing into one big ball.

Not scratching....

(And he started to slide now. Holding the blanket, holding for life.)

Not whispers....

(And he was fully falling. Hands scrambling. Panicking. Failing. Couldn't stop. Gravity had him; wouldn't let him go.)

One whisper. One voice....

"Help me help me help me help me help me...."

Mal fell. He had time for the shortest scream in the history of everything, then his head thudded on the floor, then his chest and legs followed.

His hand fell into the darkest place. The place under the bed.

The whispers stopped.

Mal froze. Just couldn't move. Not even if you'd promised him every Transformer ever made and unlimited cartoons forever and no school.

His hand stayed in the black.

Then he got his strength. A little.

He started to pull his hand back.

Something grabbed it.

And something flew out of the blackness. Something gray, something horrible, something that *wanted him*.

It took hold, it pulled Mal into the dark.

Its mouth opened wide....

Mal scrambled back....

His head hit the wall....

Wall?

He looked around.

He had slammed into the headboard.

Which meant....

I'm in bed?

Light was everywhere. Sounds of morning: birds outside; the thumping of people moving in the house; the tinny, tiny sound of pans as Mommy or Daddy got breakfast together downstairs.

His eyes fluttered like moth wings.

He looked at Jesus. He was still screaming, but the scream was to Heaven again. Not to the floor, or whatever was *below* the floor.

Mal sighed.

Looked at the door.

It was closed.

Mal shuddered.

He stayed on the bed a long time. Wondering if it would be just kind of dim underneath...

… or fully and completely *dark*.

SILENT LAUGHTER

The house still stands. Alone, quiet.

Alive.

The fact that there are plastic strips, clipped together to form a colorful circus tent over its form, does not change the sense that there is something *important* in this place.

And that is good. It is right. It is as it should be.

Things are in motion.

All this time. All this waiting. Gathering strength, bit by bit, year by year.

Waiting to begin again. As begun they have. And they will not stop.

Outside this place, three men speak. One is called Tommy. He has come to kill the things inside the house.

They cannot be killed. You cannot kill something like this.

And even if you could, he has set his sights on the wrong things. The wrong monsters. He is looking for things that slither, that crawl, that bite.

There are things far worse that hide in dark places of houses, hearts, and minds.

Two other men stand with him. One is dark and old, one is light and young. Two opposites, in age and countenance, if to represent the better and worse sides of Tommy's nature, though of course that is nonsense. As the house – the things in and of the house – knows, there is no better, no worse. There is only the weak, the strong. The ugly, the beautiful. The possessor, and the possessed.

Tommy says, Nothing came out?

The dark man says, *Nada*. Turned on the gas yesterday, left the stuff under the fans, everything like normal. Came back this morning and the gas was off, there was no smell from the warning agents. Like everything either stopped working –

Or just up and disappeared, says the light man.

The dark man looks at the light man like he is disgusted. Like he wishes the light man would not speak foolishness. Or wishes he would go away. Or just die.

The house, the things inside, almost laugh.

What do we do, boss? says the dark man.

Tommy thinks. Then he says, We start everything up again.

The other men, light and dark, agree in their expressions: they hoped for a different answer.

The light man says, Boss, I don't want to sound like an idiot, but –

And now it is the dark man's turn to interrupt: Shut up, kid!

Tommy looks at the light man. What, Troy? he says. You want to tell me the place is haunted? You think ghosts messed with the equipment?

The house shifts slightly on its foundation. A quarter of a quarter of a quarter of an inch. So minute a change that the naked human eye cannot see. But the human soul can sense a *not rightness*. A shift in the way things should be.

This makes the things inside happy. To send the men without its walls into circles of fear. Madness.

Tommy looks at the house. Even tented, he suddenly knows something *is* wrong. Call the rest of the guys, he says.

What? says the dark man. He is surprised at this turn. But also happy.

The rest of the team, says Tommy. Call 'em in. Reset everything. But everyone works in pairs. Everyone, at *all* times. No one goes anywhere alone. Someone takes a piss, he's got a buddy to hold his hand.

Tommy turns to go to the truck in which he arrived. But he freezes.

The house knows what he sees.

The covering over the house is not a single tent. It is sheets of plastic, held together by powerful metal clips.

Some of the clips have come undone and fallen to the ground.

They are the ones nearest the front door. Enough that a long slit has opened. Long enough and large enough to let someone in. Or out.

It is the spot directly in front of the front door.

And the plastic there flaps as if in a breeze. The air around the house is utterly still, but here at the front of the house, something unseen moves.

Tommy takes a step back.

Pairs, he says. Everyone, at all times. I don't want anyone going near this place alone.

The house – now part house, part things within, and part the mixing of both that has occurred over the long years – laughs. The plastic billows again.

And this time when Tommy steps back, so do both

the light and dark men. Fear runs between them like electrical currents. The house reaches out and tastes their terror. Laps it up. It is delicious. It is good.

And there will be more.

SAD GOODBYES

Alyssa loved that Blake could often work from home. It was nice having him around, seeing him in his office, or even in their bedroom or the living room. He sat there making notes on architectural drawings, on notepads, sometimes reading books full of stuff that bored her to bits but that he seemed to find fascinating. He always looked tremendously studious and cute and it was usually all she could do not to jump him.

But she also loved that he worked "offsite" – at his office. She liked that she had her own space that way – time to do work around the house, pay bills, things that she thought of as "her" workday. When Blake was home, he tended to take five from time to time, and when he did he would come over and chat, or offer to take her out to lunch, or some other nice thing that she always enjoyed – but which inevitably threw off her daily schedule.

The best thing about Blake going to work, though, was that she got to see both of her boys out of the house. Not in the sense of kicking them out; she just loved seeing them walk out together, Blake holding whatever work he had brought home with him, Mal swinging his backback around with one hand and holding onto his sack lunch with the other. Blake often rested his hand on the back of Mal's neck, and it was in those moments that Alyssa most felt like she had a family.

It was in those moments that she was, perhaps, the very happiest.

There were dates with Blake, the times they spent together making love or just chatting over a beer with some chips and salsa. There were days where she and Mal went out for "special time" – little jaunts to McDonald's for an ice cream cone or a milkshake.

But watching her boys together. Their love, their fun. They were hers, she was theirs.

That was family. That was happiness.

She hoped that would bring some normalcy back to the day. That her favorite sight would bring some sense of hope to things, even in the midst of financial troubles, a new baby they had to be on constant watch around, and a house that had won a starring role in *Bug Invasion From Hell Part II: This Time It's Personal*.

But even this thing, this favorite thing, was tainted by all that was going on around them.

"You sure you don't mind dropping him off?" she said to Blake as he walked out the door. It was what she always said.

"Nah," he said. And that was what *he* always said. "I should at least stop by the office to make sure Marty hasn't blown anything up at the jobsite."

"You always say that. But Marty almost never blows up a jobsite."

Blake laughed. "He actually might this time. The contractor's doing a demo and he's going to blow up some footings. Marty's a bit too excited to work around the explosives."

Blake walked to the car, papers and drawings clasped in hands and rolled under arms.

Mal's turn. He was waiting behind his father, and

now he hugged and kissed Alyssa. "Bye, Mal," she said. "Be good. Learn a lot."

Mal nodded, but didn't say anything. He had been withdrawn to the point of surliness all morning. Monosyllabic answers that finally drew out a rebuke from Blake for being rude. And after that: he kept on being nearly silent, nearly unresponsive. If he hadn't kissed her and, more importantly, Ruthie on the way out, Alyssa probably would have kept Mal home from school just on general principles.

He didn't swing his lunch. Didn't swing his bag around. Just marched to the car and opened the door.

Then he rushed back to her. This time the lunch and backpack both swung, but not in fun and games. He just didn't seem to notice them, didn't seem to care enough to keep them stable.

He hugged her again. Paused, still in her arms, looking up at her.

"Yeah?" she said.

"Be careful," he whispered.

Then he ran to the car. It pulled away and both her boys were gone.

She was alone.

The strangeness of the morning, the compounded oddness of the goodbye, stole the happiness she usually felt watching the two men in her life walk away together. Now there was only a sense of *offness*. A sense that all was not right. Everything was strange. Everyone was acting weird.

The receiver to the baby monitor was clipped to her belt. She had set the volume low when saying goodbye to

Mal and Blake, but now she turned it up higher. She heard only the low staticky *hissssssss* that said Ruthie was still asleep.

That and the clock. *Tick-tock, tick-tock.*

She had absolutely never heard – or heard of – a clock that ticked this loud. How could the owners of this place have slept? She had turned and twisted all night long, the sound of the pendulum like rocks trapped in her skull. She didn't want to close the bedroom door, either. Not with Ruthie in constant danger of an attack. Nothing major had happened since the hospital – thank God for that – but she still couldn't bring herself to close her door. Ruthie's, yes, or else the clock would have kept the baby up all night, too. But not hers.

Blake slept soundly. That surprised her. He was usually a pretty light sleeper. But he sawed his way through a forest's worth of logs, interrupted only by a few farts worthy of an entire logging camp of lumberjacks.

Tick-tock.

No wonder they only charge forty bucks a night. It's like living in a sledgehammer testing facility.

She sighed. Decided to get the dishes done before Ruthie woke and doing that particular chore became more difficult.

She moved down the hall.

Plik.

Alyssa froze.

The sound had come and gone quickly, not nearly as loudly as the overpowering sound of the clock. But it was instantly recognizable.

The music box. A single metallic note as the drum turned enough for a tooth of the comb to click over one of the pins.

She spun around, nearly at the same moment the note sounded.

The music box was mute. No one was near it.

She looked at the baby monitor again. The motion was automatic. Whether logical or not, a good mother's first concern will always be whether or not her baby is safe.

Hisssssss. Nothing. The sound was low and measured. The lights that were a visual cue if the baby was making noise were dim as well.

Alyssa reversed course anyway. She passed the music box. Her whole body grew so tense she worried she might seize up and be unable to move.

She passed it. Passed the clock, *tick-tock*.

Upstairs. Toward Ruthie's room. Whether logical or not, a good mother's first concern will always be whether or not her baby is safe.

Hisssssssss....

HANDS ON THE WHEEL

"You okay, bud?"

The drive to Mal's school was longer than usual. Long enough that it was impossible for Blake not to notice that his kid was acting strange. Usually it was tough to get Mal to stop talking: Blake could recite the contents of entire seasons of *Justice League*, he knew the particulars of every character in the *Diary of a Wimpy Kid* series. Even if he hadn't been listening, Mal talked about things like that so much on the way to school that Blake would have memorized them by simple osmosis.

Now, Mal was silent.

Blake glanced at his son. "What's up"

Still no answer. And Blake supposed that wasn't much of a surprise.

Giant bugs attacking him at night. A new sister with a disease that makes her much more important than even your average new sister. And he's gotta be picking up on everything else that's going on, too.

"You wanna talk about it?"

Mal finally turned to look at him. Blake felt a surge of relief that surprised him. Like the very fact that his son was going to talk things out meant that they would be fixed in the end. Or maybe like the talk meant that *Blake* would end up fixed in the end.

Mal stared at him. Stared and stared and stared.

Then turned back to look out the side window.

Sudden anger rushed through Blake. He felt like –

(*beating crushing KILLING*)

– yelling at Mal. But he tamped down the feeling. Pushed it deep down, to join the writhing mass of all the other times he hadn't yelled, hadn't screamed, hadn't –

(*slapped or punched*)

– hollered at his kid. Sure, he'd yelled occasionally, and he always felt terrible about that. Worse than most parents, he suspected. But in his saner moments, the moments when he was judging himself as Blake Douglas, architect, father, husband, business owner, member of the community, and not as Hal Douglas, alcoholic, drug addict, beater of wife and child... in those moments Blake knew he yelled no more than most parents, and less than a great many.

He loved his boy. His little girl. Adored his wife.

So why... why did he suddenly feel so angry?

His hands tightened on the wheel. He made a right turn and the cheap plastic circle actually *bent* under his hands.

"Talk to me, kid," he said. His teeth were clamped together.

Mal didn't speak.

"Bud, please don't run from me."

And now Blake froze.

Don't you run from me, you little bastard! Little shit!

The words ran through his head, over and over and over. And he couldn't be sure if they belonged to Hal, or to himself.

The question locked him up. Chained him in a cage where he couldn't be sure if he was alone, or with his father, or if being alone and with his father was the same thing.

Frozen. Unable to move.

The car ahead of him – a little red import – slowed down. Red brake lights flashed but didn't register in his mind until he was almost riding into the tiny car's exhaust pipe.

Blake screamed. He slammed the brakes but knew he wasn't going to have time to stop. He spun the wheel to the side, hand over hand. No time to even check if the next lane over was empty. Just blind terror leading to unthinking movement.

The lane *was* empty. He skidded, his tires shrieking as he braked right past the red car. The driver – a woman in her fifties with bright purple hair – flipped him the bird and sped off.

Blake managed to flip on his turn signal and get to the shoulder of the freeway.

Mal was trembling, and Blake grabbed him. Hugged him and didn't let go.

"You okay, bud?"

He felt Mal's nod. The boy still didn't speak, but the anger Blake had felt was gone. Fled with the accident. Hopefully for good.

Blake didn't let go of Mal. Both of them were trembling. Mal because of the accident.

Blake was shaking because of their close call, too. But there was more. There was the near-miss. There was also the rage and the thoughts that he had had, the words that were both his and his father's.

And then there was the other thing. The last thing. The thing he saw when he cranked the wheel, hand over hand.

For just a second, just a moment, one of the hands he saw on the wheel wasn't his.

He kept looking at his hands, gripping Mal on the back. Checking them both. Looking closely. Counting to five over and over and over and over.

Because the hand on the wheel had not been Blake's. But it had seemed so real, he must be going insane. Either that or he had actually seen it.

No... one-two-three-four-five. One-two-three-four-five.

Five fingers on each hand.

But when he was turning the wheel, just for the barest fraction of a second, it had looked like one of his hands possessed only three.

NOT SO PINK

Alyssa eased open the door. The electronic chirp of the receiver almost sent her rocketing out of her shoes until she realized it was just feedback from the baby monitor. She jerked back out of the room, an automatic reaction her body still remembered from all the days trying to get Mal not only to go to sleep but to actually stay that way. Loud noises were not only cause for grief, but shooting offenses back then.

She turned off the receiver, then went back in the room.

Still dark. But she heard the gentle sigh of her daughter in the playpen before she even took a step. She knew that sound perfectly, would have known it if she heard a hundred – a thousand, a million – other sighs from a hundred – a thousand, a million – other babies. Her daughter was here, her daughter was safe.

Still, she walked over. She had to see.

Ruthie was asleep in the playpen. The baby blanket that Alyssa had placed over her snaked between the infant's legs, halfway up the tiny chest. It was a Disney blanket, and Pooh and Piglet danced up the low hills of Ruthie's little body.

Alyssa shook her head. The baby couldn't even turn over, so how she had managed to whip the blanket around like that.... Babies were a surprise. They were a mystery and a continuing lesson and always a joy.

Alyssa smiled. She loved this part. New babies

159

didn't have the personality of toddlers, or the wonder of young kids discovering everything and really *understanding* it for the first time. But new babies could make you fall in love over and over and over again.

Just like Alyssa was doing now.

She leaned over. Didn't kiss her baby – that was a first-time parent mistake. Kissing babies meant waking babies a lot of the time. But she breathed deep, and smelled the unique mix of Johnson & Johnson soap, skin that had never seen much of the sun, diaper medicine, and whatever bits of Heaven had clung to the baby this far into life.

Then the smile fell off her face.

Another first-time parent mistake, but she did it anyway. She reached down and carefully moved the blanket off Ruthie. Pooh and Piglet danced a sideways jig, cast off their hill by an unseen goddess.

The onesie was pink. Ruthie's temp was normal.

But on the stomach, what had been barely seen under the blanket –

(*the blanket that was twisted, impossibly twisted, how did it get twisted?*)

– she thought she saw something. It faded even as she looked. Maybe she didn't see it at all. Maybe it was her imagination. Maybe it was the product of stress, exhaustion.

Or maybe it *had* been there.

Maybe it *had* been a fading handprint. Small. Blue.

Alyssa touched her daughter's chest. When she lifted her hand, her print was there. Red.

Something creaked.

She turned around. Spun so fast that she almost twirled her way right into Ruthie's playpen. She managed to right herself, though she wasn't sure if it was balance or just a mother's love acting to contravene physics. She should have fallen.

But she didn't. She ended up staring at the opposite wall.

There was nothing there.

Just empty space.

A wall.

An embroidery.

The old man still knelt. His hands were up in prayer. But the frame was slightly askew.

She couldn't remember if it was like that when she came in.

Alyssa walked to the image in a daze. She righted it with a hand that shook so badly she worried she wouldn't be able to pick up her daughter when the time came to –

(*run*)

– wake her up.

As her hand dropped, she squinted. Had the old man's eyes always been closed? Weren't they open before? A supplication to a God he knew was there – perhaps even saw?

Then she saw the other detail, and this was one she *knew* was absent the first time she saw it.

There was a black line stitched across the old man's throat. Just a simple line, not particularly thick, but it was enough to –

(*make someone think of a dead boy on a black chair with*

his eyes open and his throat cut)

– ruin the beauty of the picture.

Alyssa stepped back, her eyes riveted to the picture. To the saint whose lips no longer seemed to be praying, but pleading for mercy. Begging for the torture to cease.

She turned to the playpen.

Ruthie was awake. Her head turned, her eyes staring right at her mother through the mesh of the playpen.

Alyssa glanced back at the picture.

It was as she had first seen it. Eyes open, no dark line across the throat.

Her hand wiped across her eyes. She laughed in nervous relief and turned back to Ruthie. The baby was still staring at her.

"Hey, little girl. You watching Mommy go crazy?"

Ruthie didn't move.

Alyssa wondered if the centipedes could have followed them here. Because it suddenly felt like dozens of them were crawling up her back.

Ruthie *wasn't* looking at her. She was looking at something behind her. Behind, to the right.

Alyssa didn't look. There was nothing there. There *couldn't* be.

She picked up her daughter.

"Let's get you some breakfast. You must be hungry, and Mommy's boobs are about to pop."

She walked out of the room. She did not look back.

Why should she?

Babies can't see that far.

Even if they could, they can't tell *what* they're seeing.

There was nothing behind her.

Nothing at all.

There couldn't be.

There *couldn't* be.

ALL IN GOOD FUN

The woman moves down the hall.

She coos and whispers. The sounds might be construed as sweet, as lullabies – perhaps the woman even thinks so herself. But some would know differently. Would know better. There are sounds of comfort, there are sounds of love, there are sounds of laughter, there are all manner of good and good-hearted sounds. And all can be used to mask the deeper sounds. The sounds that matter. The sounds of fear, and longing to flee, and knowledge of death.

These are her real sounds. And the thing that watches sways to her song, and thrills to the death like a riptide pulling her closer... closer... *closer*....

The woman holds a baby in her arms, a baby that wakes so slowly. Then the babe falls asleep once more, small eyes never fully opening, never fully seeing. The family may get frightened about the infant's constant sleepiness soon. But for now they are too busy with other things. Too busy looking outward to notice the fearful things that lie among their own numbers.

Many believe that infants cannot see, cannot even focus on what lies right before their eyes.

The truth is much simpler, and much more complex.

The very young, the youngest of the world, see *everything*.

They see not just what is seen, but what is unseen: the worlds above this one, and those beneath. And sometimes they even see the things that wander in neither, but simply drift through the nothing of All.

The baby sleeps. Because in sleeping she can escape. She can close her eyes. She can *not* see.

The woman limps down the stairs.

Behind her, the door to the sewing room stands open.

Then it closes. Slowly, unhurriedly.

The latch catches in the strike plate. Solidly shut.

Footsteps. The sound of something leaning on the wall. Something shaking with silent mirth. Because what fun if the infant *had* awakened! Had seen!

What laughter and delight to watch the madness of a babe.

The woman continues to the living room. The room that is almost a well-remembered parlor or sitting room, but for the presence of a television on one wall, and a small stereo set on another.

As she walks past the clock, she unconsciously matches her gait to its beat. And what watches her laughs silently at this, too.

It is good that she walks this way. So many have walked this way. Not in step with the sound, but certainly in motion with the *time*. Heart beating down with the clock's ever-countdown.

The woman's life can be measured in the hours – minutes – on the face of this clock that has come from so far to be so close to this family.

The woman sits on a chair and turns on the television. She turns up the volume. Loud, louder. And this, like her lullabies, is the music of fear. The screaming of someone not merely calling for help, but shrieking so that the monsters in the darkness cannot be heard.

The baby finally wakes. The woman nurses.

But the baby never opens her eyes. Not once.

There is sound in the entry. A soft creak, the whispered scrape of a shoe sounding so like a mother whispering for silence during Sunday sermon.

Then a crank turns. *Tick-click.*

Music plinks out. A song from long ago, a song well known. A song that sings of good times, of smiles, of throats cut in rage, and death before and death to come.

It plays, as always, in perfect time with the clock. The syncopation of death.

And now: the scrape of shoe leather again. This time faster-faster-faster*fasterfaster*. Sound atwirl as the cylinder whirls and something dances while the woman screams her silent shrieks nearby and so never hears – or chooses *not* to hear – the singular ball taking place right behind her.

The music stops. *Tick.* The cylinder ceases. No more scrapes of shoes, no more twirls. Perhaps a silent bow, unseen but to babes and the dead.

The woman turns her head suddenly. The baby suckles. Neither sees anything, for one cannot and the other refuses sight.

The woman turns back to the television and her silent shrieks for help, screams buried in polite denial.

The footsteps run up the stairs. A door opens. Then closes. And perhaps a low giggling can be heard.

For what fun has been had, and what fun is still to

come.

UP AND DOWN AGAIN

Alyssa loved a lot of things about having a new baby: the sound of a first laugh, the first smile. The feel of the baby nursing (until that first tooth, that first bite that really hurt – then the bottle came out faster than a gunslinger could draw). She loved so many things, and each one was Heaven. And that meant that she had somehow become, for the tiniest of moments, something like an angel.

But there were also a lot of things she hated. Pulling back tiny diapers to do a toosh-check and coming up with fingers covered with poop ranked low on her list of Favorite Things. The fact that any bodily excretions would erupt (they rarely just "came out" – projectile vomiting/peeing/pooping were the norm) during fancy dinner parties or when she had just bought a cute new shirt. Maybe worst of all was the fact that babies somehow knew the worst times to wake up and start screaming and *need* attention: during fights, during lovemaking.

Each time she suffered one of those moments she felt like she had found some brand-new circle of Hell. Somewhere Dante had never envisioned... or maybe had just not had the strength to write about, because too many readers would have killed themselves. And thinking that, she *knew* she was a devil, a demon. She had been so blessed, and she hated the blessing. What kind of person was she?

She found it weird, too, that one of the things she most hated was eating. Eating was a joy when she *got* to do it. But during pregnancy, and now that she was nursing, she *had* to do it. She was "eating for two" – a cute little saying that she had grown to loathe – and that meant she could never skip a meal without guilt, and those meals always had to be at least arguably healthy or shame set in with startling rapidity.

So now she was shoving a PB&J down her throat, almost gagging on it. She had no appetite. But… "eating for two."

She didn't want to be here. Didn't want to be alone. Didn't want to eat.

And had to do all of them.

Ruthie was asleep in her arms, and Blake had the car so she was stuck here, and when she looked at the clock it was *still* only 12:46. Two minutes had passed, which meant she had fallen into a wormhole or something where time passed slower than frozen molasses trapped in amber that was itself caught in a diamond.

Ruthie snored. Usually baby snores were one of those "stumbled into Heaven" moments for Alyssa, but now the sound irritated her. Ruthie didn't seem affected by the creeping unease that Alyssa had felt since finding that damned book yesterday. Since –

(*the sounds the sights*)

– that courier kid took off after looking in the house.

She looked at Ruthie. "You'd think a kid with hair that color would have learned to be a bit tougher, huh?" she said.

Ruthie answered by tooting. Alyssa felt something bouncing off the hand that cupped the baby's bottom, so it was probably time for a new diaper. Diapers were apparently lined with gold dust these days, because they cost about a thousand dollars a box. She didn't remember them costing so much when Mal was a baby. They'd been poor then, too, hadn't they?

But they'd never been well off, either. They'd never known anything else. It was worse to know something other than poverty, then return to it... better far just to stay the way they had been. Better if they'd never moved forward.

Just me, just Blake.

She shook herself free of that idea. She had the kids, and that was hard. But it was worth it. It was a great, good thing. A work that would last.

Ruthie both snored *and* tooted.

"You are a multitasking miracle, baby girl," said Alyssa. She was talking a bit too loudly, speaking at a volume that would probably wake the baby. She admitted to herself that she didn't care. She wanted company. Not *quite* enough to blatantly tickle the baby awake, but enough to speak at normal volume.

But Ruthie just slept on. Slept and slept and when Alyssa laid out a portable changing pad and wiped her little bottom clean and slathered on some Desitin and then put on a new diaper (she could almost hear Huggies' stock price jumping), the baby just kept on sleeping.

Alyssa looked at the clock.

1:02.

"Get home, Blake."

She hefted the sleeping baby, and finally admitted two things: her arms were about to fall off from holding Ruthie for hours straight, and the baby deserved to sleep in a real crib. They didn't have one, so she should at least get the solitude and quiet and stability of her playpen.

But not in that room. Nowhere alone, but *especially* not in that room.

She took Ruthie out of the kitchen, practically running until she was halfway upstairs. That seemed strange when she realized she was running to the very place she wanted to keep her child away from. But in the next moment she also realized that she wasn't running to a place so much as she was running away from – or more accurately *past* – one.

She didn't want to be near the clock. Or the music box.

She was shivering, too. Like she had gotten a chill in the few seconds of moving through the entry. An entire winter's worth of cold had settled into her bones, ice forming in her marrow. Her teeth were on the verge of chattering. She wouldn't have been surprised to see her breath pluming like white fire in front of her.

Tick-tock.

She kept moving.

Up to the sewing room. Not wanting to take the still-sleeping Ruthie –

(*why is she sleeping so much she didn't sleep like this at the hospital did she so why is she sleeping so much?*)

– into the room with her, but not capable of leaving her alone, either. Another one of the crappy parts of being a parent, and she didn't know how single parents managed this kind of issue every moment of every day of their lives. How to leave your child in danger, or take them into worse.

She opened the door. Just a crack. Peeked into the room.

Dim. Almost dark. The sun had shifted. Past its zenith, no longer pushing through the windows on this side of the house. But it was light enough to see the tables, the chair.

The embroidered image on the wall. Saintly man praying.

There was no line on his throat.

Alyssa was relieved, but also a little worried. Was the room back to normal? That would mean something *had* been wrong... and that was beyond weird. Beyond scary.

Or had nothing been wrong in the first place? Less scary to her family. But it meant she was losing it.

She darted into the room. The movement was so fast that Ruthie finally came awake. She started mewing.

"Sorry, honey," said Alyssa, "but you aren't sleeping in here anymore."

She grabbed a blanket off the small pile of them that she had put near the playpen when they arrived the day before –

(*Has it just been a* day?)

– and tossed it out on the floor. Then she put Ruthie on the blanket and broke down the playpen. The portable crib could be folded with one hand, but it was faster this way, and Alyssa didn't want to be here a second longer than she had to.

She kept glancing at Ruthie. The baby wasn't crying, but she kept taking hitching breaths like she was *going* to cry. And Alyssa realized that she was looking at her daughter's onesie as much as she was at her daughter's face.

Looking for changes? Sure, she was worried about her daughter having another attack. Just like she *always* was.

Don't kid yourself. You're worried about seeing a blue handprint.

She finished folding up the playpen. Leaned it against the table with the sewing machine. Picked up Ruthie, who was still constantly about to cry, about to cry.

She managed to maneuver the playpen under her free arm without either crushing the baby or falling over. It hurt. What didn't? But she felt better, body and spirit, when she got out of that room and back into the hall.

She started down the stairs without thinking. Realized she wanted to get back to the living room. To the television. To the comfort of sound that drowned out....

What?

She didn't know, exactly. And didn't care. For now it was enough that it felt *better* to sit in front of the tube.

She was halfway down the stairs and looked down at Ruthie.

The baby was asleep. Again.

But this time, looking at her baby's closed eyes, Alyssa felt gooseflesh stipple her skin. She turned, certain she would see something behind her. Dark visions of claws, of talons and teeth and blood, pulsed through her mind. Her body began to ball around Ruthie. The corners of the playpen bit into her armpit and side.

Nothing there.

She stood frozen like that for a while. Not sure how long, but long enough that reality set in. She started to feel foolish. Then silly. Then ridiculous.

She turned around.

There was a dark shadow in the frosted glass window of the front door.

The front door opened.

This time she did not curl. Did not tense. This time it wasn't just a feeling. She was *seeing* something. Her body went loose. She barely managed to keep hold of Ruthie, but she dropped the playpen. It crashed end over end down the steps, each impact of plastic on wood sounding like a grenade blast.

The door opened.

The dark figure moved into the house.

It was backlit, totally blacked out by the sun shining behind it, but she knew – *knew* – it was here to kill her. To take Ruthie and perhaps kill the baby, too. But probably not.

Probably it had something worse in store for the baby.

The intruder's hand, still on the doorknob, swung out of the sunlight. Into view.

She only saw three fingers gripping the knob. For some reason that was the worst thing.

She opened her mouth to scream.

The playpen slammed to the floor below the stairs.

"Hon? What's wrong?"

Blake stepped the rest of the way in the house. He rushed up the stairs. Held her tightly. She almost sobbed into his shoulder. But refrained as he stepped back and put one hand on Ruthie's head, the other on her chest, obviously checking to make sure the problem wasn't some injury or another attack.

She saw his hands. Saw his fingers. *All* of them.

Warmth thawed the ice crystals in her bones. The warmth of relief, the greater heat of embarrassment.

It is our nature to turn outward when we should be turned inward. Not merely focusing on the mote in others' eyes, but lashing out when no mote is present, if there is the merest speck in our vision. And now Alyssa did that, shoving Blake so hard he nearly followed the playpen down the stairs. "You scared me!" she hollered.

"I can see that!" said Blake. He looked up from Ruthie, catching her eyes with his own. "What's going on?"

Alyssa couldn't answer. She just laughed.

Sometimes we cover fear with noise – television sounds, radio sounds. The beat of dance music, the blips and beeps of video games.

Alyssa did that now. She laughed, and didn't stop. She laughed so she wouldn't hear her own fear.

So she wouldn't hear the scream that hid just under the laughter.

HIDE AND SEEK

Blake got Alyssa down the stairs, and she wouldn't tell him what was going on. He got her into the living room, and she wouldn't tell him what was going on. He got her settled into a chair, and she *still* wouldn't tell him what was going on.

She picked up the television remote, and at that point he knew he wasn't going to find out. Not now, not anytime soon, maybe not ever. Alyssa could be stubborn. Usually it was a good thing. She stuck with problems, she never gave up. Whether it was pushing through her father's cancer or facing down a PTA president who had apparently decided to begin the Fourth Reich in Mal's school district, she didn't know how to back down.

But that also meant that if she absolutely decided not to talk about something – like she had apparently done now – he no longer had a say in the matter.

He crouched beside the chair and held her hand. At least she let him do *that*. Bad enough that he had gone to the office only to find out that they'd failed to land another account, and that Marty had given his notice. Bad enough they were going to be bankrupt inside of a few weeks, and it no longer looked like he could do anything at all to stop it.

At least he could hold her hand. At least he could do that. Curl his fingers around hers, make her feel safe and secure for a few moments.

The chair was a rocker-recliner, much nicer than

anything they had in their own house. Plush, a white so bright it proved that the people who owned this place had no children. Alyssa rocked back and forth, back and forth.

Her eyes started to droop.

He waited five minutes or so. Her eyes never closed, but they became crescent moons. Just sparkling slivers that he was pretty sure would see nothing at all.

He slipped his hand free and stood. He was sweaty from a day of calls and wheeling and dealing and begging and pleading. Not to mention more than a few screams about broken promises and threats of lawsuits for breach of contract.

Which was total bull. At this point he couldn't afford to hire a manicurist, let alone a lawyer.

He wanted to change his business, his bank account, his house... most of his *life*.

Since he couldn't, he'd have to settle for a change of clothes.

"Where you going?"

He started. Alyssa's eyes were wide open, but glassy. She was still asleep as much as she was awake.

"Just going to change."

"God forbid you wear something other than a t-shirt for five whole minutes." She smiled a smile so weary it broke his heart. And she sounded *so* relieved he was home. That broke his heart, too. Because what was he going to do for her, really? Other than hold her hand, what was he doing?

"You want me to stay?" he asked.

She shook her head, her eyelids sinking again. "Go

change."

Then she was out. Her arms still bounced Ruthie, even in her sleep. That was a thing both of them had found out with Mal: certain motions became automatic. You bounced a baby, you rocked back and forth. Didn't matter whether you were asleep, awake... you could be in a coma and you'd still do those things if someone put an infant in your arms.

He walked out of the living room. Suddenly dead tired himself, wanting to lay down, knowing he couldn't because Mal would have to be picked up and since he was home early today it was only right that he do it.

He was in the entryway –

(*tick-tock*)

– and realized that he very much wanted to crank up the music box. Not to dance, but just to listen. A sudden urge to hear the music, to rock back and forth without a baby in his arms. To drop into the metal sound of the old music, simply because –

(Daddy's gonna play a game)

– he *wanted* to.

How long has it been since you did something because you wanted to, Blake? Days? Months? Years? When was the last time you took the time to just watch a movie or go to a nice restaurant or –

(play a game)

– *even sit and do nothing?*

He walked on. There was no time for music. He had to pick up Mal. Alyssa was asleep because she had to hold Ruthie, who was also asleep.

178

And for just a moment he hated all of them for that. Hated them deeply and completely.

Then the moment passed, and he walked past the music box. Up the stairs.

In the bedroom he and Alyssa were using, he tossed open his suitcase and dug out a t-shirt.

"Got me on that one, Alyssa."

He thought about putting on another button-up or, even better, one of *her* shirts, just to mess with her. But he had to pick up Mal in an hour, and life was hard enough for a kid in elementary school without being picked up by a dad with serious clothing confusion.

In the end he decided for comfort over comic effect. Picked up the t-shirt again and –

Blake froze. Frowned.

He tossed the contents of his suitcase, moving everything onto the bedspread. He put everything back into the suitcase again and, just to be sure, repeated the process.

When everything was spread across the bed for the second time he smiled. He hadn't thought Alyssa would be up to dealing with the book full of dead children, but apparently she had gotten rid of it – either permanently, or just tucked it out of the way, maybe back where she found it.

Blake kind of hoped it was the latter. He had meant what he said about destroying the book. It was grotesque, offensive. He knew that people had taken pictures of their dead as tender mementos of loved ones lost, but that thing.... He shuddered.

It had not seemed like a memorial item. It had felt

pornographic. Something a twisted mind would use to satiate an even more twisted craving.

Blake was glad it was gone.

So why was he taking the clothes out again? Why was he still looking for it?

It's not here. It's gone.

"Thanks, honey. I really didn't want to touch that thing again," he said.

But he said it like an alcoholic, thanking someone for taking the wine off the table.

And he kept looking, looking, looking. Face flushing, hands trembling.

(*C'mere. Daddy's gonna play a game.*)

REACHING DARKNESS

Mal liked school. Liked it a lot. He wasn't a dork about it or anything – he got good grades, but he was smart enough not to tell anyone what they were; and even though he almost always knew the answer, he only raised his hand once or twice a day. Not like Tina Wipperfurth, who was not just a cheater at "Mercy," but also a bragger and a suck-up who raised her hand so high it looked like she had to pee.

So yeah, Mal liked school. He liked class, he liked recess (dodgeball!), and he really liked pizza day in the caf.

Still, he liked coming home more.

Some of his friends said they hated coming home. Jefferson lived with just his mommy, and Mal saw her pick him up once and she dressed like the lady on the cover of the magazine Jerry Lambert brought to school and showed a lot of people before Mrs. Augustyn found it and he got suspended. Mal wouldn't want to go home to that, either.

But Mal did like going home. To his home. He loved Mommy, he loved Daddy. He loved Ruthie.

Home was awesome. Better even than the place with wall-to-wall trampolines that Brad had his birthday party at last year.

But today, home was weird. Not just because home was at somebody else's house. He knew that people were getting rid of the king-size bugs at their real house, and that was great news. So everyone should have been happy.

But no one was. Not really.

Everyone *pretended* to be, but he felt like it wasn't true. Not a Lie, exactly, but not Really True. Mommy and Daddy kept asking "are you okay?" to each other, and then they'd answer, "fine, are you?" and then the other one would say, "fine." Over and over.

Mal felt like it was for him. Like they were acting out a TV show so he wouldn't notice something.

They kept asking if *he* was okay, too. And he almost told them about his dream a couple times. But then decided not to, because if Mommy and Daddy were this freaked out, then he didn't want to add to it. They had told him about his jobs as a Big Brother, but he also figured he had some jobs as a Good Son.

One of them was not to make things bad if they were good. Another was that if they already *were* bad, he shouldn't make them worse.

Daddy and Mommy let him watch a lot of TV, which was also weird. They made him do homework, but that usually only took him an hour or less. Then it was all "tube time." They told him he had to watch Ruthie, but again he got the feeling that was just pretend – just acting like things were normal.

He sat by her while she lay on her baby mat and he rubbed her tummy. He watched her as much as he watched cartoons. She was that cute.

Ruthie mostly slept. Boring when people did it, but babies made funny sounds and sweet faces.

He heard Mommy and Daddy talking about dinner, and that was the first "real" good time. They decided pizza.

Mal pumped his fist and said, "Yes!"

Then he got worried because Daddy mumbled

something. Mal couldn't hear the words, but it didn't sound like, "Okay, let's *do it!*"

Then Mommy said, "In for a penny, in for a pound," and Daddy said, "Okay."

Pizza came thirty minutes (or less) later.

Daddy stared at the receipt on the side of the box for a while, which was more weirdness, then Mommy pulled it off and tossed it in a little trashcan. "Enjoy yourself," she said in a "Don't Mess With Me" voice.

Daddy nodded and smiled but the smile was little and his cheeks barely puffed out at all.

Bonus time: Mommy spread out a blanket they had and said they could eat in front of the television, which was something that almost *never* happened. Daddy put Ruthie in the playpen.

"She asleep?" asked Mommy.

"Yup. You need me to get her up to feed her?"

Mommy felt her boobies, which was gross, and then shook her head.

They started to eat. Three seconds in, which was barely enough time for Mal to eat two slices, and of course Ruthie started to cry.

She was cute, but she had lousy timing.

Daddy stood. Halfway up and Mommy said, "I'll get her."

"Time?"

Mommy was feeling her chest again. She nodded. Mal tried to ignore what was happening. Especially when Mommy covered her shirt and Ruthie with a little cloth and stared under them both like the most interesting thing ever was down there. Mal knew what was happening there, and he did not think it was interesting. Gross and horrifying, but not interesting.

He suddenly realized that he had probably done that, too. Had probably....

He wondered if he would be able to finish his pizza. He felt sick to his stomach.

At least it's not milk.

Ruthie kept crying. Mal couldn't blame her.

"Latch, baby girl," said Mommy. She moved her hand under the blanket, then looked around. "She's not interested."

"Is she...?" said Daddy. Mal stopped pretending to watch TV.

Is Ruthie sick? Will she scream again? Are we going back to the hospital?

Mommy shook her head. "Her temp's fine, and her last feeding was a good one. She's probably just cranky." She looked around. "You know where her rattle is?"

Daddy shook his head.

Mommy did something weird then. She didn't stop moving, exactly. But she sorta *did*, too. Just a quick jittery stop-start, like her body was hiccupping, then she said, "I'll check in her room."

And now Mal wondered if the TV show his parents had been acting out was actually for him after all. Maybe it was for each other. Or for themselves? He didn't understand that exactly, but he thought there might be something to that idea.

"You sure you're up to that?" said Daddy. He was

smiling, but again it was that little smile. His eyes weren't smiling at all.

Mommy stuck her tongue out at him. She put Ruthie back in the playpen, still crying. Then she left.

Mal watched Mommy go. She almost ran through the entryway, then up the stairs. But as fast as she was going, she looked careful, too. A ninja cowboy deep in dangerous samurai Sioux territory.

Weird.

Scary.

Mal tried to look at the TV show, or to look at Ruthie. But neither one was real good for him right then. He couldn't focus on the TV, and Ruthie was making these creepy noises like she was worried someone was going to step on her face.

Daddy began wiggling.

Mal put another piece of pizza in his mouth. He didn't even taste it. He loved pizza, but this might as well have been a bread-and-bread sandwich. He kept thinking about how Mommy must have once fed him.

And Daddy's scrunching around on the couch was seriously making it hard to watch anything else.

Maybe Daddy's going to get up and get Ruthie.

Daddy didn't. He just wiggled around on the sofa.

"You got ants in your pants, make you do the boogie dance?" said Mal. The words were what everyone said to each other at school. They just popped out.

He was glad they did. Daddy actually smiled a real smile.

"You're not allowed to do that rhyme unless you

actually know what a boogie dance is."

Mal smiled back. It felt good. Pizza squished between his cheeks and teeth and he felt like Godzilla, crushing villagers in his mouth, *RAWR*. Godzilla was a good thing to be. Godzilla was tough and had never eaten boobie-milk.

"What *is* a boogie dance?"

Daddy smiled another real smile. "Beats me. I'm not old enough to know, either." He wiggled some more. "Something's under the cushion."

And he started to stand.

The smile went out of Mal. The moment of good feeling was gone.

Daddy said something was under the cushion.

That meant Daddy was going to reach under it. And who knew what was there, in the dark under the pillow?

Mal had a quick flash of memory, or maybe a quick flash of dream: an upside down cross, Jesus screaming straight down. Something that sounded like centipedes, then turned into whispering –

("*Help me help me help me help me help me….*")

– below him. And then Mal rolling off the bed, his hand falling into darkness.

Darkness.

And then… and then… the *thing*. The thing he saw, or the thing he dreamed. Maybe he did them both. Saw and dreamed in a place between sleep and awake.

He couldn't remember what the thing was. Just that it was black. Scary.

Coming fast. Coming soon.

Daddy stood.

He was going to put his hand into darkness.

What if the thing was there?

TOUCHES THROUGH TIME

Some things move slowly.

Some things move slowly because they must gain power, gain strength before they move.

Some things move slowly because they savor the game. The pain and the fear felt are as much to be enjoyed as the final moments where understanding enters and life departs.

And some things move slowly because it is simply the way it *must* be.

Whichever is true here, in this time and at this place, the waiting is over. The time for slow movement has passed.

Things will move fast now. Fast and fast and so fast that the blur will be all that can be seen and all that is real. Simple confusion, simpler pain.

The baby cries, for it senses what is so close.

The woman leaves, sent away by those same cries.

The boy sits on the floor. The beautiful boy, so young, so familiar.

And the man sits alone. Sits vulnerable.

Soon even he senses that there is something amiss. Things have drawn closer and closer, have taken more and more of him. He is becoming sensitive, though he may fight what is happening; though he may deny the truth of who he is, and what he will be.

But the time has come. The time is *here*.

The man makes a few jokes, but finally stands.

As he does, a hand reaches out.

It is said that time and space matter little to some things. Neither is a true statement. Time matters greatly. It passes slowly, each minute an eternity. A forever without the ability to follow desire, to slake thirsts that first ache, then anguish, then agonize.

And space matters, too. For space is the means of finding. Space can be folded, can be manipulated.

The time is now. The man feels how close *It* is, because It is below him. Space has folded, and what would have taken up the volume of a body in a time before can now curl into places much smaller.

This is part of why some things move slowly: time and space must come together, must intertwine in a way that allows both to curl in on one another. Then and now, below and above. The small and the large, the things that last and those that are ephemeral as a candle in a hurricane.

The man stands. But in the instant that he does, a hand reaches out. It reaches from a place below, beside. It seems to come from the couch upon which the man was seated, but also from somewhere else. A place beyond the ability of any to see. Perhaps the baby could see it, were it placed in the right position. No one else.

Certainly not the man.

So the man stands, and the hand brushes against him. Grazes his hip with a glancing touch that is nearly a caress.

It is not much. Almost nothing.

But in the barest of contacts, the merest of moments, time and space curl. Then and now, here and there. All come together, all begin to merge and will soon become fully one.

Before the man has fully stood, before he could possibly see – even if he had eyes with the proper sight – the hand has withdrawn.

The three fingers curl into a triumphant fist and disappear.

The touch was almost nothing.

But it was enough.

Things have been moved slowly.

But no longer.

FOUR:
SUBJECTS FOUND

One thing that stands out in these pictures – as in any old photos – is the fact that they were the result of careful planning, staging, lighting, set-up. The cost of silver-based or cellulose nitrate-based film being prohibitive, each individual open and close of the shutter resulted in a thing of tangible and objective *value*, if not beauty, and corresponding care was taken in the production of each photograph.

Modern "artists" rely on multitudinous takes made possible by the negligible costs of each individual photo. This essentially renders them little more than the proverbial monkeys, simply punching buttons until they accidentally produce a work of Shakespearean value. Contrast this to our principle subject, who took extraordinary care, even with the particular time constraints under which he operated:

> Sumtyme I dont hav tyme for a good pykcher. I wont rush the work, tho' I be fownd out. I kno my work wont be understoode and I myte be punished, but I wont rush the work.

> I luv the chyldrin. They diserve the best frum me. I wil giv them the ours for thaer most luvly selves to be seen. And my pleasur when I tuch them in the pykshers will remind mee of the pleshur I felt when I tuchd them alive.

- Silver, Charles M.
(afterword by Dr. Charlotte Bongiovi),
(2003) Berkeley, California,
Memento Mori, Notes of a Dead Man,
Western University Press, Inc.

THE FIRST OF MANY

Alyssa walked in the room only after looking at the embroidered picture to make sure it was neither hanging at an angle nor showing a man with eyes closed and a black line across his throat. It looked normal, so she went in. After turning on the light. And looking at the picture again. And counting to ten to make sure nothing happened.

And what could happen, Alyssa? What are you expecting?

Whatever it was, it didn't occur. Even so, even in the bright light, the skin between her shoulders crept and stretched and made her feel less like a mom looking for a baby rattle, and more like a soldier behind enemy lines. One looking for IEDs, but with no information, no preparation. Just a general idea and a blind hope that all will turn out for the best.

Her shoulder blades pinched closer together, but she forced herself to ignore the sensation of –

(*being watched*)

– danger.

It wasn't real. It couldn't be.

But if it isn't, then I'm crazy, right? Because I did see something. I did.

And there it was: the same problem that kept popping up. Did she tell Blake and have him put her away in a white room with rubber walls? Or did she keep quiet... and perhaps find there really *was* something wrong here?

Still thinking, she finished looking through the sewing room. She had looked here first, mostly to prove she could. Mostly to prove there *was* nothing wrong. Ostriches didn't really bury their heads in the sand to hide from things they feared: that was a human trait. Alyssa didn't want that to be her.

But she hadn't really expected to find Ruthie's toy here. She just wanted to go in and... what? Prove there was nothing to worry about? That there was, but she was strong enough to face whatever it was?

That she was just a nutcase?

She went back into the hall, then to the room she and Blake were using. It was a tidy space. Not Spartan like the sewing room, but everything put away and neat, so looking for Ruthie's toy would be easy in here as well.

She began with her luggage. Moving aside nursing bras, what seemed like the six dozen shirts she brought since she inevitably lactated right through ten a day.

The rattle wasn't in her luggage. She checked Blake's. And again, found only what he had packed. Clothes, toiletries, a book he was reading – some horror story about a monster in an insane asylum – and....

She flipped through the contents of his suitcase again. Just to make sure. Good news – even small bits of it – had been in low supply recently.

After looking three times, she was positive. "Thank you, Blake," she breathed.

The book was gone. He had gotten rid of it, just like he said he would. Not that she doubted, but it was great to actually *see* the thing out of their lives.

She decided to do something special for her

husband. He worked so hard, he did so much. He never believed it – that was one of the more insidious products of his upbringing. It wasn't just about the scars on his back, the reason he would never go shirtless in front of Mal. It wasn't about his constant terror of becoming what his father had been to *him*.

Blake's father had punished him over and over again. And it didn't matter that Blake never deserved it, not for a moment. He never talked about it – not even to her, not directly at least – but Alyssa could see that on some deep level he believed he deserved the punishments. Some fundamental place in his soul had been broken by the constant battery, mental and physical, and had come around to his father's point of view.

Blake Douglas could work every day to become successful in every aspect of his life: good father, good husband, good earner. It wouldn't matter. Not to him.

And Alyssa was powerless to fix that part of him, that broken part. It was a wound she couldn't bind, because it was in a place she couldn't find.

It was worse now that things were going tail over teakettle with their finances. Because in Blake's eyes, every success was due to luck, or someone else's hard work. But every failure, every loss: his to own, and his alone.

Still, she would try. She would try until they grew old together, died hand-in-hand together. And if Blake died not believing he was worthy of anything, he would at least die knowing that she had given him everything she had to give. That even though his "failures" she had never abandoned him. And maybe after, in Heaven – if there was such a place – he'd understand. Understand what he was, what he was worth.

Maybe that was what Heaven *was*.

The idea was enough to take her around the rest of the room without following her previous, morbid chain of thought. Without thinking of the choice between lunacy and a reality that had fallen into nightmare.

She made it to the card table Blake had set up. Flipping back a few of his work papers, her movements now cursory and dreamlike. She was barely paying attention to her present. Which was fine. One of humanity's greatest gifts is the ability to avoid the present by burying itself in past memory or future dreams.

Sometimes the present is simply too dangerous. Sometimes even thinking of it is too much.

A scream ricocheted into the sewing room. It pierced the line between first floor and second, and so pierced her as well. Alyssa felt like she was halfway down the stairs before the scream had fallen to silence. Her feet drove downward so hard that she was less running than kicking her way down.

Blake. Blake had screamed! She had never heard that, *what could have caused that?*

She ran around the stairwell. Skidded on the slick floor of the entry. Tore through the anteroom and for the first time since the family's arrival barely noticed the sound of the clock, or the pain that lanced through her as she took each step, slid around each corner.

She burst into the living room...

... and Blake was sitting on the couch. Watching TV with Mal, Mal stuffing pizza in his face so hard an onlooker might expect pepperonis to shoot out the back of his head.

Blake had Ruthie across his lap, holding her rattle over her and shaking it gently.

He looked over as Alyssa ran in, his expression surprised and amused. He rattled the toy. "Found it," he said.

"It was under the cushion," said Mal, the words barely making their way through a three-pound bite of dough and cheese.

"You...." Alyssa couldn't find words. The dash downstairs had robbed her of breath, giving her pain as a poor substitute. More than that, she just didn't *understand*. "You screamed," she finally managed.

"Dad was doing the boogie dance," said Mal. He smiled. For a moment Alyssa didn't care what happened, because Mal was smiling. He hadn't smiled – *really* smiled – since the centipedes. Seeing his face lit up with happiness, with the joy that only a child that knew a secret joke could feel... it was almost enough for Alyssa to dismiss any and all problems.

In fact it was more than enough. She smiled back at him. One hand was on her lower stomach, but it dropped away as her pain simply disappeared.

Her boy was happy.

Then Ruthie started to cry. Alyssa looked at her daughter, and saw that the baby's eyes were open. Fully awake.

Unlike babies' hearing, which develops quickly, their sight takes the better part of a year to mature. The first month they can typically only focus on things within a foot or so, and they don't even know how to keep their eyes working in tandem: cross-eyed babies or babies with one eye rolling around independently are common.

Ruthie was no exception. But at this moment she seemed to be staring at Blake. *Directly* at him, in fact, even though he had leaned far back from her.

(*like he doesn't want her to see*)

Ruthie's baby rattle – another red and white, high-contrast toy – was directly in front of her face, and it should have drawn her attention, transfixed her.

But she looked right past it. Straight up, appearing to stare directly at her father's face *almost three feet away*.

She cried and cried.

Alyssa looked at Blake, too. He was so concerned she didn't know which person was more heartbreaking. Whispering "*shhh*, baby, *shhh*" over and over, Blake rattled her toy and rocked his baby.

Ruthie screamed. Not a cry, a full *shriek*.

And for a moment, Blake's face changed. He looked angry. His mouth twisted, a writhing line ready to spit at the child, to shout at her. His cheeks reddened, his eyes glittered.

The instant passed. Ruthie stopped screaming, and Blake kept saying "*shhh*, baby" and he was simply himself again.

It all happened so fast that Alyssa couldn't tell if it was real.

Probably not. It's looking more and more like you're nuts, old gal.

Maybe it was post-partum depression, or even psychosis. She hadn't had either of those after Mal, but that didn't mean she couldn't get them now.

Blake kept whispering.

Mal kept watching TV.

Ruthie stopped screaming.

Alyssa was silent, too. But now *she* felt like screaming. The first of many screams, screams that would go on and on and never end.

CATCHING RIDES

Ralph was late. It was late, Ralph was late, the world was spinning way too fast and his wheels were spinning way too slow.

The dead were getting close.

He had missed a deadline today. The client didn't notice – Ralph was only off by six seconds, per the satellite-updated clock on his tablet. And it wasn't a beeline job, so the client wasn't all sweaty about getting the envelope into her hands.

But Ali called him five minutes later and asked if Ralph was okay. So Ali must have seen the time sig on the receipt on his software and known that it was a late drop.

"You dead, man?" said Ali. His normal voice: blunt, deep, and wrapped around a mouthful of food. Probably pulled out of the Lego lunchbox he had brought today. Ralph couldn't decide if Ali's lunchbox fetish was awesomely weird or just plain awesome.

"No," said Ralph. "Not dead." He didn't stop pedaling as fast as he could. A car pulled out of an alley and he almost got bolognafied all over its hood.

"What was that?" said Ali, his voice now blunt and deep and garbled by food and also muffled by the horn the car's owner was practically laying across.

Ralph let go of the handle long enough to engage in a bit of sign language. Most messengers preferred the middle finger, but he liked to hold up thumb, first, and pinkie. "I love you" in sign language. It kept his heart rate down and either brought out a laugh from the other person or *really* drove them bonkers. Either was fine.

This guy was a bonkers-type. The horn started stuttering as he banged it with both hands.

Then he was behind Ralph. Gone. Good, because Ralph didn't like the look of the dead woman on the guy's roof. Naked, splayed out, holding a lit cigarette whose smoke disappeared into nowhere. She gave him the creeps.

All of the dead were doing that now. Not most. *All.*

"You hear me, Hickey?" said Ali. "You okay?" He actually sounded concerned.

"I'm fine. Be in soon for another hot order." Ralph hung up. He didn't want to get pancaked, and too much phone talk was a good way for that to happen. More than that, he didn't want Ali to hear the scratch in his voice. The fear.

It wasn't a surprise he finally missed a bullseye. He hadn't slept in close to forty-eight hours. Monster Energy drinks and shot after shot of Red Bull chasers could only keep you going so long.

Then you started to slip.

Someone stepped off the curb. Soccer mom with her kid. They didn't look where they were going, and a car passed by Ralph and slammed right into them.

He screamed. Wobbled. He lost control of the bike and it veered into the lip of the curb. The tire ground against it, the spokes clicked a rapid tap dance against the concrete. Then he fell. Rolled.

Screaming still.

A few people on the sidewalk clustered around him.

"You okay, buddy?" "Someone get the license plate –" "Give him room, give him room!" A host of concerned voices, which normally would have made him smile – cities always got a rap for being full of uncaring jerks, but then a person fell and sometimes people actually noticed.

But they were noticing the wrong thing.

"Not me!" he shouted. "Help them!" He threw off several hands that pulled at him, some trying to help him to his feet while others tried to keep him down so he could recover from his fall. "Help –"

And he fell again. Nothing to do with his original crash. This was an impact of a new kind. Nothing touched his bike or his body, but he felt a hammer smash right into the gray center of his brain.

The woman and her kid were fine. The car that had run into them was still rolling down the block. Not a care in the world.

And that meant the mother and her child were not there. At least, not for the car.

Ralph could have handled that. That was the sort of thing he'd been dealing with for a long time. But the mother turned. The child turned.

Now he saw that the kid was a little girl. She'd been wearing a sweater with a hoodie, so he couldn't tell before. But when she shifted toward him he could see the long pigtails trailing down her front. He could also see that most of her face was gone, blasted away by a shotgun.

The shotgun was held by her mother. Ralph hadn't noticed it, either, just seeing them step out. But now he saw it. Saw the mother holding the wood stock, the barrel angled slightly toward the girl. The woman herself was pale. Dark circles under her eyes, blue lips. So she'd probably o.d.'d or sat in a closed garage with her car running after....

After she killed her girl.

Horrible. But again, it was something he'd seen before. This was one of the bad ghosts, one of the ones who didn't catch rides or chat about the afterlife, but just walked from place to place like a storm ready to bring a bit of devastation wherever it went.

The mother looked at Ralph. Straight, *right into his eyes*, and winked. Her blue lips widened in a long smile.

The little girl at her side did not smile. She had no face to do so.

Ralph knew that the step off the curb hadn't been just a random event. Hadn't been an accident. The dead woman had meant him to see what he did. Had intended him to believe a horror had occurred.

Maybe even tried to kill him, too. What if he wobbled into traffic instead of into the curb, after all?

The kind people were still tugging at him. He barely noticed. Just noticed that this woman was still grinning. Now tapping the shotgun against the little girl's hoodie.

Looking at him. Just like that little dead boy in the house had done. Just like no other ghost had done before.

The woman stepped toward him.

Ralph jumped back. He ran for his bike.

The dead had never touched him. As far as he could tell, they never touched *anything*.

But they had never looked at him, either. Until that little boy. And now this woman.

So things were changing. Maybe because he had seen the boy, maybe because things were changing generally. It wasn't like he got a manual or a rule book when he started seeing all this stuff.

Regardless, if things were changing, then how *much* were they changing? Would the good ghosts leave? Would the bad ghosts come ever closer? Would they try to touch him?

Would they succeed?

Would the one ghost he feared most of all finally show up to catch a final dreadful ride?

He raced away on his bike. He tried not to look at any of the blurs he passed. Most would be people, but he didn't want to take a chance. He hustled to R.I. and asked for another job. Ali said he didn't have one.

"I need one."

"Tough titties, Hickey. I just gave the last package on the boards to Lybeck."

Ralph ran for the front office. He passed the three people sitting at the desks –

(*don't look at any of them because there are only two office girls, just Malia and Ariane, so one of those don't belong, Ralph, just get out of here*)

– and found Lybeck, a guy so thin that the only thing holding him down when he rode was his pack and the massive beard he wore. The courier was just getting onto his bike, tucking an envelope into his bag.

"Lybeck! Hey! Bill!" shouted Ralph.

Lybeck started zipping up his pack. "Gotta jet, Ralphie."

"I need to take that package."

"Then ride faster next time. This is my fare." Lybeck smiled, clearly relishing the rare opportunity to be out in front of Ralph.

Ralph felt desperate. He could just get on his bike and ride, but he knew he wouldn't last. He had to be doing something. Just riding in circles would make him easier to find. It made no sense, but having a purpose kept him safer than just running blind.

He'd learned that over the years, too.

"I'll run it, you keep the fee," he blurted.

Lybeck grinned and handed over the small manila envelope he had been stuffing into his bag. Ralph ran for his bike.

"Business doing pleasure witcha!" Lybeck called.

Ralph ran ragged the rest of the day. Into the night.

Now Runners, Inc., was closed. And he was still driving. Aimless, nowhere to go. So the dead were getting closer and closer.

He passed a little old man with a walking stick. The man smiled at him as he passed, and tried to ram his cane into the spokes of Ralph's bike.

The cane went through. The spokes pierced it like smoke.

Or no... the front wheel seemed to cough ever so slightly. Like it had decided to stop, then in the next millisecond had changed its mind.

The old man ranted obscenities. Ralph left him and the curses behind.

He just rode.

Tomorrow he would go to R.I. and pick up more work. He would keep busy. That would buy him time until he could figure out how to get things back to normal – what passed for normal in his life.

He yawned. Sound tamped down as the motion closed his Eustachian tubes. When the noise of the world returned, he heard not just the sounds of a city – traffic, distant music, voices, the hum of electricity powering it all – but something thoroughly unexpected.

"Turn left up here."

The voice wasn't close. It was right in his ear.

Ralph looked over his shoulder.

The boy hanging to his waist, somehow perched on the sliver of seat behind him, was maybe thirteen. Crazed hair, even crazier eyes. Blue jeans. Black sneakers. No shirt, which let Ralph see the long gash in the boy's stomach and the intestines that drooped out.

The boy grinned widely. His teeth were beautiful, perfectly straight. But there was also a sense of sharpness. Ralph felt like he was seeing a hologram of perfection projected onto a background that was ragged and pointed as chewed glass.

"Turn up here," said the boy. "My brother said we could help him freak out some border bandits who live in a little house up ahead. Make 'em run back to Mex-I-Co." The smile got broader. "Or maybe you and I can just go back to where *I* live."

Ralph felt a hand squeeze him. Like the cane it was barely more than the implication of sensation. But it was more than any of the dead had ever managed before.

He screamed. Swerved the bike. Turned so fast that

he felt his kneecap skid against blacktop, heard a car honk as he cut in front of it. Warm air from the car's engine blasted through the front grill and Ralph could feel *that* too, warming his cheek and right arm. He was cutting it as close as he ever had.

But when he looked back the dead kid was gone. Maybe because Ralph had knocked him off the bike. Maybe because he'd gotten bored.

Maybe because some other dead soul wanted a turn with Ralph.

They'd never looked at him before. Never touched him. Never caught a ride on his bike.

Now, since he delivered that package, saw that boy with his throat cut, they had done all three.

What would they do next?

Who would do it to him?

For a moment his tattoos all burned at once. He felt hot, burning, and at the same time smothered under an ocean's worth of water. None of it real, but all of the feelings alive in his mind.

He turned left. No intention of beating up illegal immigrants, but he needed to slow down. Needed to rest. He thought he knew a safe place to do it. Not comfortable, but safe.

Unless that had changed, too.

A FAMILY'S NEEDS

Blake could tell that Alyssa was suffering, and suffering alone, under some terrible burden. And knowing that crushed him.

He couldn't tell what the problem was, and that made him feel even worse. Because that was another one of his jobs: to see what his wife needed, to help her with it, to help her in general. What was the point in being married if you didn't help each other?

But he couldn't help if he didn't know what was going on.

And he couldn't ask, either. He had been married long enough to know many of her moods. Not all of them – she was a mystery in some respects. And that was a good thing. Blake suspected that some people married mirrors: people they fell in love with because they had all the same likes, shared all the same interests. And those people probably got divorced as soon as life warped them a bit apart, as life always did.

He had married Alyssa: neither a mirror nor an echo chamber. She was kind, but firm. She had her own mind. If she thought he was being an idiot, she generally told him so. Nicely, but she told him. And if she needed to be angry she got angry. She wasn't a mannequin, she wasn't a "dream girl." She was better than that. He called her his "better than dream girl," because if he had to dream up a wife he likely would have thought of something completely different, and utterly stupid.

She was what he needed. She was no dream. She was challenging, she was scary, she was loving, she was smart. All the things a friend and lover and wife should be.

And that meant that once in a while she didn't want to talk about whatever was on her mind. So she *wouldn't*. Early in their marriage he had tried to wheedle her thoughts out of her. Mistake. He ended up still not knowing anything she was thinking, but with the added bonus of a very irritated wife.

Now he just let her work through it. She would talk about what was bothering her. She would just do it in her time. Until then, it was best to pretend that all was business as usual.

Besides, he was actually feeling good for the first time in a few days. He had worried when he got to this old place that it was just one more turd in the crapstorm that had been raining on them. And with the clock and the weird music box and the general weird vibe of the place –

(*Don't forget the way that courier took off like he was looking into the pits of Hell itself.*)

– he just got that much more concerned.

And that book. Those children. It had nearly been the straw that broke the ol' camel in two.

But for some reason it didn't bother him that much anymore. Didn't people make those dead picture things back then? Blake seemed to remember they were normal-ish. People made them to remember loved ones. Not to be creepy.

Some of the pictures had been artistic. Beautiful.

Full of... *love*.

He didn't know why everything felt better. Maybe it

was dinner. Having that pizza – even pizza they couldn't afford – had been the right move. Sitting there with Mal and Alyssa and Ruthie. He'd been nervous going in, but about the time they found Ruthie's rattle, everything just started to feel... *right*.

Like things were falling into place.

Everything would be better soon.

The family would have what they needed again.

He would *give* it to them.

He looked at Ruthie. She was sleeping in his hands. That was good. Because –

(*little bitchlet screams too much cries too much sees too much*)

– she needed her rest. She hadn't had any attacks, but that could change at any time. Best she sleep. Stay hydrated, stay calm.

He kissed her cheek, then bent over to put her in the playpen. Alyssa had moved it into their bedroom and he could tell from the look on her face that there would be no discussion: the baby would be sleeping with them from now on.

He remembered trying to keep a secret from his father once. He read a science fiction book. His father didn't like science fiction. Didn't like *books*. His father suspected something was happening, something was being kept from him.

Blake told him the secret after only one strike with the bamboo cane his father kept for serious offences. But the rest of the strikes – the punitive ones – kept him out of school for two weeks. To say nothing of the softer and more terrible strikes of flesh against flesh.

He glanced at Alyssa. She was sitting on a plush chair in front of a vanity against the opposite wall. Drawing a brush through her long, blond hair.

He wondered absently if she would tell her secrets after a single strike of the cane. Probably. Most people would.

He lowered Ruthie into the playpen. Put a blanket over her. She sighed. Beautiful sound.

He smoothed the blanket over her.

As he straightened up, his hip twinged. It felt like it was about to go out on him, as though when he sat on Ruthie's toy during dinner he had really bumped into some deadening agent. He slid to the side, barely managing to right himself without hitting any of the walls of the playpen.

Then the moment passed. His hip felt fine again. He straightened.

He heard the low *clink* of plastic. To the side, Ruthie's mobile was moving slightly. He must have grazed it with his elbow when he fell.

How? You fell the other way.

But that was what must have happened. Ruthie couldn't have done it, that was certain. And there was no one else around.

He glanced over his shoulder. Alyssa was looking at him, minor concern on her face.

He smiled. Winked.

Damn, he felt good. His hip didn't hurt. Just warm now. Almost pleasant. He'd check it out later.

For now, he was going to chat with his wife. She

needed that.

He was going to give her what she needed.

He would give them all what they needed. That was his job.

RING AROUND THE ROSIE

Alyssa brushed her hair.

The smooth motions were familiar and hypnotic and comforting enough to drive back the emotions that tore at her. At least, they drove them far enough that she felt like she might be able to think straight. Before, she had been feeling so many different things that she couldn't concentrate on any of them. It was overwhelming, and that didn't lend itself to clear thinking or good decisions.

She had finished dinner with Mal and Blake, and it was a good one. Mal loved the pizza – like he always did. He would have polished off the entire pie if they'd let him.

And Blake....

Tears pushed at her eyes. She resisted the urge to wipe them with the back of her hand, blinking them to oblivion instead. She didn't want Blake to see her cry. Didn't want to wreck whatever spell had fallen over him.

Dinner had been more than just good. Because Blake had seemed like *himself*. Like the version of him she fell in love with, the man who ran away from abuse, but who never ran away from challenges or his own fear of the future. The man who struggled with self-worth, but could always find it in himself to value others.

The man he was when they married, the man who fathered Mal and raised him up.

The man whom she had lost in recent years. Who had lost *himself*.

Blake smiled and laughed during dinner. Tickled

Mal, and Mal laughed, too. Not just smiles, but *laughter*. The last few days, the bugs and the fleeing and the fear, disappeared from their little boy's eyes.

Alyssa watched it and enjoyed it and filed the images away in her mind where they could be viewed and savored whenever she wished.

She herself remained silent. Loath to break the mood. Enjoying the sight of father and son playing.

Fighting the fears that still gripped her.

There are events in life that can never be properly explained. The moment when you look in a person's eyes and realize you love him. The first touch of your child in your arms. Curling up in a warm bed with a lover while a winter storm rages outside. Moments so sublime that words fail and only feelings have the depth to contain them. U*nexplainable*, and so merely *relatable* by those who have gone through those same moments.

But Alyssa knew there were also dark mirrors of those moments. And she had known it for years: ever since the first time Blake told her what his childhood had been like, and her own realization that as much as he told her, as much as he dared open up and she dared listen, she would never comprehend the fear he lived with, and his longing for an existence *without* that fear.

These last few days, they were like that. The centipedes, the flight to an alien home. The book of dead children. The things she had seen – or perhaps hadn't.

She didn't know how to explain them. So she was alone. Because what could she tell Blake that would make him understand what she was feeling?

She kept brushing her hair. Brushing, brushing.

Repetition a substitute for action, motion without thought that had become a final refuge taken up in the darkest parts of the mind.

She looked at herself in the vanity mirror sometimes, but mostly she looked beyond herself: Blake, the playpen, the open door and the hall beyond it. As though by seeing as much of her world as possible, she might be able to control it. To keep it safe.

That's impossible. A lie.

Blake put Ruthie in the playpen. He stumbled suddenly, nearly fell, and her heart stopped because –

(*what if he drops her what if she falls and hits her head and her skull cracks and her blood splashes across the floor and*

oh my dear Lord we're going to die

going to die

going to die

GOING TO DIE)

– Blake had never stumbled before. Never. He moved like a man carrying spun glass whenever he held the children, especially when putting them to bed. But for a moment it was as though he had lost control of himself.

And not in the way that most people said it – "He lost control of himself" meaning "he fell" or "he got angry." No, Blake moved like he had suddenly ceased being the owner of his body. Like something else had stepped in and in the split-second of the change his muscles relaxed and he nearly fell.

Alyssa turned around to see him righting himself, the mobile swinging.

Blake winked at her. And that was strange, too. She

didn't know why: he had winked at her before. But there was something in his eyes....

She turned away from those eyes. From that look. Back to the mirror. To the world beyond herself. And she saw in the mirror: a reflection. A shadow flitting past the door. Low, small. Headed toward the stairs.

She sighed. At least this was a moment of normalcy: Mal had always had a habit of sneaking out for snacks, for drinks of water. Anything to eke an extra five minutes out of his day.

"Mal's out," she said. She put the brush down and got up from the vanity.

"I thought you put him down," said Blake. He sounded annoyed. Tired and almost angry.

"I did," she said.

Metallic notes drifted into the room. The music box playing its tinkling, lifeless dance.

Blake was moving toward the door, and Alyssa followed him. Frowning. Because snacks and water were Mal's go-to device for staying up. Not playing with antiques.

And she'd gotten the distinct impression that the old box disquieted her son.

No, it doesn't disquiet him. He's scared of it. Scared.

Blake stumbled again.

Alyssa almost said something, but then her husband was out of sight, padding into the hall. She crept out behind him, both of them swerving slightly aside to miss the accent table that sat in the middle of the corridor. Alyssa was wearing loose sweats and one of Blake's t-shirts, and she pulled the cloth tight against her as though afraid she might contract some disease if she touched the table.

It was where that book had come from.

The music box kept playing. Singing the old, staccato song that men and women waltzed to once upon a time.

But the dancers are all dead, and the box should be still.

"Mal?" Alyssa called. Blake twitched in front of her, and that was strange, too. He should have expected that she would call their son.

He shook himself visibly, then shouted, "Bud?" as they continued moving toward the stairs.

The music played.

No voice called back.

"Mal, answer us!" Alyssa shouted.

The music box stopped. She heard the solid thump of the top closing, the mechanism shutting off.

"Whassup?" Mal finally said.

Alyssa froze. So did Blake.

The voice was sleepy. Confused.

And *behind them.*

They turned. Mal stood farther down the hall, in the door to the bedroom he was using. He rubbed his eyes, blinking his way out of sleep and dreams.

"I dreamed I was dancing," said the little boy.

Alyssa looked at her husband. He was already staring back at her. The light in the hall was on, and so was the one in their room. His eyes caught both sources of illumination and seemed to go transparent. For a moment she could see behind them, directly into the raw terror that was trying to take him over.

Or just take *him.*

Blake blinked. A mask fell over his countenance. A tough expression that couldn't completely hide that terror.

"Who's –?" she began.

The phone in their bedroom rang. And now she knew it was her eyes that were clear, that showed nothing but unadulterated fear.

There was someone in their home. But that wasn't the scariest thing right now. Because she had heard of people being in others' houses. Home invasion was something understandable, if hardly desirable.

But not this. Not a phone ringing.

Not a *single* phone.

There were phones in the kitchen, the living room, even one in the entry. And then the one on the second floor: the one in their bedroom.

But the only one that was ringing now was the one in the bedroom.

"Maybe the other ones aren't connected," whispered Blake. So he was thinking the same thing. *Afraid* of the same thing.

Mal had crept to them. He didn't know what was going on, but he was clearly afraid. Because Mommy and Daddy were afraid.

Blake grabbed Mal's hand and pulled their son into the bedroom.

The phone kept ringing. Ringing, ringing....

They stared at it like it was a viper.

Alyssa wondered if they should go looking for whatever was in the house.

Now it's not who*ever, it's* what*ever.*

But she knew she wouldn't. None of them would. If things were normal, they would call 911 – and that was something they needed to do with the phone. If things *weren't* normal….

Blake picked up the phone. Like everything else in this place, it was old. A rotary-style phone with a tall cradle and forks that splayed out like demon fingers plated in gold.

The phone cut off mid-ring.

Ruthie sighed in her playpen. The sigh of a baby asleep, but for a moment it sounded like a sigh of resignation. Of someone who sees death coming and accepts because it cannot be outrun.

"Hello?" said Blake. "Hello? *Hello?*" He slammed the receiver down on the cradle.

And another phone rang. Somewhere else in the house.

They crept down together. Into the hall and down the stairs, Mal, Blake, Alyssa, all holding hands….

She froze. Her arm lengthened out as Blake kept walking forward, and Mal bumped into her at the same time. Then Blake jerked to a halt as well.

"What?" he said. The word spat out like steam escaping a ruptured piston.

"Ruthie. I forgot…." Alyssa couldn't even finish. How could she have left her baby behind? Alone. What kind of mother –?

"She's better off," said Blake. He yanked her down another stair. "Come on."

She wanted to protest. But something seemed to bind her tongue. Maybe the fact that Blake was probably right.

But if that was the case then why was Mal with them?

The phone in the living room was still ringing. Another old-fashioned one, rattling its machine gun chimes through its brass casing on an end table by the couch.

Blake picked it up. "Hello? Who is this?" A pause, then, "*Answer*, dammit!"

His face curled, but before he could slam this phone down as well, another phone rang. He stared at the one in his hand in shock. How could another phone ring if this one was still off the hook?

Blake dropped the receiver. It fell against the wood of the end table with a dry clickety-clack, a painful noise that drew Mal closer to Alyssa.

The phone in the entry was even older. Not a rotary, it was a tall crank phone attached to the wall, an earpiece hanging from its side, a microphone jutting from the middle of the wood case. The mic looked like a mouth, open in a silent scream – a picture helped along by the twin bells, eyelike and staring, that hung directly above it.

She had assumed the phone was ornamental.

The bells chimed again. Fire bells, old sirens. Sounds of warning. *Run, run, danger, danger.*

This time *she* picked it up. Her hand felt as on a

string, moving slowly through the suddenly thick air.

She put the earpiece to the side of her head.

The music box played. Not behind them. Not in the entry way. On the phone.

She dropped the earpiece, her hand going over her mouth.

"What?" said Mal.

And Ruthie started to cry upstairs.

Alyssa ran.

The stairs tore her. Her crotch felt like she was giving birth again, she felt a trickle on one leg. Blood. Fear.

Ruthie.

Mal and Blake were right behind her. And still she thought she could hear the music box playing, metallic notes rendered even tinnier by their rendition through phone lines that shouldn't –

(*couldn't didn't*)

– exist.

Mal actually pushed past her in the hall. He was in the bedroom a half step ahead of her. His small voice quavered out, dancing back to her. "Ruthie, Ruthie, you okay?"

She made it into the room, and her son was already peering over the top of the playpen. "Ruthie!"

Alyssa joined him there. One hand on her lower belly, the other on her heart as though ready to keep it from leaping out when she saw the inevitable tragedy of…

… Ruthie asleep. Silent and apparently content in the middle of the playpen.

Mal looked at his mommy with open eyes. "What's going on?" said the eyes.

Her eyes had no answer.

She jumped as something touched her back. Her shoulder.

She spun.

It was only Blake.

Alyssa's breath caught at her throat. Half in and half out, like her soul was trying to flee and to hold tight to her body at the same time. Blake was so close he was almost looming over her, leaning in to look at the baby, leaning *over* her like a malignant shadow.

Click.

Her eyes, which had been glued to Blake's, tore loose and flitted sideways. The wardrobe. Large and dark and beautiful, scrolled sides and gilded edges – it looked like something C.S. Lewis might have stared at while writing about Narnia.

It was open.

Not far. Just a crack. A quarter-inch of darkness between the two heavy slabs of wood that were the thing's doors.

Blake reached for the doors. For the darkness. His fingers fell into the crack, and he pulled. The doors swung open on perfectly oiled hinges that made no sound but still somehow pounded a new beat in Alyssa's heart.

Inside the wardrobe, clothing hung in neat rows. There was something wrong about it, but it took her a moment to figure out exactly what it was. There were no reds or blues, no greens or yellows. All was gray and brown and black. Tweeds and twills that looked soft but firm, clothing built partly for comfort, but mainly for protection – mainly to last.

None of the clothes dropped more than a yard from the closet rod. Another strangeness, another jarring sensation that Alyssa couldn't quite place until she realized that she was looking at a closet full of children's clothing. Clothing that looked like it belonged to another age, another time: a time when gunfighters were on the wane and textile mills on the rise, when cities and factories began blotting out sun and sky in earnest.

A time when children were born, and children died, and when they died their pictures were taken in books of the dead.

Below the clothes, shoes piled atop one another. Wood, cotton, leather, linen. Laces and buckles. All small. Some so small that only toddlers – perhaps only infants – could have worn them. And with that realization came the new comprehension that not *all* the clothes were dim. Some, tucked away between the others, were light and airy. Gowns made for christenings or baptisms… or funerals. Tiny things that seemed so delicate and ethereal they might blow away on a breath, might disappear into nothing – if they even existed at all.

Do they? Are they really here? Is any *of this?*

But it was. Blake was reaching for them.

Clothing above. Shoes below. Between them nothing.

And beyond?

She couldn't see. The wardrobe was deep, and past the clothes the light from the room seemed to fade. Far too quickly, in fact, as though it dared not intrude into the holdings of whatever thing had put the clothes there in the first place.

Or perhaps that thing was hiding there itself. In the dark. In the permanent night in the back of a wooden box. The coffin that held the clothing of the dead.

Blake was still reaching. He didn't know. Or didn't care.

"Don't," she said. The word wasn't a whisper, but it had no strength. Blake ignored her. He pushed aside the small clothing.

And still the back of the wardrobe couldn't be seen. Just a thick darkness, a horizontal tumble into nothing. Blake's hand fell into that abyss, and Alyssa felt certain he would be yanked off his feet, torn away from her and Mal and Ruthie and flung into –

(*his past, our future*)

– some place too horrible to understand.

He reached…

… reached….

… reached…

And the phone rang.

Alyssa gasped in shock and terror, and Mal coughed and fell into her arms. She clutched him to her legs without thinking, fear binding them more perfectly than any glue could have done.

It was the phone in the bedroom, and again it was the only one that rang.

Blake jerked his hand – still attached, still part of his body – out of the wardrobe and turned to the phone. Terror seemed to stretch his face, pinching his skin and making him seem thin and worn. Then the terror turned to something else. Something Alyssa didn't understand. Something terrible.

He moved to the phone. But this time it didn't give him a chance to answer. The ringing cut off and they heard the downstairs phone – the one in the parlor – ring. Two staccato chirps, then the phone in the entry began clanging its old fashioned bells.

Then the bedroom phone again. One ring this time, then downstairs. Upstairs, downstairs, upstairs, downstairs. A circle that went top to bottom, top to bottom like a trail of notes dancing an angry descent to Hell.

The rings came faster, faster. Faster faster *fasterfasterfaster*.

Mal moaned and clapped his small hands to his ears. Alyssa realized her own hands were in the same position: the ringing wasn't just coming faster, it was getting *louder*.

How? How is that possible?

Blake grunted. Not in fear or even surprise. Anger. His eyes seemed to flash, and once again Alyssa saw something alien there. Angry.

He grabbed a lamp off a bedside table. Tall and sturdy, green glass that looked almost like jade, it fit in his large hand like a blown glass club. His other hand yanked the cord out of the wall. It came loose with a dull thud that somehow made its way between the pealing tones –

(*ringringringringringringupdownupdowntoptobottomtop tobottom*)

– of the ringing phones.

"Wait here," he said. His voice was low and husky. The phones clipped the words and made them fade in and out, disappearing and reappearing like they were pushing in from somewhere both terribly close and even more terribly far away.

"Where are you going?" she shouted.

"Daddy –" Mal began.

"Someone's messing with the phone junction."

He headed for the door. As if responding to his action, the phones quieted. Didn't stop, but the volume dropped enough that Alyssa let her hands fall from her ears.

"Don't," she said. Her voice pleading, almost as high as the bells that rang around them.

The light that had flashed in his eyes now sparked even brighter. "They're messing with us, Lyss! Someone's doing this. Whoever owns this place has some perverted sense of humor – that's probably why this place was so cheap. Maybe we're on a reality show for sadists." His fingers grew so tight around the lamp that his knuckles glowed and she thought she could hear the glass crack. "I'm going to find out who's doing this. I'm going to stop it."

Alyssa didn't understand what was going on. Not just with the phones, but with her husband. What had him acting frightened one moment, loving the next, then with a look in his eyes, an expression she had never seen there and that –

(*was alien different unbelonging other someone ELSE*)

– almost scared her.

Blake left.

This time Alyssa didn't forget her daughter. She picked up Ruthie –

(*Still asleep? Through all this how is she still asleep?*)

– from the playpen, grabbed Mal's hand, and followed Blake out of the room. She stopped in the doorway, looking after where he had gone.

He must have been running, though. Because by the time she got into the hall he was out of sight.

She heard the front door slam. A chill writhed its way up her spine, a centipede with its hundred legs climbing the bones.

Had Blake left?

Or had something come in?

FLIGHT INTO DARKNESS

The dream had been happy. Dancing to a tune he knew, a happy sound. Mal was alone, alone in a small place. A place just big enough for him to turn around, to spin like a helicopter. Fast and fast and fast until he was so dizzy he had to laugh because if he didn't laugh he might barf.

Then things turned dark. He didn't know where he was. Not exactly. But it *had* been happy. Good. Now his spin got faster and faster and then too fast and then scary-fast. He wasn't dizzy, he was afraid. His feet kept slipping on a smooth floor that was impossible to see.

And he realized he couldn't even see *himself*. He could *feel* himself, but when he looked down in the middle of the spins, there was nothing there.

Darkness, blackness, fell all over him. Like when he hid under blankets. But this wasn't safe. No help from the monster. The dark *was* the monster.

Something whispered. Something he couldn't hear.

And then… his name. Not coming from the thing in the dark (the thing that was the dark). It was from somewhere beyond.

Mommy. Daddy.

He ran on legless legs. Clawed with hands that were nowhere. Pulled through black that fell into a mouth he could feel but that could not scream.

And then sat up in his bed. Well, not his. The bed in this new place. The cross on the wall. Froo-froo bedding wadded up all around him like bizarro quicksand.

Mommy and Daddy calling him.

He went to them.

They were afraid. He didn't know why. But soon he got it. The music box was playing, and he recognized it from his dream. His dancing where he was there, but also wasn't.

Then they went into the room, and Daddy looked into a closet full of old clothes, and the phones rang, and now Daddy was gone.

Daddy was gone.

Mommy had Mal under her arm, held against her legs. Ruthie was sleeping in her other arm, and Mal could hear his sister's gentle breathing behind him.

The phones were still ringing. It scared him. Scared him even worse than the dance. He wanted to run, and wanted to scream, and wanted to go to the bathroom right there in his PJ's right in front of Mommy.

He did none of those things. Daddy had run away and Mal was the man of the house. But he was a man of the house who didn't know what to do.

They went into the hall, and then something made a noise behind them. Mommy turned a little, and Mal also pushed his way around her, just enough to see.

Ruthie's mobile was spinning. Dancing just like he had done, round and round and he wondered if it would all fall down like the ashes to ashes.

Then it stopped. So did the ringing phones.

And a voice screamed. "*LEAVE!*"

The voice was like his dream-self. It was real, but it

was nowhere. Louder than loud, louder than the phones had been. Coming from right next to the mobile. And also right in his ears.

Mommy's body went hard behind him, all her muscles getting stiff like his hardest plastic toy. He wanted to pull her far away from the mobile, far away from the room. But he was stuck to the floor, too. His muscles were so tight he felt like they might just ping apart: rubber bands pulled too far.

The mirror on the desk-thing – what Mommy called the vanity – cracked. A long line in its center that made Mommy look like two different people when he looked at it.

Then it fell. The glass exploded in a trillion tiny pieces. But the explosion happened *before* the mirror touched the floor.

In the next second something hit the big bed with a *whud* sound. So hard the bed slid a good foot.

Mommy moved. Grabbed him and ran.

The bedroom door slammed shut behind them. It hit so hard that Mal's teeth slammed shut, too, and the shockwave of the door bounced his feet an inch off the floor.

Mommy held him tighter and they ran.

Inside the closed-up room, it sounded like a fight was happening. An angry thing – a thing he knew must be a ghost, like that *Poltergeist* movie Daddy showed him and Mommy got angry about – smashed into all the walls.

They ran.

The door slammed open.

Paint flew off the walls around them. The little table in the hall turned over as they ran past. It almost hit him in the leg, but he dodged. It hit Mommy and she shouted.

"Mommy!"

"Run! Don't stop!"

The music box started playing below them. *Ahead* of them. The big clock ticked, faster and faster. His heart beat faster with it, and he wondered if the clock could make it beat so fast that it exploded.

He thought maybe it could. And that maybe it would.

Paint and wood were like a snowstorm. He had to close his eyes to tiny lines, barely could see. The storm danced to the music box, like he had danced in the dream. He knew it wasn't the box making the storm, it was something in the hall. Something following them. Something that wanted to hurt them.

They went down the steps. Mommy pushed him. Too fast. He fell. Mommy grabbed him and actually pushed him back to his feet. Pushed him down the stairs and up to standing at the same time, and he wasn't quite sure how she did that. But she did and they made it down the stairs and he was sure that he heard not four feet but six bamming down and that was impossible because it was him and Mommy and that was four and yes there was Ruthie but she didn't walk she was just a little burrito-wrapped baby in Mommy's arms so who was the other person who was behind them who –?

He didn't look back. There might be someone. Or there might be *no one*. He didn't want it to be either.

They ran to the front door. He knew it was gonna be

locked.

Mommy let go of him. He shivered. She just let go of him long enough to try the door, but it was a forever and that was way too long.

She clicked it. It *opened*.

They ran. Ran into the dark outside. And the dark outside seemed so much brighter than the lighted house inside.

The door slammed shut behind them. He heard the music box stop tinkling, the big clock stop beating his heart to explosion.

He relaxed. Mommy's muscles got a bit softer at his back. She kept pushing him away from the house, but he knew they had beaten it. For now at least.

Then Mommy got tense again. He thought for a second the thing was out here. Had made it outside its house and was going to destroy them right out in the open. Maybe because they were still on the property, so it could get them just fine.

But no. That was impossible, wasn't it? There was no clock, no music box, no dark feeling.

What was Mommy worried about? What was out –?

Daddy.

Daddy had run out here. And was probably *still* out here. But that was good news, right?

So why did Mal suddenly feel cold? Thinking of Daddy's eyes in the bedroom, the eyes that were usually so warm and loving, but were somehow different when he ran away.

Like they belonged to someone else.

Someone not nice at all.
Why am I worried?
Where is Daddy out here?
Is *Daddy out here at all?*

GIVEN IN

Blake didn't find anyone. Not a thing, not a trace. He ran around the house, tripping over planters and ornamental walls that seemed to spring out of the ground at the last moment solely to obstruct him. Each time he almost went down his rage increased.

He finally slipped and fell. Dog crap or just a wet patch of grass. Whatever it was, he went down and the vase he'd been clutching flew from his hand. It shattered with a tinkle that was almost merry. A sound far too bright for a night so dark.

The sound carved his rage to pieces, slashed it away like a coat that had been torn down to its barest threads.

He stood, dusting himself off, picking a large pebble from his palm. Wondering what was going on, what had just happened. Not just with the phones and the wardrobe.

With *him*. The anger. The fury that he hadn't felt since that last night –

(*C'mere, kid. Daddy's gonna play a game.*)

– that final night –

(*Don't you run from me, you little bastard! Little shit!*)

– that night he couldn't take it anymore. That night he fled. Not from his father but from himself. Running with blood on his hands, and for once it wasn't his own.

He turned and, like the night he had left his childhood home behind, the night his father died, he ran.

But this time he wasn't fleeing, he was searching.

Where was Alyssa? What about Mal and Ruthie?

Why did I leave them? How?

He didn't understand what was happening. Could barely remember the last few minutes. He knew the phones had been ringing. Remembered a distant sense of anger. A need to find out what was doing it and –

(*punish them punish them good and proper*)

– put a stop to it. But he'd left his family. How could he have done that?

He ran to the front of the house, and with every footfall he pictured a new death they might have suffered in his absence. At the side of the house he realized he was picturing the many ways he himself had been torn, had been hurt. Only it wasn't him this time. It was his wife, his children. And they weren't just bleeding, they weren't just breaking bones and skin.

They were dying.

He turned the corner. Ran around to the front of the house. And there they were. Standing, shivering, waiting. He was sure for a moment they weren't real. Just the ghosts that were all that remained of his family, his joy. Memories of happiness forever lost, which are the worst kind of damnation.

"Blake!" shouted Alyssa. And Mal screamed, "Daddy!" at the same time.

Not dead. Not dead. Alive.

(MINE.)

He tried to ignore the last word. Tried to ignore the other ghost that kept pushing through. The ghost of a father long dead but ever present.

Alyssa reached for him, then her hands curled back like withered plants. Just a second – she reached for him again almost instantly – but that second tore him apart.

For that second she was afraid of him.

He fell into her arms. Held her and Mal and Ruthie. Held them so tight he knew he was trying to force the fear from between them. And knew that it wouldn't work.

She was afraid. Afraid of what had happened, yes. Afraid of what was going on around them.

And he was one of those things.

Alyssa breathed in to say something, and he feared it would be, "We're leaving you." His heart stopped.

"We can't stay here," she said.

His legs turned to reed, he almost fell against her. Only the fact that she had to be hurting, that her postpartum body could barely be holding up, kept him upright.

"Yeah," he managed. "Yeah, I know."

They got in the car. They didn't go back in the house for their things. They would do without.

He drove. Everyone was silent, and he himself fell into a mindless daze, almost a fugue. When he finally came to himself enough to take stock of where they were he saw that he had driven them to the worst part of the city.

And that was the only place they *could* go. That was the only place left to them, because it was all they could possibly afford.

The place they pulled into was simply called "Motel." And it was a truism that the less creative the name of an establishment like this, the less you could expect from it.

Alyssa eyed it warily. The cheap paint job splashed directly onto the bricks, the air conditioning units hanging below the windows that looked like they dated back to the Revolutionary War. Still, she glued a smile on her face and looked at Mal and said, "You've never slept at a motel, have you?" He shook his head. His face was white. "This'll be fun for you, then!"

Blake loved her. Maybe more than ever. She was so strong, so good. Everything he'd never known before, and everything he'd never thought he *would* know, but knew he didn't deserve.

They got out of the car. He tried to get Ruthie, but Alyssa squeezed in front of him and got the baby out. She did it smoothly, but it was still pretty obvious: she didn't want him holding the infant.

Blake stood still as his family went to the office. Battling a slew of emotions. Trying to focus on the love he had just felt, to cast out the irritation –

(*anger*)

– that tried to force its way in.

He walked after them.

The night manager was almost as old and cracked as the desk he sat behind. Nursing a cup of coffee that smelled hot and cheap and necessary in a place like this. But his smile was pleasant under gray whiskers as he turned to the family and said, "Hey, folks, how can I help you?"

The question flared an ember of anger in Blake. He wanted to answer, "How do you think?"

Again, Alyssa got between him and what he

wanted. "A room," she said.

"Double occupancy is sixty-nine a night. Two forms of identification."

"What about the kids?" asked Alyssa. "Are they extra?"

The manager winked at Mal. "What kids?" he asked innocently.

Mal winked back. A little boy's wink, the kind that squinched the entire side of his face and nearly shut the other eye as well. It made Blake feel a little better.

Blake fumbled his wallet out of his pocket – thank God he hadn't gotten undressed for the night, thank God Alyssa slept in sweats and a shirt and was wearing slippers – and slid over a card and his driver's license.

The manager slid the credit card through a slot on the side of his register. The noise was barren. The sound of dreams come to die.

A moment later there was a double beep. The manager turned a sad smile to Blake. "Sorry, but...."

He didn't have to finish the sentence. Blake had been waiting for this to start happening. But knowing it was coming didn't make it any easier. Didn't make the shame burn any cooler in his cheeks and ears as he accepted a worthless rectangle of plastic and shoved it back in his wallet.

One more way he was failing his family. One more way he had proved himself less than a man.

His father was right. Had always been right.

(*you can't escape this, won't escape what you are!*)

Blake fumbled another card – his only other card,

out of the wallet. He gave it to the manager, and his hand trembled. Not just because he didn't know what they would do if this didn't work. It was more than that. This card represented his last worth.

The manager slid the card through. Dry snick, barren motion, dying dreams.

The moment stretched out. Out, out. The manager frowned, slid the card through again. He tapped the corner of the card against his chin.

The register beeped. "We have a winner!" he said.

Another wink at Mal, and Mal again winked with most of his head.

Blake felt no relief. The pit in his stomach grew a bit deeper. When would this card stop working as well?

One of poverty's meanest tricks is to replace the mundane pleasures of the present with the grand worries of the future. It is never about smiles and small moments. It is about looming debt, about Final Notice and Amount Due and Shutoff Date. Past problems steal present joys because of future fears.

The manager was talking about a "continental breakfast" – coffee and Nutri-Grain Cereal Bars that went out every morning from six to nine. Then it was out the door, up the stairs and into a room that smelled of cigarettes and sweat and a few other unidentifiable things that no amount of cheap cleaner could mask. Two beds – singles – and barely enough room between them for an adult to walk sideways. An original Philo Farnsworth television with an actual VHF knob on it.

"It's smelly," said Mal.

"Yep," said Alyssa. She spoke brightly, as though

this was part of the grand adventure of it all. "You want a bath – shower?" The last word changed as she walked into the "bathroom." Blake followed and saw a shower that looked like something out of an exceptionally bleak dystopian future. A whitish pod with a plastic tentacle sticking out of one wall, reticulated so that it could be used by lodgers of any height.

"Cool!" said Mal. He started stripping and grabbed at the tiny bar of wrapped soap on the floor. Blake couldn't be sure if he was more excited about the sci-fi shower or the tiny soap. It didn't matter. Hardly anything did.

Mal showered. Alyssa put Ruthie – still asleep, which was only one more in a long list of the night's strange events – down in the middle of one of the beds. The newborn sighed, stretched. Alyssa unwrapped the light blanket that swaddled Ruthie, and pulled the girl's onesie away from her leg. Apparently there was nothing in the diaper, because Alyssa just rewrapped her and let her lay quietly on the bed.

Alyssa moved to the edge of the same bed. The television was within easy reach so she turned it on and spun the wheel through varying levels of static before finally turning it off again.

She didn't talk.

Neither did Blake.

He leaned on the door, not sure if he was doing it because the floor there had the largest square footage or if it was a subconscious effort to keep out unwanted visitors. Either way, he didn't want to chat. He sensed Alyssa *did* want to, but also knew that she would wait until Mal was asleep. Probably in the other bed.

Blake wondered if she'd trust him to sleep with one of the kids or if he'd just have to sleep in that shitty crack between the beds. *That* would be fun.

Mal came out of the bathroom, preceded by a puff of clean-smelling steam. Dressed again in his pajamas and smiling. Then he stopped smiling as he looked at Blake. Blake tried the manager's winking trick. It didn't work. His son just looked at the floor.

"Do I have to go to bed?"

"We'll be right here," said Alyssa.

"I'm scared."

"Nothing will happen."

She guided Mal to the bed nearest his father. She didn't look at Blake.

A moment later she was singing a low song to Mal. It was "Twinkle, Twinkle," which the kid hadn't wanted to listen to for years. But he didn't seem to mind now. His brow smoothed out, his eyes closed. His breathing leveled and deepened.

Alyssa waited a moment, softly rubbing Mal's arm. She looked at Blake and he thought they were going to talk about whatever she had on her mind. Instead, she picked up Ruthie and placed her gently beside Mal. There was plenty of room for both of them in the bed.

Blake smiled. Just a little. Because Alyssa clearly meant for him to share the other bed with her.

Unless she wants you on the floor.

The smile fell away from his mouth.

"So we'll stay here a few days, then we can go home," said Alyssa.

The statement, delivered firmly and without offer of discussion or compromise, took him off guard.

"What?" he said. "We can't afford to do that. We can't afford to stay here that long." He heard the words, heard them coming from his mouth. Knew they made no sense – what else *was* there to do? They didn't really have any friends or family – none who lived close enough to help, or who could put up an entire family. But at the same time, staying was impossible. *Everything* was impossible. There was nowhere to turn. "We can't afford to stay here!"

"Just two nights," said Alyssa.

"Not even that."

"So what, you want us to go back? To that place?"

He pushed away from the door. Crossed his arms over his chest. Angry now. Because she was pushing him.

No she's not. She's just trying to help –

(*Help herself, not you.*)

She's worried –

(*She's telling you what to do. She's telling.*)

She's just –

(*She's just a bitch.*)

"We're not going back, Blake. We're not."

That was it. It was clear now: she was trying to force him into a decision, trying to make him do what *she* wanted instead of what *they* agreed on.

"Whoever did all that is probably gone," he said.

Her eyes bulged and her mouth fell open. "You actually think someone did that? Our landlord pranked us? Some local kids just got a wild idea to stage the most elaborate joke in the history of the world? Are you insane?"

241

He moved toward her. A single step, but it felt like he had put his foot down in a swift current. A riptide that might yank him away, somewhere deep and dark.

"Don't call me that," he said.

"If the shoe fits."

He hit her.

FIRST BLEEDING UNBLED

It all happened so fast. So fast, and she wasn't really sure what happened.

She knew he hit her. Of course she knew that, it felt like she had been slammed with a burning anvil. It was just a flat-handed slap, but her teeth ground into the inside of her cheek and her lip split. She rocked back and to the side. Her head hit the wall beside the bed, and she felt a cut open on her forehead as well.

So, yes, she knew she had been hit.

But she didn't understand what had led to it.

Blake had never touched her before. Never raised his hand, never even clenched his *fist*. In fact, there had even been a few times in their relationship when she wished he was a bit tougher. Not meaner, but a bit more willing to stand up for himself. Sometimes it seemed like he was so afraid of becoming –

(*his father, his genes, his destiny*)

– something awful that he shied too far the other direction. Sometimes she wondered if that was why the business was failing. His work was exemplary, but maybe he couldn't land clients because he just didn't know how to fight for them. Because fighting was something he could never, ever do.

So what happened here? How had he gone from afraid to angry to violent so fast? Where had her husband gone?

For that matter, where had *she* gone? What made her

say those cruel words to Blake. He *had* been acting irrational, but why did she call him insane? Why did she poke him in a place she knew would always be so terrible and so tender for him? It wasn't like her.

None of this was like *them*.

Was it the fear? The exhaustion?

Did it matter?

The instant after she bounced off the wall Blake was on top of her, falling on her with all his weight, his hands clutching her and flailing at her.

She tried to scream, couldn't. Then realized that he wasn't attacking her. He was trying to pull her up, trying to pull her *to* him.

"I'm sorry, I'm sorry, baby, so sorry."

She pushed away from him. Shoved with both hands and then managed to get a foot between them. She put it on his chest and levered him away. He was so big he barely took a step. Instead she ended up sliding back on the bed while he remained nearly stationary.

"Get away from me," she said. Her voice was low. Quavering. She didn't know if she was more afraid or enraged. She knew who he was when she married him. Knew what he had gone through, and knew what he had done to get away from it.

But she had believed he would never do something like that again. She had believed she was safe.

"I'm sorry, Lyss," he said. His hands reached toward her. Halted when his arms were only half-outstretched. "I'm sorry, I won't do that again. We'll do whatever you want. I'm sorry. I won't leave you alone. Ever. Promise."

She pushed herself into the corner of the bed, far away. Staring at her husband. Wondering what she should do. His hands dropped. His shoulders slumped.

"I don't know what to do," he whispered. His voice was so low, so pitiful, she almost went to him.

He's never done this before.

But he's done it now.

He's been a good father and husband.

But he hit me.

She stayed put.

He lifted a hand again. "Can I...? You're bleeding. Can I...?" He looked disoriented, turning his head from side to side as though searching for something that would make all this right. He took a step, going to the small sink that stood outside the bathroom. He grabbed a towel off the wall and held it out to her.

If he'd tried to help her with the wounds – tried to touch her – she didn't think she would have let him stay. She would have made him leave, or called the cops. But his face was so pitiful when he handed over the towel that she just took it.

She didn't know what she was going to do. She still might kick him out or call the cops. But not this instant.

She mopped the blood off her mouth. Not much. Worse was her head. Head wounds bled like crazy, so she wasn't *too* worried, but she thought based on the amount of blood on the towel that she might need stitches.

She looked at Blake. He still stood there like a beaten puppy, lost and forlorn. His gaze finally raised to meet hers, and his expression went from grief and remorse to concern.

"Lyss?" he said. "Lyss, you okay?"

"What do you...?"

She didn't have to finish the sentence. Thunderclouds gathered around her field of vision. They spat lightning that coursed through the rest of her sight. She slumped.

The last thing she saw was Blake leaping forward, his big hands reaching out. The hand that had struck her open again, this time to catch her as she fell...

... fell...

... fell...

... and then her eyes fluttered. Opened.

She saw squares. Dots.

Ceiling tiles.

Something moved beside her. A large, warm thing that shifted and rubbed against her. It breathed deep as a dragon.

Blake.

She was still in the motel. Still with Blake. In the *bed* with him.

She rolled over, nearly falling into the crevasse between the room's two beds before managing to get her feet under her. Looking over she saw Mal and Ruthie asleep on the other bed. Mal had his arm over his baby sister, a protective older brother doing his work even in sleep.

And Blake... her husband hadn't taken her to the hospital. Must have been worried about the questions. So he had just put her in bed, which was terrible. Worse: he had crawled in bed beside her.

She stood. Her body creaked, ached. Not just the site of Ruthie's birth, but everywhere.

And standing, she happened to see the mirror over the small sink.

Like everything in this room the mirror was cheap, ill-used. Scratches clouded its surface and made it nearly a parody of reflection, but she thought....

She moved toward it. In front of it. Her face so close to it that she could see fingerprints and smudges that showed how long since it had been cleaned.

So close she could see her face.

And so close she could *not* see the blood.

Her lip, which should have been swollen, was normal-sized. She opened her mouth as wide as she could, and there was no trace of blood inside.

Her forehead, the spot she remembered hitting the wall, was whole. Unblemished skin stretched from temple to temple.

Blake sighed. The dark wraith-image of his legs that she could see in the mirror shifted slightly. He coughed.

And Alyssa stared at herself. No wounds. Not a mark.

"Did I dream it?"

She must have.

She *must* have.

But in that moment she didn't know whether the knowledge came with joy or dread.

Blake hadn't hit her.

But she remembered it happening. Just like she remembered the changing embroidery, the voice in the room, the hallway exploding around her and Mal.

What was happening?

Was anything happening?

She got back into bed with Blake. After all, he hadn't hit her.

But it took a long time. She stood at the sink and stared in the mirror, watching the dark ghost of her husband as he moved and made small sleep-noises. Watching and waiting and wondering what was real.

She finally turned away from the mirror, away from the image of herself that made no sense, and went back to her family. The children kept sleeping. Blake slept with his face away from her, and she had the strange feeling that if she turned him over he would have no face at all. Just a blank stretch of flesh, inhuman and incapable of humanity.

One hand lay on his side. The cheap motel cover bound it up so that he looked like he only had three fingers. And now he was a faceless thing that had been maimed in some cruel accident... or perhaps a well-deserved attack.

She stared at the three-fingered hand, perhaps even longer than she had stared into the mirror. Listening to the breathing all around her, but suddenly unsure if anyone in this place was really alive.

Then Blake's hand unclenched. All five fingers appeared and he rolled over and he had a face and that face was smooth and open and kind. He couldn't have hit her. He never had, he couldn't have done such a thing –

(*even though he did once he did much worse to his father*

248

to his own blood)

– and she was safe with him.

She didn't remember sleeping that night, or the next night. They did stay in the motel, and the credit card didn't bounce. Not even when they got some food and diapers at the nearest small market. She hadn't bled much after Mal, and that was repeating, thank God. Even so, the emergency pads she kept in the glove box weren't going to last the night, so they had to pick up a package of those as well. Each purchase made Blake visibly cringe. Each cringe made her quake.

What if he hit her?

Would it be the first time or the second? The third?

What was she remembering that wasn't real? And were there perhaps real things that she was forgetting?

Mal hated the television situation in the motel room, but he did like Pop Tarts for breakfast, Lunchables at midday, and Jack in the Box for dinner. He played with Ruthie. It was all a strange dream, a family packed in a box like a present waiting to be opened on Christmas or some birthday.

And then the day came to leave. The box opened. They went home again. Not the rental. Their *real* home.

Blake had called ahead, had verified that the place was ready, but Alyssa didn't really believe it until she saw the house. Its familiar lines and angles were open to the morning light, the plastic tent gone and no sign of the exterminators.

Blake squeezed her hand before they got out of the car. She managed not to recoil, wondering if he noticed that this was the first time she had let him touch her since they left the rental.

"Home sweet home, huh?" she said. The words fought their way out. But saying them actually made her feel better.

Mal's voice chirped out from the backseat. He sounded equal parts happy to be out of the motel and worried to be back.

"Is it over?"

Alyssa looked at Blake. He was grinning at their son. "Well *I* certainly don't have any plans for going back to that place again."

He sounded upbeat. Hopeful. She had to smile as well. "I think so, Mal," she said. "I think it's over."

Blake took Ruthie inside. Mal ran in after them.

Alyssa went to the mailbox. The door hung open on its hinges, days of mail wedged inside and spilling out. It was such a thick wad that most of them fell from her fingers. Maybe not a bad thing since most were either junk mail offering useless coupons to places she had no intention of ever visiting or bills threatening a variety of repercussions if not immediately paid.

She bent to pick them up. Her center hurt as always, but maybe a little less. She was getting better. Maybe things in general were getting better.

She picked up the mail in a single scoop. Straightened. And this time when she dropped the mail it *all* fell tumbling from her hands. All but a single envelope. The one that had somehow found itself on the top of the massive pile.

It was oddly shaped. Square, but not quite even. As though not made by machine but by hand. It was yellow in the center, the paper browning slightly toward the edges. Old.

It felt like parchment paper.

She tore open the envelope with fingers that shook so badly she nearly dropped it again and again. Then she yanked out what was inside.

The paper that came out was parchment, too. Just like the envelope. Just like the paper had fallen from between pages of death and told her to run.

This one had writing, too. The same thick, black strokes.

I wont leave you alone. Ever.

The shaking in her hands moved to her arms, then took control of her entire body.

It was here.

And not just here. She had seen – heard – these words before. In a dream that perhaps hadn't been a dream. When Blake had struck her he had said those same words. "I'm sorry, I won't do that again. We'll do whatever you want. I'm sorry. *I won't leave you alone. Ever.* Promise."

Promise.

FIVE:
PICTURE PERFECT

Finally the time comes to actually take the picture. And for some it is beyond anything. It is ecstasy. It is sublime.

> Poppa found me doing bad things wunse. He did what Godlee Poppas do, and I never did it again.

> But when I take the picshers I feel lyke that agin. Things get fast and fast faster I cant help it and I hope Poppa will forgiv me and wont hit me no more even tho he is ded and gon a long time.

- Silver, Charles M.
(afterword by Dr. Charlotte Bongiovi),
(2003) Berkeley, California,
Memento Mori, Notes of a Dead Man,
Western University Press, Inc.

HOME SWEET HOME

Alyssa walked. She knew she should run, but her feet refused. Or perhaps her feet were willing, but her mind was not. Her mind did not want anything to be wrong, did not want whatever had happened at the rental to have followed them here.

Though she suspected –

(*knew*)

– that it might actually have followed her family to the rental. That what had seemed to start there might actually have been set in motion before that. With –

(*Blake?*)

– the centipedes. With her son.

She ran.

When she got to the door she didn't know what to expect. But she slammed it open so hard it bounced right back and almost hit her in the face.

Blake's gonna be pissed when he sees the mark on the wall.

She expected blood. She expected death.

Ruthie was on a baby mat on the floor in the living room. Mal holding a toy over her head, reflecting a warped image on a bent plastic mirror. The baby gurgled. The onesie was pink. All was well.

"Where's Daddy?" she said.

Mal didn't look up. Totally engrossed in play with his baby sister. Or just avoiding her eyes. "In my room," he said.

"Is he... did he seem okay?"

"Yeah, why?" Now he looked up. Disquiet in his eyes, rapidly shifting to fear. "Did something happen? Are we –?"

"No." She smiled. What she hoped was reassurance on her face, what she suspected was merely a confused mask that conveyed nothing but a macabre mix of her own fears. She tried to smile a better smile, then just turned away when she realized she would only make him more worried by standing here.

It was only a few short steps to the entrance to her son's room. Just behind the stairs, "Below the Ascension" Blake had always said. As though Mal was a demon in their lives. Silly, since he was the best kid ever. But now the bedroom seemed like it *might* be a portal to a deep and dark place.

Mal's door was shut. She opened it. The doorknob was bitingly cold under her palm. She was oddly pleased when it only rattled a bit in her hand.

Blake was under the bed. His long legs stuck out like he was a mechanic inspecting the chassis of a classic car. They jerked as she entered. He slid out.

"Geez! You scared me to death!" He smiled brightly at her. A smile totally like *him*. Bright, cheerful. No trace of worry, not even the money concerns that had driven his shoulders down in the past year or the fears about Ruthie's health.

So why didn't she feel better looking at him?

Blake moved to Mal's toybox.

"You...," she said. She felt a thousand questions

bubbling up behind her lips. Why did you hit me? *Did* you hit me? Did any of it really happen?

And the one that finally escaped was the most banal, the least important.

Or perhaps the most important. Because the banal, was, after all, real life. The mundane moment-to-moment moments were the ones that comprised reality and made existence worthwhile.

"Any bugs?"

Blake moved to the closet. He pulled Mal's clothes apart one at a time, searching between each.

Little boy's clothes. They look like the ones in the wardrobe.

Will Mal die?

Blake shook his head. "Not a one. The exterminators were expensive, but it looks like they did a good job."

He started to turn from the closet, then stopped. For a moment his smile dropped away. Behind it Alyssa saw something strange. Not the fear she had actually expected, the terror that had become a constant companion in the last days. The opposite.

For a second, Blake looked ecstatic. She thought of their wedding night. The look on his face as his fingers danced across her, as he whispered to her that he would love her, would stay forever.

Blake reached out and touched a piece of molding on the side of the closet. He pulled at it, turning so Alyssa could no longer see that strange, terrible happiness.

The molding wiggled a bit.

"Looks like this got knocked loose," said Blake. He

looked at his watch. His face looked normal again. Even businesslike, as though he was on a job. "I'm going to fasten this down before I start work for the day."

He winked at her. A completely normal wink. Just the right mix of lover and husband and friend. But her belly felt loose, her wounds twinged.

"Mom?"

Mal was in the doorway. His face white.

"What?" she said. She turned from Blake. Blake didn't move. He was engrossed in the molding, gently pulling it farther away from the wall. "Where's Ruthie?"

"Could you come here?" said Mal.

And he left. Walking herky-jerky, a poorly manipulated marionette. Pinocchio before the Blue Fairy set him free.

She hurried after him, and again her mind threw terrible images at her eyes. Her baby, dead. Her house, invaded.

Get out. You have to get out.

Where can I go? It's not here, it's everywhere.

She followed puppet-Mal into the living room. Ruthie was, again, still on her mat. Gurgling. Happy.

Everything in the living room was where it belonged. But there was a plus-one. An unwelcome party crasher.

Alyssa pitched sideways. Clutched at a wall to keep from falling to the floor.

"What is that, Mom? Where did it come from?"

Alyssa stared. Couldn't speak. Just like the boy she stared at. The boy long-dead, throat cut and blood streaming over his tall white collar, sitting on the strange black chair.

"What is it?"

The book sat beside Ruthie. Open to the boy's picture, but she knew if she flipped through the pages each one would be full of other dead children posed on that terrible chair.

"Where did it –?" Mal began again.

Alyssa waved her hand. She didn't want to hear the rest of the question. Even though it was the one ringing in her own mind.

Where did it come from?

Why was it here?

How was it here?

She looked at Mal. She needed to answer. If not the truth – a truth she didn't know – then *something*.

Her mouth opened.

And the doorbell rang.

The sound prickled her skin. The hairs on her arms stabbed into the air. She turned to the door.

The frosted glass window showed a silhouette. A dark outline. Featureless, silent, unmoving. A thing on the other side of a glass darkly, and one that held her frozen.

"What is it?" said Mal again. She didn't know if he was asking about the book or the thing beyond the door.

She couldn't answer either question.

A BIT OF CHANGE

At first he was mad. He had paid through the nose, dammit! Through the nose! When you handed over the last money you had you didn't deserve a good job, you deserved *perfection*. Not "close is good enough" or "just about perfect." Per-damn-fect.

And the bug guys had nearly gotten it.

Bugs dead: check (apparently).

Bugs gone: check (absolutely).

Molding banged up: shit shit shitty shit shit (yep).

Blake held back his irritation while Alyssa was there. Important to keep a happy face after everything she'd been through. But inside he seethed. He wanted to find the good gents of Pest in Peace and stick them in one of their own tents. Give them a blast or two and see how they liked it. Mess up their houses and see how they liked it. Kill their kids and their wives and see how they liked....

He shook himself.

What was I thinking?

He couldn't remember. Not for the life of him. He thought it had been something about his father. And that was something better left unthought.

Though it was nice to think about leaving. To think about beating the shit out of him, after all the long beatings Blake had endured. To finally outgrow his old man and his own fear.

The blood had been so warm on his hands.

He hadn't stuck around to make sure he killed the bastard. And they didn't tell things like that to fourteen-year-old boys who had been beaten and molested for their whole lives.

That made him sad. Not to know. To know for *sure*.

The blood had felt warm. Good.

He pulled molding away from the wall. He wasn't mad anymore. He thought there might be something underneath it, and that was interesting. Maybe he wasn't mad at the exterminators after all. Maybe.

He heard something. Or felt it.

He turned. The door to Mal's room was swinging shut. No one there, but it moved evenly until it clicked firmly into place.

Blake turned back to the molding.

The blood had felt so warm.

And there was something underneath the wood. Something interesting. Like brains under bone, like a heart under ribs.

He was smiling.

A moment later he heard/felt something new. Not the door this time. He knew it was closed, and that it would *stay* closed until he was done with whatever it was he had started. That was fine.

The sound came from the back of the room.

He turned to Mal's bed. Below the window where it had always been, the brightest and most beautiful spot in the room.

The shade was drawn –

(*Was it drawn when I came in here? Is that even*

important?)

– and the bed crouched in shadow. The darkness deepened the lower it fell, and below the bed shadow ended and pure darkness held sway.

The sound/feeling came from the place of greatest black.

Blake waited. After a moment he saw a faint shine. A glimmer so dim he might have imagined it. Then it grew. It multiplied. It became two and four and then so many he could not count it.

The centipedes came, and he was not surprised, not afraid. They spewed out from under the bed, raced across the floor.

He turned back to his work. He gave up teasing the molding free and began yanking it, tearing it. Soon his fingers were bleeding, his nails hung in bloody shreds. He moved from molding to wallpaper, his motions jerky and ragged. He wanted to move faster, faster, faster. But his hands weren't listening properly. One hand moved those jerky motions of a poorly driven machine. One felt like several of the fingers were asleep.

He pulled the wallpaper away. It was blue with small airplanes flying around it, tiny men in parachutes between each plane.

Beneath the paper: bare wood, smeared with gold glue that looked like snot. Below the glue the remnants of old paint, half-scraped and grayed by the glue, looked like flaking skin.

Something tickled his ankles. The centipedes began crawling up his legs. He had to bite back a laugh. Not because he cared about laughing in and of itself, but because laughing might slow down his work.

His fingers yanked the wall that was Now, revealing layers Before.

The centipedes covered the room, and crawled higher and higher on his body.

Blake did not laugh. But his smile grew and grew. And that was fine. That was right. It felt good. Felt like blood.

GONE JUST LIKE THAT

Mommy walked toward the door and Mal thought that was crazy and wanted to go to her. But Daddy's words kept banging through his head. The words when Ruthie was born. "What do I do?" "You be a good example. You take care of her. That's what big brothers do."

Daddy had also told him to take care of Mommy, but Mal was pretty sure that was just when Daddy had to run off after Ruthie. And Daddy was in the other room now, so Mal should stay with his sister, right?

He didn't know. He had to guess. Do his best.

Mommy kept moving to the door. To the shadow behind it. The scary shape that a few days ago would have been just *a* shape but now Mal was sure it was a ghost or a werewolf or maybe that girl from the movie about the killer videotape that he saw at Kel Pedroso's house and Mommy got so mad at Kel he wasn't allowed back there for a month.

Not any of those. Worse.

And Mommy was going toward it.

"Mom, don't," he said.

A faraway part of him realized he had never called her "Mom" before. That maybe he was Growing Up a bit. And maybe that was sad. But it wouldn't matter if everyone died.

Mommy put her hand on the door. She looked down at her hand like she thought it might jump off her arm and bite her face. That was why she didn't see the shadow disappear.

She pulled the door open and gave a little yell. Not a scared one, more like a karate yell, like she was going to try and ninja-chop whoever was there.

No one was.

Something fell into the house with a hollow *tuk* sound. It was a tube like Daddy got all the time from work. Probably full of plans for whatever building he was designing, dropped off by a courier because it was too big or too important to send in normal mail.

Mal felt like pudding. He probably would have drooped all over the floor, except Ruthie was right there and that would have meant he drooped all over her and he didn't think she would like that. He kept straight up, but was so glad it was just a courier and not a mummy or a dead girl he almost giggled.

Mommy didn't seem happy. She looked at the tube for a second. Then she stepped out onto the porch. Then she screamed, "Hey!"

And then she ran away. Gone, just like that. He said her name. "Mommy" this time. But it wasn't a yell. Maybe not even a talk. Just a whisper, and then he was alone except for Ruthie who didn't count because all she did was make funny noises and need him to protect her.

Thinking that he wondered if he should do more. Mommy was gone. Daddy was... well, he was in Mal's room. But when Mal had gone back there, Daddy had looked weird. Like he wasn't interested in Mal. Or anything else, other than that piece of the wall he was pulling at.

He had a look in his eyes that scared Mal.

No, Mal was on his own. Just him and Ruthie.

He sat down next to her. She was too little for him to pick up the right way. Her neck was all floppy. Mommy and Daddy had let him hold her – a bunch of times, and he was really proud of that. But he wasn't sure about picking her up himself. Still, he wanted to get close as he could. Like he was her shield.

He sat behind her. And as careful as he could he lifted her little head into his lap. He kept his hands behind her floppy neck and her big head. She looked up at him, and he thought she was smiling. He thought maybe he was doing the right thing.

Then her smile went away.

Her onesie changed. It wasn't pink anymore. It was blue. Not just one place, either. All over. Ruthie started to shiver. Her little mouth opened and closed so fast it was blurry.

Mal started breathing fast. What was he supposed to do?

He heard something then. Something behind.

Daddy!

He felt lighter, instantly better. Daddy was back. Back with them, back to normal.

Mal turned. Smiling.

Then not smiling. His mouth opened to scream.

It wasn't Daddy. Not really.

THE ONE WHO KNOWS

When she saw the shipping tube, Alyssa realized that only one person had seemed to know instantly that there was something to fear. And if he had known that, what else might he know?

That was why she stepped out of the house: hope. Hope that she would see the same courier delivering this package that she had seen a few days before. Hope that he might be able to help. And that was why, when she saw the scrawny form and the red hair of the kid who had delivered the package to Blake at the rental, she ran down the porch steps.

She had to follow him, because she knew he could help. And she needed help; they all did.

"Hey!" she shouted as soon as she saw the red hair, so vibrant it was almost an attack; heart and teddy bear and My Little Pony tattoos just as glaring and strange as they had been before.

The kid didn't look back. He ran. Streaking toward the stripped-down bike on the curb.

Alyssa ran after him. She didn't think about it. Didn't have time. She had to catch him: she had no other idea where to go or who to turn to.

The courier got on his bike. Started peddling. He was fast. The back wheel of the bike turned so hard it didn't even catch at first, just spinning against the street before it finally grabbed the asphalt and launched the bike forward. The front wheel came up a few inches before slamming down, and the courier jolted ahead.

"Hey!" she shouted again. "Hey, what's going on? Do you know what's happening? What's...?"

The courier moved away. And she felt answers, understanding – safety – move away with him.

She watched him until he turned a corner and disappeared. Her only hope for understanding, gone as fast as it had come. She didn't know what else she could turn to. She didn't know any mediums, didn't know what she could search for on the internet that would provide real answers about what she might be going through.

She went back up the steps. Her footsteps were solid, final, each one seeming to say "This is the end, nowhere to go."

Someone screamed. A tiny shout, cut off before it bloomed into the shriek it wanted to become. High-pitched and instantly recognizable. Mal.

Alyssa ran back to the house. Her steps lengthened to the point that she feared she might trip, but she pushed herself still faster.

"Mal! Ruthie!" she shouted. She cursed herself for leaving them alone, tried at the same time to convince herself there was nothing wrong. Nothing to worry about.

It was a lie, of course.

She ran into the house. The living room.

The mat was one of those thick cotton blankets specially designed for a new baby to rest on. To sleep on and look at the world from and someday roll over on.

Ruthie was doing none of those things.

Ruthie was gone. So was Mal. The book, too. And

somehow that only made it worse. To know that wherever her son and daughter were, the death-tome might have followed –

(*been taken*)

– along with them. To know they couldn't escape it.

The toy Mal had been holding – the squishy little toy with a plastic mirror sewn onto one side – lay mirror-side down a few feet from the mat. Like it had been thrown there, or kicked. Other than that, there was no sign that either child had ever been in the room.

She had the strong impulse to turn over that little toy. To look into the mirror as though it were really a recording a device that might show her what had happened in here. But of course it wouldn't.

Or perhaps it would. Perhaps that would be worse.

She didn't touch it. It stayed on the floor.

"Mal!" She ran from room to room. The living room was empty. So was the entry, the dining room. No one hiding under the table.

"Ruthie!" She knew it was foolish to call for a baby – the infant could hardly call back. She did it anyway. And again: "Ruthie!"

The kitchen was empty as well. She opened the pantry, even went so far as to yank open the under-sink cupboard space. Mal could squeeze into that dark little place.

But he wasn't there. No little boy, no baby girl.

She ran upstairs. Room to room, faster and faster, calling their names as she went from her bedroom to theirs. No answers, no sign of them.

Then there was only one place left. The place she had left for last, and she realized that in all her calling she hadn't once called for Blake. Neither wondering where he was nor calling for his help.

Because she *knew* where he was.

And she didn't think he was going to help.

She went to Mal's room. The second she rounded the stairs and set foot in the thin corridor that led to his room and the kitchen, she heard something. Each step toward her son's room made the sound louder. Low, but insistent. Sliding. Rasping.

Familiar.

She kept moving toward the room, but her toes felt like they were turning inside out. Trying to keep as far back as they could.

The sound was one she had heard on the night her boy had awoken in a sea of centipedes. Millions of legs and bodies tangled around him, ready to bite and kill and drag him down to wherever they had come from.

That same sound came from his room now.

She was no longer running. Her mad dashes from room to room had been arrested by this sound, by her own fear.

She pressed forward. "Mal? Ruthie?" she said. Her voice was a wheeze, a gasp.

Then she stopped again. Just for a moment. Because a new sound joined the angry chittering. A plinking counterpoint that turned their hordes into a huge insectile waltz.

It was the music box. Singing its song, and she knew

that this was where it really belonged, that this was the party for which it had really come to play.

She was crying. Fear for the children. Fear for Blake. And as good a mother and wife as she liked to think of herself to be, she knew she was terrified for her own safety, too.

She knocked on the door. The rasping dance of insect feet didn't cease or even stutter. It went on, as did the music.

She knocked harder.

Blake's voice answered the knock, so quickly that it interrupted her motion. Like he was waiting for her to do this and waiting to give his response.

"Leave us alone."

The words were low. Almost friendly. But there was no mistaking the darkness below them. Or the fact that the rasping chitters rose with his words. It wasn't just a request. There was threat buried in the sentence, and the grave was a shallow one.

Alyssa reached for the knob. She knew her kids were in there. She had to –

"Don't."

Her hand jerked just as it touched the doorknob. The contact itself seemed to cause an electric shock to jump from metal to skin, numbing her fingers.

This time the speaker wasn't Blake. It wasn't coming from Mal's room. She turned her head to look down the hall. The small entry, the open front door to the house.

Did I leave that open, or did he open it?

The courier stood in the doorway. He looked

around, observing the living room, the dining room. But she noticed he didn't come in. He didn't cross the threshold.

He finally looked at her. His skin, like that of most redheads, was fair. But now it looked whiter than it had before. He was pale as snow, and his acne and the red freckles that could still be seen around his many tattoos were so bright they looked like laser targeting dots.

"Come with me," he said.

"I can't," she answered. Her hand rose toward Mal's door again. "My kids –"

"They're not yours. Not now." The courier looked around again, his eyes contemplative. "It's still happening. It's not done." He refocused on Alyssa. "There's still time to get them back. But you have to *know*, or all you'll do is die first, probably right in front of them."

The courier didn't look at her again. He turned around and disappeared from the doorway. Gone.

She wanted to follow him. A moment before she *had* followed him, had fled after him in a moment of unthinking decision that may have gotten her children killed. But now that she had an actual invitation to do so, she didn't want to leave.

She turned to Mal's room. The chittering and the music box had been joined by deep pounding. It sounded like Blake was beating the walls down with a sledgehammer.

"Blake," she said, not really sure how she would finish the sentence, "I –"

"*WE'RE WORKING!*"

This time there was no attempt at friendly tones.

Rage and hatred were all that she heard in her husband's voice. And his scream drew the chittering to a fury that was so loud it drilled into every crevice of her mind and made her scream.

She finally ran. Not because she wanted to, but because to stay would be to fall into an abyss of insanity and be dashed to pieces at the bottom.

And what could she do for her family if she was insane?

Or dead?

DARKFIRE

Ralph didn't know what day it was. He just knew he'd been working at working – working at surviving – for what seemed like forever. Starting work at sunup, finishing after sundown. Sleeping where he could.

So far *those* places were safe. So far.

But he hadn't thought beyond that. He hadn't changed his clothes, hadn't showered. Ali and the other couriers had made some comments – even a group that was as determinedly ill-groomed as some of them were had started feeling he cast the profession in a poor light. But he barely heard them. He was just moving. Keeping ahead of the hands that kept clutching at him, the smiles widened by razor gashes, the bloody holes where eyes once were, an infinitude of misery.

And anger.

These dead were so angry.

He ran job after job, and took no thought of what else he might do. Because he didn't know if there was anything *to* do. No one had ever taken him aside and given him a crash course in spirit evasion. And he was tired. So tired, so incapable of thought. Becoming almost an animal, a thing that existed only *to* exist. A beast for whom survival was the end-all and be-all.

So he took the jobs because that gave the beast purpose. The last remaining shield, however pitiful, that might protect him from the things that were now far too present, far too close.

Ding-dong.

It wasn't a job that needed a signature, just a drop. So he dropped it and ran/stumbled back to his bike. Heard the door open behind him but didn't stop. He had nothing to say to the client.

And what if it *wasn't* the client? What if the wraiths had learned to open doors? Something new... and every new thing had, thus far, been bad.

Then he heard someone scream, "Hey!" and he knew that it was one of them. They *had* grown stronger. Not just hanging to this world, but somehow coopting the trappings of life itself. This ghost had a house.

That makes no sense, Ralphie. What would a ghost do –

Don't argue, just run.

What if someone needs you?

RUN!

He ran. Crashing down the porch, nearly tumbling face-over-feet as he stumbled to the bike, the only thing he really trusted.

He fumbled with the bike as well, managing to get it upright after a few fractions of a second during which he grew old and died a thousand times. Then he was astride the seat, the worn leather under his right buttcheek as his left foot clipped into the pedal and then pushed down as hard as it ever had.

The bike jumped forward. He heard more screaming, more words. A woman's voice. A woman-*thing*'s voice.

"Hey! Hey, what's going on? Do you know what's happening? What's...?"

He turned a corner, and her voice died out. She might have stopped talking, she might have disappeared. But he couldn't slow down, because maybe she had just moved ahead of him. That had never happened before... but it would hardly be the first new thing to happen these days.

He pushed the pedals. Down, down, down, down. He wasn't moving nearly as fast as he usually did, but even middle-speed for Ralph Hickey was pretty-damn-fast for most. He would put as much space between himself and this latest attack –

(*think, Ralphie, think what she actually* said, *man!*)

– as he could. He would get back –

(*think, Ralphie, think what she actually* said, *man!*)

– to R.I. and get another fare. He would –

(*think, Ralphie*)

– stay ahead of these things –

(*think what she actually*)

–until he could figure out –

(said, *man!*)

He skidded to a stop.

She had been asking what happened. What was going on.

Or had that been a dream? Some kind of psychosis brought on by too much caffeine, too much work, too much exertion, and too little sleep? Ralph had heard of things like that. R.I. had its own urban legends about riders who went until they saw dragons flying behind them and their bladders exploded. Ali called them "Model Employees" but they were a cautionary tale about couriers misusing their most important equipment: themselves.

Or maybe it was a trick. Could it be the things were getting subtle? Trying to fool him with pleas for aid, like that woman had done yesterday –

(*or was it the day before or the day before that?*)

– when she walked in front of the car?

He stiffened.

He wasn't moving. Wasn't rolling or running for the first time in days.

But when he looked around, he saw he was alone. No one – nothing – near. No hands reaching for him, no voices taunting him.

"What's going on?" he said. His voice sounded tired, even to himself, and his head was packed with sawdust.

Had the ghosts gone away?

No, he didn't think so. They were still around. Just not here. Not in this particular place.

"Why not?" he said. Talking to himself wasn't what he thought of as a great sign of mental health, but that ship had probably already sailed. "What's here?"

He looked around. Houses, lawns, hedges. Some kids' toys on a few properties. Normal neighborhood, close to downtown, where fairly well-to-do folks lived. Nothing interesting. Nothing suspicious.

"What's going on?" he said. Realized it was what the woman had been screaming. And now he wondered if she hadn't been another one of the specters that had come so close of late. Maybe she was real. Maybe she needed help.

Maybe she could help *him*.

He pulled out his tablet. Brought up the delivery

history. The last address he'd delivered to was at the top. Not one he recognized. He had a good memory for places, so if he'd delivered there before he probably would have remembered it.

But the recipient name... that was familiar. He stiffened on his seat.

Blake Douglas. That had been the name he delivered to when he saw the dead boy. The poor kid with his throat cut to pieces.

And after that, everything started to go to Hell. Literally.

He put his tablet back in his bag and started biking. The wheels turned slowly, the pedals were bricks under his feet.

He didn't want to go back there. Whatever was going on to him, it had started with the Douglas delivery.

But he had to go back, didn't he? Because the dead were getting bolder, getting stronger, getting closer. If they kept it up he'd be one of them before long.

He didn't want to see that little boy with the slit throat. Worse, he didn't want to see whoever had done that *to* him, like the woman who carried the shotgun around to tap on the daughter she had blown to pieces with it. He didn't want to face the malignancy of a monster that would kill a child.

So, fine, he wouldn't go in the house. He'd stay out on the porch and hope the thing that killed that boy wasn't around.

But he had to see the Douglas woman – if it was her that he had heard calling to him. Because that was the only way he might find answers.

Ralph could see the dead. He had other skills, too.

But it didn't take a prophet to know that if things didn't change he was dead meat. Then maybe it'd be *him* catching rides, talking to a few freaks who could see into the beyond.

Maybe his mom would be there.

That thought made him feel like he was drowning. But it got him moving faster. Back to the Douglas house. To the people who had brought this darkness.

Hoping that the darkness would illuminate his way.

When he got there he dropped his bike at the curb and walked to the door. R.I. policy was that if you were delivering to a residence you left the bike at the curb. The other couriers said it was because that showed courtesy – no leaving skid marks or grease stains on a client's sidewalk or driveway. Ralph followed protocol automatically, but halfway there realized he would have that much farther to run to get to his bike if he needed it. He almost turned back. Didn't.

He needed to know what was happening.

The package was gone from the porch. The front door was open. Not things that normally caused his nuts to tuck right up into his chest, but that's what they did now.

He pushed forward.

At the doorway he let himself stop moving. He wasn't going in, no matter what. And he didn't have to. He could see the woman clearly. It was the same woman who had been on the stairway at the other house, standing like she was exhausted or tired or maybe both. She was about to grab a doorknob to someplace down the hall.

"Don't," he said. She jumped, but she wasn't any more surprised than he was. He hadn't intended to speak.

But when he saw the doorknob, it was like looking at a fire. Only fires were bright, usually cheery. This was a thing that looked dark. All of the burn, none of the comfort. Touching the doorknob would just hurt this woman.

She looked at him, and he saw instantly that his life wasn't the only one that had fallen to pieces in the last few days. The pain in her eyes wasn't just physical. It was mental, emotional, and spiritual. She was being hammered to pieces by something bad. Something... *evil*.

"Come with me," he said to her.

She looked back at the door. "I can't," she said. "My kids –"

And again the words jumped to his lips. "They're not yours. Not now." He didn't know what the words meant, and that frightened him, too. Seeing the dead was one thing. To have your voice hijacked, to speak words that were true but unknown even to yourself....

It had happened before. The day he told a young woman to get to the hospital because she had an aortic dissection and would die within the hour if she didn't. A time he gave five dollars to a bum and told him to go buy a lottery ticket at exactly 6:02 pm.

The day he heard his own voice telling himself to run away because his mother was finally going to kill him.

It had happened before, and it was always terrifying. The voice that knew more than he did using his own lips to speak.

"It's still happening," he said. And now he wasn't sure if it was himself or that *Other* who spoke. "It's not done." He looked at the woman. "There's still time to get them back. But you have to *know*, or all you'll do is die first, probably right in front of them."

Those last definitely weren't his words. And they were too much. He ran from them. Ran from the woman, ran from the house. Wishing he could run from himself.

He was at the bicycle in a second, holding it up, trying to keep himself from running even farther, riding into day until it turned to night and then perhaps just riding off the side of a freeway overpass and being done with it all.

A moment later the woman left the house. She stumbled down the walk to the sidewalk the same way he had done, and he wondered how long it had been since she had slept properly.

Same as me.

He started walking the bike away. Moving fast enough to show her he had no intention of stopping to wait, but not so fast that she would have to run to keep up.

"Come on," he said. Even exhausted he could have left her behind in a moment, since he trained his legs and lungs all day every day. But as badly as he wanted to get away from this place and the darkfire he had seen leading to that room, he needed her with him. She was his only hope for peace.

She kept up better than he expected. No panting, no murmur of complaint. She simply fell in beside him, both of them walking in the street, hugging tightly to the curb.

"Who are you?" she said. "What's happening?"

He didn't want to answer that. "What's your name?" he said. "The last name's Douglas, right?"

"Alyssa." She answered quickly, but wouldn't be swayed from her question. "What's happening? Who are you?"

He fixed his gaze straight ahead. Wondered if maybe this was why so few of the dead would look at him: maybe they all had things to say they knew he wouldn't want to hear. Sobering thought.

"My name's Ralph," he said. He opened his mouth to say more, but something flitted through the edges of his sight. He snapped his head to the right and saw... nothing.

Another shadow moved. This time when he turned toward it he saw a man in a bathrobe standing on one of the lawns. Nothing unusual about that, but the lawn was being watered, the sprinkler *tchk-tchk-tchk*-ing as it wetted every inch of green.

The man was dry.

He smiled at Ralph.

"Here's not the place to talk," said Ralph.

"I need –"

"Come on," he said. He didn't want to let her start her questions. Starting here would be bad. Another shadow flashed, another specter appeared. A woman dressed in a poodle skirt, holding a wriggling bundle in bloody hands.

Another shadow blinked into this reality. Another.

This was another new thing. Another *bad* new thing. These specters weren't merely following him as he passed, they were gathering.

How many would come?

What was calling them?

He moved faster. "There's a place. We should get there."

"My kids," said Alyssa. "They –"

"I told you *they're not yours!*" Ralph shouted. The force of the words stopped him, and again he wasn't quite sure if they were his words or those of the thing that sometimes spoke through him.

The shout vibrated through the neighborhood, seeming to shake leaves in the trees and causing a trio of jays to erupt from a bush before they evaporated in the daylight.

Alyssa fell back, terror and despair on her face.

One of the ghosts – a cherub-faced man with a bloody third eye where a bullet had gone through his forehead – clapped approvingly at Ralph. The clap made no sound.

Ralph swallowed. He held out his hand. Alyssa shied away from him. He remained motionless so she would know he wasn't going to hurt her. "They're not yours," he said softly. "But maybe you can get them back."

The bleeding cherub stopped clapping. That made Ralph feel good.

"How?" said Alyssa. Still pulled away from him, wary.

"Come on," he said again. And started walking to what he hoped would be a safe place to talk. If such a thing still existed.

THE SAFETY OF THE GRAVE

Sometimes when a nightmare has you tight, jammed between its claws and ready to cram you into its mouth and chew you to pieces, sometimes you just can't move. You twist and turn and struggle, but nothing happens. Your body is immobilized, wrapped in dread that locks every muscle in place. This is the last thing a fly feels before the spider sucks it dry. This is how Alyssa felt as she walked after the courier, the man-boy who seemed to know something, but who said nothing.

She felt her feet pacing forward, was incidentally aware of the ground moving below her, the slight breeze around. But still she still felt like something held her motionless. Or perhaps like she was floating in a void where the only realities were herself and the things made real through the raw power of her fear.

She was walking, but standing still. Moving, but not toward anything she understood.

The courier remained silent. He looked around, his gaze never stopping to rest on anything, his head on a constant swivel. She tried to follow what he was looking at, but there was nothing there. And there was something in his gaze – the stare laser-focused on specific places, but those places completely bereft of anything but the wind – that unnerved her.

Not as much as what was happening back home, though. Not as much as what could be happening with her family.

She didn't know how long they had been walking. She looked around and didn't recognize where they were. Not in her neighborhood. Miles away.

Why am I walking when my family needs me?

And the answer to that was simply that she didn't know what else to do. She didn't understand what was happening, only that it was real, strong, and evil. And it apparently had something to do with Blake and Mal and Ruthie and her. Something specific.

She felt ashamed that she wasn't slamming through the house, looking for the children. That was what Momma Bears did, and she had always prided herself on being a Momma Bear among Momma Bears. Someone who would defend her cubs from danger no matter the cost.

Yet she was running away.

Not running away. You have to know. He even said that. Said you have to know or you'll just die.

But know what?

"Who are you?" she asked. Her mouth seemed to crack as she spoke, and again she wondered how long, how far, they had walked. She was awake, but in a dream. And in a dream distances passed in a blink though you barely moved at all. Time was nothing, and distance just another part of the dream.

The kid – he was a young man, but his face was so boyish and his energy somehow so *light* it was easier to think of him as a kid – didn't stop looking around. "Told you," he said. His voice clipped the edges off each word, left them smooth and tumbling out of his mouth. "Ralph. I'm Ralph."

"No, I mean –"

"I know what you mean." Still biting the words off, still flicking eyes left, right, up, down, from one empty point in mid-air to another. But now she also heard exhaustion in his voice. He sighed, the sigh turned into a cough. She got a whiff of bad breath and wondered when he had last brushed his teeth. He stank, too. Like he hadn't showered in days and days. "I'm a guy who sees things sometimes."

"Like a psychic?"

This time the sigh ended in a snort. "I said 'a guy who sees things,' not 'a guy who cheats people.'"

That seemed like a conversation-ender. She was quiet again. Knowing that she should be asking questions didn't mean she could think of any to ask. Simply saying "What's going on?" hadn't gotten her anywhere yet, and she didn't understand enough to ask anything else.

Some people said there were no stupid questions, but she suspected that only stupid *people* actually believed that. Anything she asked would be stupid. And she didn't want to risk pissing off or scaring off this kid who looked like he was on the verge of jumping off a mental cliff of some kind.

They walked. No talking.

The kid stopped. So quickly she was a full ten feet ahead of him before she realized she was walking alone.

"What?" she said.

"We're here," he answered. He turned his bike. Started walking in the new direction.

Alyssa laughed. Not a belly laugh, not a chuckle. It was the craggy laugh of a person who has gone to church and found an orgy in progress. A laugh substituting for every sound of disbelief at once.

"You've got to be kidding me," she said after a few moments, after the laugh wore away and speech returned.

Every town, no matter how small, has one thing in common with every city, no matter how large. All of them are places where people live, and so they are also places where people die.

Most of the dead travel to cemeteries that, like hardware stores and restaurants and grocery markets, have become the province of big businesses. The dead are tagged and stacked and embalmed with modern efficiency, then entombed with whatever religious ceremony the family desires and can afford.

After that it is just a matter of determining which landscaping service can mow the lawn for the cheapest rate.

Some of the dead, though, pass into other places. Less organized, older, longer on history though shorter on curb appeal. Here the dead rest in small graveyards tucked away behind old churches, across from what had once been county seats, or simply parked on unexpected blocks in unlikely places.

Alyssa remembered seeing this small cemetery a few times, though her dream-soaked brain couldn't bring up when that had been or where this place lay. A wood fence surrounded it, posts and crossbars that were so old they were splintered and graying. Old headstones so weathered they barely retained a shape sat next to several ledger markers – flat slabs that covered the entire grave. A few small obelisks, a stone angel with one wing chipped away to nothing. Some tufts of grass that were all that remained of beloved dead.

Three trees crouched protectively over the area, willows whose branches swept lightly across stone and swung in the breeze. It was a graveyard that had clearly housed the most prestigious members of this area a hundred years ago and more, kept intact by historical societies or relatives or just the ties of tradition.

Alyssa had always liked passing the place. It bound her part of the world to the past, gave it solidarity. But it was not the place she would have chosen to go under the present circumstances.

Now she realized: it was miles away from her house. Six, seven – maybe more.

Ralph was already passing between the two tall posts that marked the cemetery entrance. His footfalls were silent, the wheels of his bicycle made no sound. But he seemed a clumsy intruder, a sneak thief in an unfamiliar room. And she wondered whom he might awaken.

She hurried after him, though. The last rays of the sun pushed through the willows, and that only heightened her sense of anxiety, the sense of *un*belonging.

Sunset? How long have we been walking? How much time do I have left?

The realization brought another. She was alone. Not just separated from Blake and the children, but from everyone else. She had her sister, but Heather was a continent away, living in a cramped apartment with Xanthe and Teresa and still trying to make it as a drummer.

When she and Blake had moved into this house, they hadn't reached out to the neighbors. They knew them, but didn't have phone numbers. Didn't have friendships.

Didn't really have anyone but each other.

That had seemed enough.

It wasn't.

She skidded on something. When she looked down she saw something brown and red and black. Bits of fur and bone, soft things that she had ground underfoot. Rot that had found its way aboveground in this place where such was supposed to be safely buried. Just a dead squirrel. It seemed profane. It seemed portentous.

In the daylight this place was cozy, charming. Now, in the in-between time of sunset, the charm gave way to something else. Threat, a sense of malaise that might be her own fear imposed on her surroundings.

But what if it was real?

Ralph dropped his bike next to a ledger marker. The flat slab was inscribed at one end, though the letters were so worn she couldn't see them in the dim light.

"Pull up a shair," he said.

She looked around. The trees seemed to reach for them. "This is a safe place?" she said.

Ralph shook his head. "No place is *safe*. But some are safer than others." She noticed he had stopped looking around like he was aware of an invisible mob – an attacking horde that only he could see. Some of the tension had left his wiry shoulders.

Still, she didn't believe that a graveyard, of all places, would be a place of refuge.

Ralph saw her disbelief. "Forget what you've seen on TV. It's all crap. The least likely place you're going to be bugged by a spirit is at its grave."

Alyssa looked around, a large part of her expecting to see a green specter rise out of the ground in front of one of the tilting headstones. But nothing rose, nothing lurked. "Why?" she said.

"It's all hallowed," said Ralph. He took his pack off, dropping it on the flat gravestone. "By prayers, by tears, by love." He chuckled. "Plus, would *you* want to stick around in a place like this for hundreds of years?"

Alyssa looked around. "No, I guess not."

"It'd get boring."

That wasn't what she had been thinking, but she let it go. "So what are *we* doing here?"

"I'm going to tell you what I know, and we're going to find out what we can find out." He sat on the edge of the stone. It was fairly low, only about a foot above ground, but the grass looked too damp to sit on and Alyssa realized that every part of her body ached. She dropped down near Ralph, the kid's pack between them.

"When I delivered that first package, to the other house, I saw a boy," said Ralph. He looked hard at her, gauging her reaction to his next words. "That mean anything to you?"

She shook her head. "He's my son, he's just –"

Ralph cut her off. He shook his head so hard she thought it might fly off his neck. "Not unless your son dresses like an extra from *Anne of Green Gables*. And he has a slit throat. And is very dead."

Alyssa felt the blood drain from her face, from her whole body. She weaved a bit, and gripped the edges of the tombstone to keep from pitching forward. "He was haunting that house? But what about what's happening now? What –"

Ralph shook his head again. She was already hating when he did that. It meant things were going bad to worse, or worse to worst. "Definitely not. He wasn't tied to the house, he was following *you*. Your family." He leaned in close. "Any ideas why?"

Now it was Alyssa's turn to shake her head. "No."

Ralph sighed. "That's too bad."

"Why?"

"Because you're dealing with some big nasties." His gaze flicked to the cemetery entrance. A bit of that desperate look returned to his eyes. "And the only way to deal with them is to know what they want. If you don't...."

He was quiet. She knew he wouldn't finish. But she needed him to.

"Then what? If you don't, *what*?"

He looked at her. His eyes were empty. "I don't really know. I think you'll probably die."

APPEARANCES AND BECOMINGS

Struggle and death.

The legs moved like waves, a writhing motion so perfectly organized as to seem impossible. Sickening. Beautiful.

The centipedes rolled over one another in a squirming mass. They could see, but they moved as if blind. Groping in all directions, tearing at brothers and sisters with venom-filled fangs.

And consuming. Consuming everything. Carnivorous, cannibalistic.

Lovely.

Blake would have watched them forever if he could. He would have sat among them on the floor that had disappeared under a carpet of their bodies, alive and dead, whole and half-eaten, and watched until death claimed him and then he fell and they ate him as well.

But he couldn't. He had work to do. Games –

(*C'mere, kid. Daddy's gonna play a game.*)

– to play.

The centipedes were everywhere. Ceiling, walls, window, floor. Covering what had been, and Blake sensed they were doing more than just tearing at each other. They were also finishing the job he had begun.

And now it was time. Now it was ready. He didn't know how, but he knew it was his turn in this great work.

He raised his hand. It had changed. There were no longer five fingers, but three.

Blake shuddered. He sensed – understood – for the first time what was happening –

(*You can't escape what you are.*)

– and what was going to happen.

"Please," he said. His mouth seemed like a stranger, something faraway and not under his control. He wanted to scream, but all that came was a whisper. A sound swallowed by the susurration of the millions of feet, the soughing of millions of fangs plunging through exoskeletons and into soft flesh beyond. "Please, don't –"

The words ended in a gurgle. A strangled noise that ended his awareness.

No, not ended, *made whole*. A voice whispered to him, and it was familiar. Like his father's voice, but kind. Loving. One that would never hurt him, because it *was* him. His own voice, and being his own he had to trust it.

This is you. This is me. *This is us and who we are.*

He looked at his three-fingered hand. Now the change did not seem strange, it seemed right. A maiming, but Blake felt more whole this way than he had before.

He felt a phantom hand across his cheek. The last beating his father had given him.

(*You can't escape what you are.*)

His father had been right. And it was finally happening. Blake was *becoming*. Finishing the transformation he had begun those long years ago, when he turned away from the pain inflicted and instead inflicted pain of his own. The day he ducked his father's drunken strike, knocked his old man down, kicked him, kicked him, punched him.

The social workers, the police – they didn't tell Blake if he killed his old man. But Blake knew. He'd always known. You couldn't be alive when your head was shaped like a new moon and blood came out of the one eye you had left and your throat was flat as a tire with the air left out.

So much blood. So much warm, delicious blood.

Blake had started to *become* on that day.

And on this day, he would finish. The three fingers on his hand showed him that.

He brought the hand forward, slamming it against the wall of centipedes directly in front of him. The insects split apart like the Red Sea, so not a one was crushed below his palm. There was only the wall beneath his skin.

And when he touched that wall… it was like a sonic boom went off in the room.

The centipedes poured off the wall in a tidal wave. Millions of creatures with tens of millions of legs, crashing against him, washing over him so that he was baptized by their bodies. He opened his mouth, spread his hands – one whole, one with three fingers. His eyes stayed open. They fell against him, and some pinched and bit as they passed over him.

It was beautiful, all so beautiful.

He was becoming who he must be. Becoming who he truly was.

He heard the millions and billions of tiny clicks behind him and knew that the centipedes on the other walls and on the ceiling were pouring down as well.

Falling from the work they had done. Some dead, some alive. They had come to do this, to help him change and to give him a place. *The* place.

The place that was, the place that now is.

(*I'm back!*)

For a moment Blake felt fear. There was someone else in his mind. Someone else in his head.

Then fear disappeared. Wonder replaced it.

Where the centipedes had been, the walls were now unmarred. And they were no longer covered in planes and parachutes, the funny images of childhood. Now the walls, like Blake –

(*and the other*)

– had *become*. Had become what they were, and what they should be. The drywall was gone, and now the wall was plaster, painted bright yellow. A dado circled the room about six feet above the floor, and above that the wall was painted dull red. Many of Blake's peers had wallpaper done in the latest styles of the Orient –

(*no that's not right what's –?*)

– but he couldn't afford that. Not with all his money going into his hobbies, his obsessions.

Still, modest though the walls might be, they were *his* again. The way they had been. Should be. His place of repose, and where he could do his work.

Tick-tock, tick-tock, tick-tock.

He smiled. Didn't turn yet, savoring the sound before the sight. The clock was a gift from his father-in-law, given on his wedding day. "As long as you keep it wound, your marriage will not wind down," said the old man.

Blake kept it wound. And the old man had been right – his marriage didn't wind down. It simply stopped, the day Laura died. The day his son was born. He supposed he should have hated the clock, just as he supposed he should have hated his boy. But he loved them both. Adored them both.

"My son...."

(*Mal's my son, isn't he?*)

(*No.*)

He turned. A slow turn that let him see the room that had come back to him. The wallpaper was not all that had disappeared. The window was gone; now four blank walls enclosed the room: perfect for his purposes.

He kept turning. The clock was there. So tall it nearly touched the ceiling, dark wood that matched the dark numbers on its ivory face. A moon dial that he had broken on the day of Laura's death, so always it was midnight. Always the count of his life was dark, at least in part.

Next to the clock was the music box. Another gift from his father-in-law. "So that you will dance with my daughter, because a marriage must be play as well as work."

They had danced. Had danced many times. And though the dances had ended, he still played the music. Played it at his happiest times, his times when he felt the greatest love.

And that was when she died. When the music played and she came from her bed, newly bled from birth and found you. Found you and what you were doing....

He didn't like that thought. Didn't like what he had

done. But he had had to do it. He had seen the look on Laura's face and knew she didn't understand and never would. So he had to stop her from telling others about it.

He couldn't *not* do his work. It was too important. Too beautiful. More beautiful than him, than her. She had to be stopped, and she was.

She left him alone that day. Alone with a son.

Blake –

(*Am I even Blake anymore? I don't think....*)

– kept turning. Walls, clock, music box. All his. Just as the chair was his. The chair with its beautifully scrolled legs, its rich, red upholstery. This had not been a gift. This was something that Blake had saved for himself. Saved penny by penny from his earnings clerking for Mister Mason. It was one of his two most prized possessions. It was the reason for his existence.

His son sat on the chair. And for a moment he didn't understand what was going on, because the boy was his son, and wasn't his son.

It *was* his boy. That beautiful mouth, that tousled hair.

But it wasn't Matthew Jr. So how could it be his boy?

And who was the little baby? The infant with the bright red outfit?

(*Ruthie*)

Blake stared at both of them. The boy who was his son –

(*Mal*)

– had his legs pulled up high, away from the centipedes that had fallen from ceiling and walls but still obscured the floor. The little baby started sliding off his lap, toward the insects. He hauled her higher on his lap. She was shaking, twitching, and now she started to wail. To scream.

The boy's face was miserable. "Please, Daddy," he said. "Ruthie needs to go to the doctor."

Blake – barely Blake at all, nearly *become* who he must be – felt something prickle at his neck. Felt something new enter the room. He saw something fade into the world, standing beside the clock. *Tick-tock, tick-tock.*

Soon the music box would play. Soon the dance would begin.

He turned to the boy, recognizing him at last. Not his son, but something greater. Something far more important.

He tousled the boy's hair with his three-fingered hand.

This was not his son.

It was his subject.

His model.

FUN AND GAMES

Ralph could tell Alyssa was on the verge of wigging out. He couldn't blame her. He wasn't far from that himself.

Getting here had been awful. He had never been to New York, but he'd seen plenty of movies and television shows. Images of walking along crowded sidewalks or through subway stations during rush hour were as much as part of his visual lexicon as they were anyone else's. And until the last blocks he'd experienced pretty much just that walking to the cemetery. Only instead of lawyers and secretaries and housewives and homeless, all the pressing bodies had been bloodless corpses, gray and grasping.

It hadn't been too bad at first. Just one or two of them leering at him from the shadows when he first dropped off the package at Alyssa's place. That was the fewest of the creepies he'd seen in days. He wondered if they were afraid of whatever was going on in that place. If they had been drawn out by whatever evil was about to occur, but at the same time didn't want to get too close.

As they walked toward the graveyard, more and more of them started showing up. Some just walked toward them – toward him. Like idle pedestrians who had seen someone they know, they just kind of shifted their angle of passage until they were walking right alongside.

Others… others just appeared. Those were always the worst. To be walking alone one moment, then have someone with a knife sticking out of her face right in front of you, or maybe a kid whose torso has been mangled by a car tire strutting alongside you all of a sudden. It was enough to give Ralph a series of heart attacks every time it happened. He figured each time took a week or two off his life.

And what happens when I reach T-minus zero? Just poof and I'm gone? Or do I become one of them?

By the time they got to the cemetery he was afraid to take a step. He didn't want to touch the things, didn't want to be touched by them. But it was going to happen, and maybe worse.

At least they didn't follow him and Alyssa into the cemetery. It must have been a good one. Full of good people, full of people whose families loved them. That's what Ralph thought, at least. He wasn't sure that was what actually what kept the ghosts at bay. He wasn't sure about very many things. Just lots of guesses. It could have been that the spooks were simply allergic to moss.

But it made him happy to think they couldn't stand hallowed ground. Not like churches hallowed by ritual prayers and holy water, but ground hallowed by love and good feelings. His mom had always talked about good feelings, especially when she had him strapped down on the board and was covering him with the tattoos. He screamed a lot – hard not to when you were four and five and six – but he still heard her talk about love. She screamed about it so he always heard, no matter how bad he hurt.

Not sorry to see the last of her. But her words remained. Some of them were even good, no matter how bad she might have been.

"We're wasting time," said Alyssa. Her voice pulled

his eyes back to hers, his thoughts back to the present. "I need to find my kids."

He sympathized. He almost told her to go ahead; to run back. After all, what did he know? What did he *really* know?

But something stopped him. Sometimes he had to tell someone something – a lottery ticket or a heart about to fall to pieces in someone's chest. And sometimes he had to *not* tell them something. So he didn't tell Alyssa to go back home. Instead he said, "Again: run home and you'll die." He chewed his lip for a second and added, "So will they."

She blanched like he had just hit her. "How do you *know*?"

"Whatever is behind this isn't just here to bother you. It wants to kill you all." He reached for his bag. Grabbed the zipper for the main pouch.

"Then what do I do? I have to do something."

He opened the bag. Pulled something out. It was night now, but there was enough of a moon to see what it was. A long box, about sixteen inches by six inches, maybe two inches deep.

"Now we play," he said, and set the Scrabble board on the stone marker between them. He scattered the tiles, turning them all face-down, and chose seven for himself.

He had to try not to shrink back: Alyssa looked like she was going to take a poke at him. "*What*? You say something wants to kill my kids, then you –"

"Relax." He saw she wasn't going to take any tiles, so he chose for her, not looking as he put seven tiles in one of the racks. "Some people use runes, but they're too iffy. Some people use dice, but they're too limited." He pushed the rack in front of her. "This way gets *results*: a mixture of what we know and what we're given."

Ralph could tell that Alyssa didn't really understand what he was talking about. And truth was, like everything else, he didn't fully understand it himself. He had done this a few times, to mixed results, and it always scared the crap out of him. But they needed answers. Both of them. Whatever was happening to her was pulling the dead like a magnet. And they were the worst kind of dead.

"You first," he said.

She looked numb, but chose two tiles and placed them in the middle of the board: IT.

"Interesting," he said.

"What? What does it mean?" asked Alyssa.

He shrugged. "Beats me." He put THANKS down, working off her "T."

They played. He could tell she was agitated, and getting more so. Again, nothing he blamed her for. And nothing he could do about it.

That was part of how this worked.

It happened about five turns out. She held out longer than most.

Alyssa screamed and smashed her open hand into the game board. "This is *useless!*"

The board swept off the ledger stone, bouncing into a headstone nearby, then fluttering off like a wounded bird before coming to rest on the grass.

"I can't just sit here and –"

Ralph cut her off with an upraised hand. Then slowly dropped it as he said, "First we do the part we know

– we arrange the letters we have. Then we find out what we're given...."

His fingers ended pointing at another ledger marker, the twin of the first. Probably the wife of whoever was under this marker, because it was set in a good six inches lower: the chauvinism of the past hard at work.

Some of the Scrabble tiles had fallen on that marker. Most of them were face-down, but a few had fallen face-up.

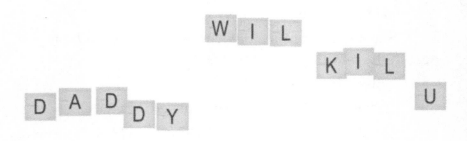

Alyssa gasped. Ralph felt about the same, but he managed to put on what he hoped was a sophisticated expression. "Awesome, huh?"

Alyssa tore her eyes away from the tiles to look at him. "'Daddy will kill you.' What does it mean?"

Ralph's attempt at urbanity faltered. "No idea."

Alyssa's eyes widened; he couldn't tell whether in surprise or anger. "Is there ever a point where you *do* know something?"

Ralph rolled his eyes. "Why my generation gets a bad rap as being so focused on instant gratification, I'll never understand. It's a *process*." He moved to the other slab of stone. Motioned for Alyssa to join him and as she did he touched the Scrabble tiles with a flat palm. He shivered as he made contact with the message they held. "And it's not important that I understand."

"Then how can we –?"

He shook his head. "Not important that *I* understand. Only that you do." He leaned close to her. "But you gotta know… understanding isn't always fun."

And before she could move away, he touched her forehead with his free hand.

Alyssa stiffened. Her mouth opened to scream.

No sound came. None from her.

But beyond the entrance to the graveyard, he heard a thousand voices shriek. The dead knew what he was doing. Knew, and were not pleased.

"Good luck," he whispered. "Wherever you are."

And he stayed like that, touching a woman with one hand, the message she and he had brought from God-knew-where with the other. And the terrible song of the undamned all around, trying to lull him into a forever sleep.

He thought he heard his mother among them. Singing a song, waiting with a needle to paint another picture on his back, his arms, his genitals. And this time he wouldn't be able to escape from her.

"Hurry back, Alyssa," he whispered.

FLASHES IN THE DARKNESS

The first thing she understands is that she is nowhere. She may be watching a place, but she is not *in* that place. She may be near a person, but she will never *touch* that person.

The next thing she understands is that the place she watches is one she has never seen before. And yet it is familiar, utterly known to her.

This is Mal's room, she says. And the words, spoken on lips that have no more existence than a dream, can be heard by none but her.

Mal's room, yes. But it is also not his room. She sees her child's space, with its familiar furnishings and bright colors, but over it, like one photograph superimposed over another, she sees something else. Something older and infinitely darker in every sense of the word. As she watches her son's room fades, and the dark one waxes strong. Soon it is the only one she sees.

The new place – the place that is in the same space, but wholly different in time and meaning and purpose – is the same size as her son's room. But these walls are yellow, with a rust-red strip along the top. In the corner sits a chair. Red with dark wood legs that are intricately scrolled.

She shudders, though she has no body to shiver, no muscles to twitch. She has seen that chair. She did not know it was red – she saw it in black and white, grayscale yellowed with age – but she recognizes the legs. Wood with intricate scrollwork that can be seen even beneath the dangling legs of dead children in an obscene book.

The lumpy black covering she saw in the pictures is nowhere to be seen.

Another difference between this place/time and the one she knows: there is no window. The light that she treasures whenever she helps her son clean in here, whenever she comes to wake him in the morning – it is gone. This room is made to be closed, to be dark. It is a room for hidden things.

But though enclosed, someone has taken care to illuminate it. Dozens of kerosene lanterns blaze throughout the room. Sitting on the floor, mounted on wall brackets. They flicker and make the air itself seem to writhe and dance in pain.

A clock she knows well sits in the corner opposite the chair. An equally known – equally dreadful – music box is beside it. The clock ticks its loud heartbeat, and the box is closed and silent.

The door to the room is open, and now a man enters. She knows his name though she has never seen him before. He is Matthew Hollis, Sr. Tall, with a barrel chest and a face that has seen been broken by long ago fists. He wears a dark brown vest buttoned nearly to his neck, with a watch chain hanging from one of the button holes. A bowler hat sits atop his head.

His arms are strong and they easily carry the child he brings into the room with him. It is a little boy, and though the watching woman cannot tell how he died his gray face and blue lips leave no doubt that dead he is.

Matthew Sr. swings the door shut behind him, then puts the boy down. Not on the chair, but on the floor. The watcher is surprised at this, but perhaps even more surprised at the tenderness the man displays. He moves slowly, holding the boy's body so his head does not strike the wood floor. As if he would notice a fall, as if he might suffer a bruise.

The man kisses the boy's closed eyes. It makes the woman's insides curl. She would vomit if she could.

The man draws back and she sees he has only three fingers on his right hand. The other two are missing. She cannot tell if it is a birth defect or the result of an accident. But the sight makes her again twitch her bodiless shiver, and she remembers the sight of her husband in the hotel, his hand bound up in the sheets, looking similarly malformed.

She closes her eyes, aware that to do so is folly: she has no eyelids. She cannot shield her sight from evil.

Still, when she closes and then opens her eyes-not-eyes, things have changed. The child no longer lays on the floor. Now he sits on the chair, which has been covered with that lumpy, almost grotesque sheet.

Though dead, the boy sits erect. His eyes are open, and she cannot see if they have been glued or sewn or something worse. She is glad not to know.

The wicks of the kerosene lamps have all been trimmed so they are at highest flame. The room is now bright, and she sees why it must be: a camera sits across from the boy. Old and boxy, a jutting cylinder of a lens at the front and an accordion-like structure in the middle.

A flash mechanism sits beside it. More light for what will be the best possible picture.

And the music box plays. It plays, and for some

reason the sound is more frightening than it has ever been before. Because what kind of dance can there be when the only dancer present is dead?

The flash flares with a loud *POP*, brightening the room. She didn't see Matthew Sr. come in to trigger the flash or take the picture. But she was looking at the dead boy. She is not surprised she missed it.

What else did she miss? She can't miss things. If she does, she senses her family will pay. Will suffer.

Will die.

She has to watch. Has to attend. Has to *know*.

When the flash dims Matthew Sr. is bringing another child into the room. He wears a different vest, a forest green jacket covering it. No hat.

He holds another dead child. Another boy. Another lifeless body.

The pop sounds, the flash pulses, and again the woman cannot see all that happened. Again when it dims the man enters with another burden, holds another child, places another little death on the floor, closing the door behind him each time so none can see his most private moment.

POP... a boy on the chair, ten and lovely even in death....

POP ... a girl this time, a cleft pallet marring her face, the cheeks still red and flushed with once-life....

POP ... a baby, dressed in a christening gown, too young to sit upright, laying across the black covering, eyes closed as though too innocent to witness this moment even in death....

POP ....

POP ....

POP ....

Child after child after child.

And then another child. A last child. A girl. Larger than the others, nearly a woman. Matthew Sr. spends more time with her, pulling her into his lair, laying her on the floor.

He does not notice the whistling. Or that it comes through the door he has, for the first time, neglected to close.

The Camptown ladies, sing this song, Doo-da, doo-da....

The whistled tune is jaunty, light. It pushes into this dark place as an unwelcome guest.

The Camptown racetrack's five miles long, Oh, dee-do-da-day....

But Matthew Sr. still does not notice. He is kissing the girl's eyes. Another kiss for her cherry lips.

Goin' to run all night, Goin' to run all day....

The song cuts off suddenly. And this silence is what finally alerts Matthew Sr. Not music, but absence. He turns slowly, even as another sound pushes into the room.

"Daddy?"

Even as she knew that this man was Matthew Hollis, Sr., so the watching woman knows that this is his son. The boy is beautiful, even in the writhing light of the lamps. Even with the black eye –

(*the size of a father's fist*)

– and the finger marks –

(large fingers, strong fingers)

– that ring his neck. His eyes widen. "What are you doing?" asks the boy. He looks at the girl on the floor. "That's Missus Tate's girl. She was missing... wasn't...?"

He looks at his father. And just as the watcher knows, so does he.

He runs.

Matthew Sr., who was holding the girl's head as he kissed her, lets it fall. It knocks against the floor as father runs after son.

A moment later the woman finds herself in a new space. A space even darker than the one she was just in. Not just the spiritual darkness of death too soon, but an actual blackness that clings to all. Impossible to see, though she has a sense of what is here. What is near.

There is someone with her. This place is little more than a hole. A tunnel, a crawlspace. So small that even Matthew Jr., as small as he is, has to work to flee through it. Barely enough room for him to crawl, and no hope at all for him to stand. Which is the way his father wishes it. He is on hands and knees, crying and bleeding.

He is not the only thing that crawls down here. Many-legged creatures writhe over his hands, into his clothes, through his hair. He can feel them touch his skin, feel them bite his flesh. Centipedes.

His clothes are a torn mess, shreds with bloody edges. Blood drips from the boy's nose and mouth as well. From the new cuts on his face, the ones on forehead, cheek, above his blue, blue eyes. The blood splashes on his hands, rolls into the hungry soil below.

He crawls forward. Whispering, whispering. So low

that even the watching woman – who is right beside him in this impossible place – cannot hear him. It is just a murmur of terror.

Then whispers turn to screams as the wood above the boy's head shatters. The three-fingered hand punches into view. They fumble for a moment, then grab the boy's thick, blond hair. Yank him through the wood planking above. Through a hole too small for his skull, but one that the hand pulls him through nonetheless.

The screams end. Though the blood still flows from above.

The woman follows the boy. Up through the floorboards, to the room where the dead are caught on film. She realizes that the place he is pulled forth – from one grave to another – is the exact spot her son will one day sleep. Where the centipedes will burst forth.

The boy bleeds, his skin peeled free. But he finds his voice again. "Please, Pa, don't hit me again. I'll never tell. I promise!"

"I know, son. I know you won't. Just like your ma never did."

And *POP* ....

One more child on a shrouded chair. One more picture to go in a book. The blood has been cleaned from his face, the bruises covered with makeup. But the throat, slit in rage, is clear to see.

The clock ticks. The music box plays.

Then one final moment. One final understanding.

Matthew Sr. comes in again. Shuts the door one last time. This time, though, he bears no child in his arms. This time *he* is the one bleeding. His face wounded, his clothing ripped.

He locks the door. It begins shaking, the wood pounding at his back and voices slamming through with the same violence.

"Open up, Hollis!"

"Open up, baby killer"

"Monster!"

"We'll kill you!"

"You took my baby!"

The door rattles harder, harder. Matthew Sr. looks for a place to go, a place to run. But there is nowhere. Not in this most private place. This most secret place.

Until he spies the hole. The broken spot where he pulled his own son forth in a mockery of birth, only to send him to his death.

The man rushes to the hole. Pulls it open a bit wider. Wide enough?

He looks at the door. It is splintering. Falling apart. Fingers reaching through.

He pushes himself into the floor. Scraping his way in, his own skin flaying from his flesh just as did his son's. Crawling to earth like the vermin he is. Has always been.

The watching woman follows him down. Down, down, down. Forever down as he crawls. Crawls forever, but not long enough. Crawls so far, but not nearly far enough to escape the vengeance of those behind.

Something crashes at his feet. It shatters, and wetness touches his legs.

Then another crash.

Another.

The third tinkling object – the third lamp – is still ablaze.

Matthew Sr. screams. And burns in his hole until only singed meat and black lengths of bone are left.

The woman watches. She does not burn, and she has no flesh to char. But she screams silent screams as well. And looks in a dead man's eyes until they pop and ooze out of a skull that no longer houses thought, no longer houses life, and never housed a soul at all.

Then the woman leaves. She is gone from this house, this time, and returns to herself and weeps in the arms of a man-child who whispers that all is well though both he and she know it is a lie.

ALONE IN THE DARK

Alyssa was gone a long time, and all Ralph could do was watch. Sometimes that seemed like all he could ever do.

He watched all those times his mother hurt him.

He watched when the televisions showed her plane had gone down – in the middle of the Atlantic, no less, so there was going to be nothing but an empty casket to bury.

He watched the dead and didn't have any way to stop them save one by one. And that would have been futile, because more would have taken their places.

Even on rare occasions when he saw people whose futures were going to be destroyed by some terrible event – adultery of a spouse, death of a child, an accident for themselves – he had learned long ago that most warnings just got him strange looks at best and suspicion by the police at worst.

He just watched.

At least this time he was helping someone find their way to answers. He hoped. He didn't know for sure. Couldn't, he suspected. He was just a conduit. Alyssa was the focus of whatever was happening, so she would be the focus of greatest understanding.

Alyssa twitched.

Then shuddered.

Then she screamed. Perhaps a word came out of her mouth. If it was anything, it was,

"Burrrrrrniiiiiiiiiiinnnnnnnnnng!"

She fell into him. Shivering and sobbing. He held her and didn't know what to say because he didn't know what she had seen. He just rubbed her back, stroked her hair and told her it would be all right, would be okay. Hoping that was the right thing to do because it was the only thing he could think of.

She spoke at last. He didn't know how long had passed. "His daddy killed him. Killed all those children, and now he's going to kill mine." Alyssa looked up at Ralph, her eyes shimmering, face glistening with tears, snail tracks of snot running down her chin.

Now Ralph got a little shot of what she'd seen. Not full force, just an echo. It was enough. He almost started screaming himself.

No wonder the dead were out in such force. No wonder so many of them – all of them – were so malevolent. Something deeply evil, completely twisted, was alive after a long, long time.

Not alive. Worse. Far worse.

"How do I stop him?" asked Alyssa.

Ralph saw an empty casket in his mind. Felt the terror he felt every night when he went to sleep and feared who he might see when he woke up. The fear that he might see *her*, because the one person he most wanted to forever rid himself of was one of the few who was truly beyond his reach.

"You stop ghosts by putting them to rest. Giving them a proper burial. Priest. Real mourners. Loving family, if there is any. A proper grave."

"There isn't time for that."

314

"Then you destroy the remains. If you can find them."

If they aren't in the bottom of the ocean, under tons of water and whatever hasn't been eaten by sharks mixed with four hundred other sets of bones.

"How?"

The word didn't register. Didn't make it through six hundred feet of water that he carried with him all the day, every day. "What?"

"How do I destroy them?"

"Fire."

"Like, toss the bones in a fireplace?"

"No, the remains have to be turned to ash."

Alyssa nodded. She swiped an arm across her eyes, then stood and walked toward the entrance of the graveyard. She wasn't aware of the ghosts gathered there, didn't hear them sigh and a few of them reach hungry arms for her. But Ralph saw. He felt it must be an omen, and knew she was going to die. Maybe tonight.

"Wait!" He hurried after her. "What –?"

She didn't stop walking. "I can't wait any longer." She looked over her shoulder. She was smiling. Her face was sad, worried, afraid. But the smile was real, and some of the things waiting to embrace her moved back a half-step, as if afraid of the genuine goodness of the emotion. "Thank you, Ralph," she said. "Thank you so much. But my family needs me."

He ran after her. Caught her arm. "How are you even going to do it?" He expected that to give her pause. You couldn't just burn a body to nothing, not unless you had a crematorium in your hip pocket.

Alyssa didn't even blink. She just responded, and her words carried the weight of a winning lottery ticket, of a heart rupture predicted and avoided. The weight of fate. "My husband works at some places that use flammable materials and explosives. I'll take the remains there."

"Do you know where to look for the remains?"

He was still holding her arm. She nodded and he again saw nothing real, but felt that *echo*. A moment of trapped fury –

(*Who are they to do this to* ME? *To* ME?)

– followed by fear –

(*... way out, way out, where is the –*)

– followed by pain.

(*Burrrrrrniiiiiiiiiiinnnnnnnnnng!*)

Alyssa nodded. "I think I know where to look. I hope so." Now she was the one holding him. "Can you... can you come with me? Help me?"

Ralph looked beyond her. At the things reaching out. Not just for her, but for both of them. "I've helped enough. And I'm not getting any closer to what's going on than I already have." Alyssa's expression fell. So did Ralph's. That sense of fate was still there. He knew how she was going to respond before he said the next words. He said them anyway. He had to. Had to try. Maybe she'd surprise him.

"It'll find you. It'll kill you before you get close to its remains."

Fate was the winner. It always was. Fate was a prick that way. Alyssa shook her head. "I have try," she said.

Ralph couldn't be sure whether he was witnessing amazing bravery, perfect love, or gross stupidity. Perhaps all three. Maybe this was what mothers were supposed to be like.

He wouldn't know.

He let go of her, but gestured for her to stay. Then ran back to the gravestone with the scattered Scrabble tiles. The one next to it still held his pack and he ripped it open. After a moment he found what he was looking for inside. He brought it back and held it out. Something he had carried with him for his entire life, had never once gone without.

Now he would give it to her. It was time someone else hold it. That was the weight of fate.

Alyssa took the lighter from his palm, looking at him quizzically. A simple Zippo, steel and sturdy. Something made for lighting a lifetime's worth of cigarettes. Or sterilizing a body's worth of needles.

"I won't come, but maybe this'll help you start the fire at least," said Ralph

She turned again. This time she didn't walk, she ran. The wraiths opened like a second gate as she left. One that only allowed passage in one direction.

He shouted after her as she passed through the cemetery entrance. The final line between safety and danger.

"Hey! Some ghosts are stupid – all they want is the evil crap they wanted in life. But some get craftier, more powerful, more twisted. They make plans." She was disappearing in the night. In a moment she'd be out of sight. "Watch your back!" he screamed.

And then she was gone.

The dead followed. A few looked at him as they left. But for now they were not interested in a man – a *boy* – who cowered in a cemetery. They were only aware of a woman who fled toward something darker than any of them might ever hope to be.

Ralph thought he might be able to leave.

But he didn't.

He gathered his Scrabble pieces and sat alone in the dark. The only light he always carried with him – a Zippo lighter he'd swiped off his mother's nightstand when he left for no reason at all, just because it seemed right – was gone.

Seemed appropriate.

SIX:
FINAL EXPOSURE

Many know that *Memento Mori* is an appropriate title on several levels: both for its subject matter and the fact that Dr. Charles M. Silver died soon after finishing the manuscript. It is fitting, then, that this book end with the words, found written at the scene of Dr. Silver's death (the details of which have been gone over in disgusting detail by the news media and shall not be repeated herein). As with so many of the words he spent his last months with, these are a quote from the "work notes" of Matthew Hollis, Sr., recently revealed to be one of the 19th century's most prolific mass murders and, more importantly, one of its most gifted photographers:

> I dont no if I kin do this much mor. I dont no if I kin evr stop. I seen things no one else nevr seen, and they will stay with me forevr, even beyond the grave. All the smiles and kisses of the childrun will be with me alway. My boy is one of them, but they are all my boys, all my gurls.
>
> They ar mine forever. And I guess that makes me theres, to. God rest my soul.

\- Silver, Charles M.,
(afterword by Dr. Charlotte Bongiovi)
(2003) Berkeley, California,
Memento Mori, Notes of a Dead Man,
Western University Press, Inc.

INTO THE UNDER

The door opened before Alyssa touched it. But the motion didn't strike her as haunted, it struck her as hungry. Still, she walked in. Prey that had not only sought its predator, but had pried open its jaws and insisted on being eaten.

She passed into the place that had been a home. And as she did she understood that it had ceased to be such a long time ago. Not with Blake's possession – if that was what it was. Not with her children's disappearance. Not even with the centipedes.

It happened when Blake stopped being a father. Stopped being a husband. When his concern for the bills and the business outweighed his concern for her and for the children. When his fear of the future outweighed any chance he had to enjoy the present.

His father had beaten him. Blake had never passed the favor on to them. But his fear of the event had paralyzed him over time. Had pulled him away from his family and his business and eventually turned him into the victim he had fought so hard not to be.

Blake's father had reached out from his grave long before Matthew Hollis Sr. ever had the chance to do so. And maybe that was why the old murderer finally had the strength to rise again. Maybe the dying of the last embers of their home allowed him to come close, like a beast in the night who would only attack when the campfire has dimmed.

All of it was academic. She wasn't here to figure out the whys. She was here to end it. To destroy the bastard who was taking her family.

Whoever that might be.

She stepped through the door. Shivered. It was cold in the house. Not just because the heater wasn't working, but a bone-cold chill of deep places, of a longtime grave unhallowed by tears or time.

It was dark. She flipped the switch by the front door. The light in the entry should have turned on, but nothing happened. She knew that would happen, but she wasn't about to be one of those idiots who goes into the darkness without at least *trying* for light.

So you tried. Now get going.

She moved down the hall. Expected to see the clock and the music box. But of course they wouldn't be here. Not out in the open. No, they would be hidden. In their places where they counted down the last moments of existence and made music as the images of the dead were burnt into forever.

She flitted her way to the bedroom. To Mal's room, to *Hollis's* room. The place where this would have to end.

She reached for the doorknob. Steeling herself for anything.

The door flew open. And Alyssa bit back a scream as someone barreled through the darkness at her.

But even as her body recoiled in terror, she also reached out. Because it wasn't a threat. It wasn't anything she had expected to find... at least, not so easily.

"Mal!"

Her boy was holding Ruthie. The grasp was awkward, but he knew to keep one arm behind her head so her head didn't loll forward. Still, the little girl was crying and Alyssa instantly started to look for places she might be injured, ways the carry might have hurt her.

It wasn't the carry, though. Her onesie was bright red, and as Alyssa watched her little body began twitching in the same seizure motions Alyssa had seen in the hospital.

And as bad as that was, it wasn't her priority.

Mal's eyes were wild, like he was somewhere else. "Where's Daddy?" she said. She had to shake him to get his eyes focused on her.

His head thrashed from side to side. "I don't know. We were in there, and I closed my eyes, and when I opened them the door was unlocked and he was just gone."

Ruthie's body unlocked, then went rigid again. Her pain-sounds grew.

Alyssa felt torn. She wanted to do the right and good and *normal* thing. But doing so would leave a doorway open that had to be slammed shut. *Nailed* shut and the door burned down.

She couldn't help her daughter. Not the way most mothers would.

"Mal, I need you to be a super-big boy." He managed a wide-eyed nod. "Take Ruthie to the Thayers next door and tell them to call 911."

"What about you?"

"I'll be right behind you."

He didn't move. Bouncing Ruthie the way –

(*Blake did, the way a Daddy would do*)

– someone much older would do. "You have to stop it, don't you?" he whispered. "The thing in Daddy? You have to kill it or he won't go away."

Alyssa tried to smile. Little boys should stay little boys forever. They shouldn't have to learn about death or violence or sex or leaving home or killing murderous ghosts that wanted to destroy them.

She failed at a smile. Had to settle for a kiss on her son's head. She stifled a wild urge to offer him a cookie for being so good.

"I'll be right behind you, honey."

She watched him go. The stairs. Passing the open space that led to the living room. She tensed, waiting for something to erupt from there, to grab him and Ruthie and drag them screaming into a nothing-night that would last forever.

It didn't happen.

Mal left. He closed the front door behind him and Ruthie's screams faded away.

Alyssa turned back to her son's room. The door was already open. She just had to go in.

She did.

This time there was no fade in from the reality that was *now* to the history that had *once been*. Past had fully usurped present, and Matthew Hollis Sr. ruled in this place. The room bore no resemblance to the place her son had slept and played and laughed and sometimes cried. The window and bed and toys were gone. In their place: walls with old paint, kerosene lamps with flamelight that crawled on every surface.

A clock.

A music box.

A chair. It was covered with that black pall, uneven and strange.

The room was empty of anyone. She didn't know if she expected to see Blake or Hollis himself. Perhaps there was no difference at this point. She thought that was probably the case.

In the space where her boy slept, a crack marred the wood floor. The edges jagged angrily around a dark hole, and now she knew that the door to the room was not the mouth of this house. No, this *hole* was the maw, the splintered wood its teeth. The crawlspace below was a long gut, and any who entered would fade and disappear.

Matthew Jr. – dead.

Matthew Sr. – dead.

Come in, come in.

The void seemed to call her, and that scared her so badly that she couldn't move. But the paralysis only lasted a moment. Hollis wasn't here, but how long would he be gone? How many minutes would she have to find his bones and take them away and destroy them?

Was there time to save her family?

She moved. She was a wife, a mother. Momma Bear's family was threatened, and she wouldn't let anything get them.

The edges of the crack were just as rough as they looked. Simply running her fingers along them drew a half dozen splinters into the pads of her fingers. She tried to pull a few of the boards up, to widen the hole.

No go.

She looked into the darkness.

She couldn't see much. The darkness swallowed the lamplight only a few inches down. But the light was enough to see – sense – something down there. *Many* somethings. Teeming motion, masses of movement.

The centipedes. Soldiers defending their most important turf. What had started out as insects that hid in dark and damp places, feeding on smaller insects and perhaps on each other, had grown to be a part of the thing that held this house in sway. Bigger, stronger, in every way worse than they should be.

Alyssa went in. Pushing like a babe returning to the womb. Only there was no comfort to be found. Just darkness, pain.

The centipedes fell on her immediately. They dropped to her clothes, braided themselves into her hair. One twisted along the curve of her ear, and another felt its way into the hollow of her neck. A thick taste filled her mouth, acid burned her nostrils. She gagged. Vomit rose in her throat.

She didn't vomit, because the pain that came next constricted her esophagus.

The centipedes were biting her. Each bite felt like a bullet hitting her at point-blank range, and made all the worse because it happened in total darkness, preceded by nothing but disgust and terror. She thought she could feel a minute quiver before each bite came, as though the centipede was gathering strength, or perhaps experiencing a climax of pleasure as it delivered its venom.

The pain, the revulsion, should have stopped her.

My family.

She pushed forward. Eyes and nose burning, vomit rising and she biting it down, biting it down.

Mal.

No room for hands and feet.

Ruthie.

She had to push with her tiptoes.

Blake.

Reaching with fingers.

She pulled forward inch by inch in the dark. Didn't know how far she had gone, how far she would have to go. Forever forward, which also meant she would have to go forever back.

After long years of pain, though, she realized that the darkness was brightening. She thrilled with excitement, then with fear. Someone was coming! Hollis was here!

No. Neither was the case. It was just the light from the kerosene lamps in the room above, filtering down through the break in the floor and into the crawlspace. What had appeared perfect black now brightened to the last moments of sunset, the final seconds before nightfall, as her eyes adjusted.

She thought she had crawled miles. It had only been inches.

She pushed forward. And the trip was even worse now because she could actually see the centipedes that covered everything, that covered *her*. She plunged elbows down on them, her palms squashed them as she pulled forward. But as soon as she crushed them under her hands, those hands would disappear under a new carpet of the biting creatures.

She was slick with ichor. With her own blood from the bites.

Can't go on.

Have to.

Why?

The kids.

They're gone. Safe.

You know they're not.

Could be.

And Blake?

She felt forward. Sliding over slime. Trying not to scream in pain, but whimpering now as she slowly lost that fight.

She reached out again to pull herself forward, and this time felt something new. Not dirt, not writhing bodies.

Bones.

They were wrapped in bits of barely-there cloth. The charred remains of an outfit she had seen before, in a memory of a vision of a dream.

Her hands closed on the bones, and as they did the centipedes withdrew. She pulled the bones to her, and something fluttered out of one of the rags that bound them.

A photo.

She picked it up and brought it close to her. For a moment she barely noticed the burning in her flesh, her eyes, her throat.

The light down here was barely enough for her to make out what she was seeing. Barely.

It was another photo of Matthew Jr. Like the one that she had already found, the one in the book of the dead that the child's father had kept as a memento of his victims. But this one wasn't the same as the one that had found its way into that book. Not an exact copy. Something was different about it, though she couldn't tell what.

It made sense that there would be two pictures of Matthew Jr. – after all, this was the killer's son, a person that might matter more to him, a child whose image he might want to keep close at all times. But what was it about this picture that made Alyssa's stomach knot?

What was she seeing, but not understanding?

She brought the image closer. Looking hard, trying to understand, to know.

What is it?

And then she did see. She did know.

And the fear that came was worse than any that had come before.

UNSTOPPED MOTION

There is a place that once stood in time. Then it shared several times, and now it is a time apart.

The candles send dancing lights across the walls, over the ceiling. The lights grow frantic, frenetic. It seems they must blow themselves out.

Then, suddenly, they cease. The *lights* remain, but the *motion* ends. The lights become static. They hold themselves impossibly in place, painting unmoving abstracts across the clock, the music box, the black-covered chair... and the camera that has just appeared.

For a moment, nothing moves. The world hangs still on her axis, not a grain of sand falls through the hourglass of creation.

Then motion returns. The flames dance.

And the black cloth on the chair *moves*.

SELF REALIZED

Move.

Move.

Move.

MOVE.

But she couldn't.

Alyssa had bones in one hand, as many as she could hold tucked under an arm already cramped under her by the coffin confines of the crawlspace.

The other hand held the photograph. Matthew Jr., dead on a chair. His mouth closed and straight but a second smile below his chin that was wide enough to more than make up for the lack of one on his lips. Black blood from the wound stained his white collar. It colored his clothing, made his propped-open eyes seem dark with rage.

None of that mattered. All that mattered was his pose. His upright position, sitting sturdily in the chair.

Alyssa had thought the children wore a harness that kept them upright. Perhaps bound – even nailed to wooden frames.

She was wrong. So wrong.

The picture she held was different than the others. More honest, showing the tragedy and the anger and violence of the deaths. No chance to pretty up the death, and the death itself had not been pretty. Perhaps the others had been smothered or poisoned. But Matthew Jr. had been caught by his father. Hunted down, captured, slaughtered. A dog already wounded, finally put out of his misery – though from what Ralph had shown her, the misery hadn't really ended. Just shifted, just changed to an eternity of abuse at the hands of a father who gloried in hurting those too small to save themselves.

Is that why he went for Blake? Because of what Blake's father did to him?

Or what Blake finally did back?

Either way, the further truth was beneath the boy in the picture. The posing was not because of straps or harnesses or frame. It was because of that strange black covering.

Matthew Jr. sat atop the shroud. And this time, for the first time, there was a mistake in the picture. A glimpse at the truth behind the cloth. A three-fingered hand, barely visible under a fold of the dark fabric, holding Matthew Jr. upright.

The pictures weren't just of the children. They were also self-portraits.

And that meant…

PLAYIN' A GAME

... when the cloth fell from Matthew/Blake/Blake/Matthew, it felt both wonderful and terrible. As always. It was birth, it was death. Under the cloth was where he-Matthew held the children, the place he-Matthew allowed himself the greatest pleasure. His-Matthew's ecstasy was under that darkness. Leaving was agony.

But the only way to find more happiness was to leave the darkness, to explore the light. Always the way.

So Matthew/Blake stood.

Looked at the hole in the floor.

They had no idea what the woman was doing in there. Nor did they care. They sensed – a small part of them even *worried* – that she was scheming something. That she intended something dangerous.

But what could hurt *them*? The only thing that had ever done so was their fathers. With whips and belts and ping-pong paddles and kisses and caresses secret and scorching and painful in the night.

And look what happened to those men. Those bastards, dead both, gone both, unmourned and damned both.

Blake/Matthew walked toward the hole.

(*C'mere, kid. Daddy's gonna play a game.*)

Only it was barely Blake at all now. More and more just Matthew Sr. But he liked that last fleeting thought.

C'mere, kid. Daddy's gonna play a game.

He had never played a game with a full-growed woman. He bet it would be sweet.

He smiled. Smiled big, and felt himself stand tall and tough like his Pa always stood.

"Daddy's gonna play a game," he said. And smiled like a centipede about to breed and then eat its mate all up.

He looked behind him.

Nothing there just a moment before. But now… a familiar camera. He knew there would be a film plate, loaded and ready. A mechanism he had designed hisself that would allow him to take the picture while sitting in the chair and holding a child in his lap. Feeling the love for them, the warmth replacing their coolness.

Only this time it would not be a child. It would be a woman. The only woman he'd ever had was Matthew Jr.'s momma, and she'd failed him in the end. She'd threatened to turn him in, to tell on him. She hadn't loved him at all.

This woman, though… she would love him. And he would love her. Forever.

His centipede smile got bigger and wider and his face near split in two. Maybe it *did*: things were different now, and he could do things he never done before. He was bigger and stronger and nothing were goin' to leave him now.

Toward the hole he went. Toward pictures and love and soft black cloth.

"Daddy's gonna play a game."

SETTING THE LIGHTING

Alyssa hoped she was wrong. Knew she wasn't.

Didn't matter.

There was no way out through the crawlspace but one: back the way she came.

Maybe he's not on the chair.

Maybe it's just the black cloth.

Maybe there's nothing else.

She pulled herself and the remains of Matthew Sr. backward as fast as she could. Hoping it was fast enough.

Hope was all she had, so hope would have to suffice. Hope was a thin thread, but even thin threads could be enough sometimes.

What if he is there?

The thread frayed.

What if this won't even work?

It popped a bit further.

What if it does work, but I don't have all this bastard's remains?

And it separated.

A three-fingered hand slammed through the hole in the floor of the room above – the ceiling over her head – and grabbed her feet. She had almost made it out of the hole, but she had never had a chance to get out of the room. The whole house was a pitcher plant, designed to allow unwary creatures entrance. But once in they slipped deeper and deeper into the cuplike shape and were digested within.

The hand on her calf had fewer fingers than it should have, but they were incredibly strong. They yanked her out of the hole with ease. She slammed backward, her body pinballing back and forth on the sides of the hole, leaving bits of flesh behind with every impact. Then the sideways motion switched to vertical as she was yanked upward into the room above.

She came out still clutching bone, screaming as the fingers flipped her over and yanked her to her feet.

The remains of Matthew Sr. fell from her hands. She was numb with terror. The burns where the centipedes had bitten her, the abrasions and cuts from the crawlspace, even her plan to take the bones away – all were forgotten in that moment. Fallen into the deep crevasse of insanity that opened before her.

The man standing above her was Blake. But it wasn't. Her husband, but not.

His hand had changed. Three fingers, the ones she had seen in the picture, had thought she saw in the motel. The fingers that pulled her out of the crawlspace. Those were the ones on *his* hand, on *his* body.

But that wasn't all that had changed.

His clothing had become a weird amalgam of his normal wear and the late eighteen hundreds outfit of Matthew Sr. Jeans melted into wool pants. T-shirt and vest were woven roughly together. Not *sewn*, but woven, as though they came from the factory that way, the deranged invention of a designer gone mad.

Two times came together on the man she had known

and loved, and where they joined there was a crust, a suppurating excrescence that reeked of corruption. It was all that should not be.

The face had traces of her Blake, but as she watched, her husband faded away and the face became wholly that of Matthew Sr. His mouth open in a smile so wide it unhinged his head and tilted back the top half like the lid of a trash can before slamming closed with a loud clack of crashing teeth.

"You should have stayed out of my business," he said.

He didn't sound mad, though. He sounded happy. Thrilled.

He slapped her, the same place Blake had done/not done in the motel. Only this was worse: a vicious smash that sent her reeling against the wall. She didn't know where she was, what she was doing. No terror any more, just the radical disorientation of someone who has suffered a sudden concussion.

Then she felt her scalp yanking away from her skull. She screamed as Matthew Sr. grabbed a wad of her thick hair and threw her face-down on the floor.

"Please! Blake, please, don't do this!"

"Blake's gone, missy." Matthew Sr. knelt on her back. He leaned toward her and his cold breath washed over her cheek. It stank. Rotten meat, a rotten soul.

"And you'll be gone soon, too," he said. "Just your picture left to love."

His knee stayed on her back, but she felt his weight shift as he moved. There was a low click, then her body felt warm and cold at the same time as she heard the music box

336

begin to play and remembered it playing as he took each and every picture.

He wrapped his hands around her throat. Pressed them together.

It felt like every atom of oxygen disappeared from her body all at once. In movies, television, books, all manner of media, people always gasped out last words when being choked. She realized now those people weren't *really* being choked. Because *really* being choked meant not a sound. Not a whisper, not a gasp. She couldn't pull in the smallest wheeze, couldn't push out the tiniest hiss.

Her vision blackened. Not just at the edges, either: someone took a thick brush and started painting directly over her eyes. Watercolor at first, stuff she could see through, but rapidly thickening to acrylic.

She had seconds.

She bucked, trying to get the dead man off her.

He rode her like a horse. He would break her.

Gonna kill me.

Picture me.

Bury me with the bugs.

Exterminator did a lousy job.

Get your money back, Lyss!

Her thoughts spiraled.

Full refunds from Pest in Peace!

She shoved herself forward. Choking, losing consciousness. Her hand thrusting under her body and only gradually realizing what she was doing.

Pest in Peace. Shitty bugs.

Bug on top of me.

The hole was nearby. She thought.

She kept bucking. Pushing. Blacking out to the sound of Matthew Sr.'s mad laughter.

Having a grand ol' time, you monster?

Her vision disappeared. She was moving by touch.

No sight, but she saw…

… herself loading up the kids.

Blake arguing with the exterminator. Older guy. But firm. "I've already cut it to the bare minimum for you. We're going to saturate your house with phosphine. You want to come home to everyone puking and explosive gas pooled on your floors?"

And still pushing forward, remembering the taste in her mouth, the gagging as she fought her way forward in the crawlspace. She had thought it was revulsion, terror, rot.

But what if it wasn't? If there was more to it?

She bucked forward another inch, one hand still groping beneath her. Hard to do with Matthew Sr.'s weight on her.

The other hand swept in front, wide arcs that supported her worm-like motions. But also searched.

She found something. Hard, long, wrapped in cloth.

Bones.

Which meant she was near the hole.

Something writhed on her hand. More than one. The

centipedes. They knew what she was going to do.

And then Matthew Sr. knew as well.

He let go of her throat. Air blasted back into her body with such exquisite joy it hurt. But she had her strength again, so when the weight above lurched forward she was able to keep pace.

"Don't!" shouted the thing that had stolen her husband. Tried to kill her family. To kill her.

"You died in there once," she said. Her voice sounded like it had been run over a cheese grater. She didn't care. She knew she had him.

Her vision flooded back to her. And it was her turn to grin as she shoved the bones back into the crack. Back into the hole, back into his grave.

Ralph had said she could bury him properly – mourners, priest, proper grave.

She had none of that.

But she did have pooled phosphine.

She opened her hand and showed Matthew Sr. the lighter that Ralph had given her. The flame was already dancing.

"And you can die in there again," she said.

She threw the lighter into the hole. Matthew Sr. dove after it. He was halfway in and she wondered if there was enough of the gas – or any. Wondered if he would snuff out the flame.

Wondered if any of this struggle was worth it.

WHOOMP.

The explosion tossed Matthew Sr. into the air. Slammed him against the ceiling, even as the floor beneath rose up to meet him.

Alyssa heard a soft, high-pitched whistle.

What's –?

And she knew. The centipedes. Screaming as they turned to ash. Impossible for such things to make a sound, but for creatures kept alive for centuries, kept so long as guardians to the damned…. Perhaps they were given this last moment to scream their anguish.

Or maybe it was final relief. Ultimate release.

A second explosion lifted the floor again. This time it was under Alyssa. It tossed her back and she knocked into the camera. The heavy contraption – wood and metal – toppled. She was on her back, watching helplessly as it fell toward her.

The lens stared at her angrily as it fell. Black with rage and the souls it had captured. A silent eye that had been blinded at last.

The camera box fell on her head.

And with that Alyssa, too, fell silent and sightless and knew no more.

EXPOSURE

Alyssa woke up screaming.

At first it was the moment of memory that clings after a terrible dream that cannot quite be remembered.

Then it was a moment – worse – where she *did* remember.

And then it was the demon leaning over her. Large, backlit by fire. All she could see was his eyes, bouncing with reflected flame, the lights nearly in time with the notes of the music box that played on in endless circles.

The notes began to warp. The demon leaned toward her.

She screamed.

"It's me! It's me!"

And she knew the voice. Blake. Bloody, bruised, singed.

Alyssa screamed again. "Show me your hand!"

He did. Five fingers. Normal. His clothes had returned to normal. No afflicted melding of old and new, just the usual too-casual-for-work outfit he always wore as though to subtly say he didn't ever want to leave his family.

He helped her up. His fingers curled around her hands, and as soon as she was upright he held her. Tight. The aches that played her body like a melting music box disappeared for just that moment.

Then a blast of heat hit them. "Come on," said Blake.

341

"We have to go."

The room was Mal's again. Bed, toy box, small desk, window. But fire blazed everywhere.

It spouted from a hole in the floor. Rolling out from under their son's bed, consuming all.

Blake guided her toward the door.

Out the hall. Flames following them. She looked back and knew the house was going to burn. What had started there would only truly end when it was all ash.

"Think insurance will cover it?" she said.

"I don't much care," said Blake. He smiled as he spoke. Her pains disappeared again. Just for a second. Just enough for a bit of hope to filter through and give her the promise of light in the future.

"What about the other one?" said Blake suddenly.

"The other one?"

"The little boy."

Alyssa was about to say, "I don't know," but then she did.

Phone ringing: bedroom, living room, entry. Bedroom, living room, entry.

"He was leading us to the front door," she said.
"What?" said Blake.

In the bedroom, Ruthie's mobile was spinning....
And a voice screamed. "LEAVE!"
The mirror on the vanity cracked. Then fell. The glass

exploded in tiny pieces. But the explosion happened before the mirror touched the floor. In the next second something hit the big bed so hard it moved a good foot.

Alyssa grabbed Mal and ran all the way into the hall.

The second they were out, the bedroom door slammed shut behind them. They ran.

Inside the closed-up room, it sounded like a fight was happening.

Alyssa looked at her husband. "I don't think the boy was ever trying to hurt us. He was trying to save us."

A single word on the picture that fell from the memorial book.

"The whole time, he was trying to lead us out of that house," she said. The heat at their back was stronger now. But she felt it as a comfort. Every degree was another ash made out of the bones of the man who had done all this. "Trying to save us from his father."

They were at the front door. Blake opened it.

"Mal!"

Their boy was waiting. Standing just at the bottom of the porch, looking up at the house. She could see light reflecting into the night, firelight already crawling through the walls and into the upper floor of their home.

Blake ran out of the house, arms outstretched. Mal cringed.

"It's okay!" shouted Alyssa. "It's okay, Mal. It's him, it's Daddy again!"

Blake enveloped the boy in a hug, and she was only a step behind. Both kneeling, both holding their son. Feeling him, realizing how close they had come to losing each other.

"What happened?" said Mal. Still trapped in Blake's embrace, but looking over his father's shoulder at the house. Alyssa could feel heat at her back. They'd have to move farther away in a second.

"It doesn't matter," said Blake. "It's over."

"You stopped him?" said Mal.

"Stopped him for good," said Alyssa. She looked around, though she knew what she would – wouldn't – see. "Where's Ruthie?"

"Safe," said Mal.

"With the Thayers?"

"Safe," he repeated. His voice was strange.

His skin felt cold.

Alyssa was about to ask him again. Something trilled inside her. Something was wrong.

Blake coughed.

Blood dribbled out of his mouth. He looked down. So did Alyssa.

A knife stuck out of Blake's stomach. Something big, judging by the handle, but she couldn't tell for sure because the entire blade was completely buried in her husband's flesh. A moment later even the handle was obscured by spurts of blood, pumping out in time with Blake's heartbeat.

She looked at Blake, her mind blanked by what had just happened.

What did *happen?*

Blake was looking at Mal. Eyes wide.

Alyssa followed her husband's gaze. And realized what she should have seen, what Blake had long known....

"One-third of abused children grow up to be just as bad as their parents," he said. And, as always when he said it, he sounded half ashamed and half... what?

Hopeful.

And in a vision, given to her by a boy who was so afraid, so deep in darkness himself she now suspected he had also known this kind of fear....

Matthew Jr., pulled out of a crawlspace. Skin peeled free, crying, bleeding.

"Please, Pa, don't hit me again. I'll never tell. I promise!"

Don't hit me again.

Blake began to crumple. Alyssa tried to hold him. He was too heavy. Mal – what had been Mal – smiled.

"'Daddy will kill you,'" she whispered. Mal's smile grew. "It's not what your father did," she said to him. "It's what you wanted done. You never wanted us to get away.

Not from him, not from *you*."

The letter in her mailbox. From Matthew Jr., not his father.

I wont leave you alone. Ever.

"You wanted us to kill your father," she said. Mal – Matthew Jr. – still hadn't spoken. But now he began to laugh. The laugh was low, a rumble that was completely out of place in the body of her boy. Old, twisted, evil. "That's why you saved us," she said. "We got it wrong. The Scrabble pieces didn't say 'daddy will kill you,' they said, "will kill you, daddy."

Her boy reached out. His *hand* reached out. The hand that now belonged to another.

She shrank back, but he touched her. Just like Ralph had touched her, and just as when the courier had lifted her into vision, so now she saw. But this was not a lifting, it was a descent. A fall into Hell, into damnation.

Matthew Jr. crawls through the darkness. Bleeding. Terrified.

But also angry.

The blood is new. Some of the bruises.

But not all. Not by a long shot.

Pa wants to kill him. The day has finally come. And the anger that sparked so many times now explodes into a final, consuming flame.

He crawls, he bleeds. And he whispers.

"I'll kill you someday. I'll kill you, Daddy. Kill you. Kill you."

Still half in vision, barely aware of her husband's body finally completing its slow tumble to earth, Alyssa said, "You wanted us to kill your father."

Mal – already changed, even though she didn't see it in her panic – left with Ruthie in his arms. Pretending to wide-eyed fear. Hiding cold calculation as he said, "You have to stop him, don't you? The thing in Daddy? Or he won't go away?"

Another small push in a series of shoves, all of them toward a final outcome.

"You wanted *me* to kill him."

Matthew Jr. stopped laughing, though the levity was still in his voice when he said, "Not just that. Not just him."

"They aren't just born monsters," said Alyssa, sitting on her good husband's lap. "They learn to be that way." She reassured him, and hoped he heard her....

And later, Ralph told her, "Whatever is behind this isn't just here to bother you. It wants to kill you all."

Alyssa looked at Matthew Jr.

Beside and below them, Blake sighed and then was silent.

"You don't have to be a monster," she said.

Matthew Jr. grinned and giggled. "But I *want* to be," he said.

He began to whistle.

Goin' to run all night, Goin' to run all day....

Alyssa never got a chance to run. Though she did get to scream. And scream and scream.

TWISTED

Ralph sat on the bike. Sat and sat and sat.

Watched.

He could see the Douglas house in the distance. It was a bit taller than most of the others on the block, the kind of house you might purchase if you were finding a bit of success and wanted the world to know about it.

That's what Ralph figured, anyway. Not that he would really know. He'd never had that kind of success. Never wanted it. Just wanted to ride, and to be left alone by the dead.

The closer he got to the place, the more ghosts there were. On the sidewalks, on the street, in yards and on rooftops. All of them moving slowly toward that house in the distance. That house where something evil was happening. Something so very bad that it drew all maleficent things to it.

Ralph had no chance of finding his mother. He had no chance of finding her body and turning it to ash and ridding himself of the forever fear he took with him everywhere he went: the terror that she would return and one day be his mother again. And that this time she would never leave and he would never be able to escape.

But this woman, Alyssa… she had a chance to stop her family from falling prey to something like that. Maybe something even worse.

That was why Ralph got off his butt and left the cemetery. That was why he peddled through silent streets full of silent figures that ignored him but that he knew were as aware of him as he was of them.

Maybe he could help. Really help, just this once.

The closer he got, though, the slower he moved. He felt his uncertainty chip away at what might be the one fully good decision he'd ever made.

Soon he stopped biking. Just sat in the middle of the street. Watching the top of the house, wondering what was happening there.

Come on, Ralphie.

He didn't move.

Be a man.

Still nothing. Just fear that emptied his legs of strength.

Do something. For once.

The things around him opened their mouths. All at the same time, they opened wide and began to moan. Not waves, not up and down sounds like a person might make while suffering pain. This was a single note coming from each mouth, combining to make an almost deafening chant.

She's winning.

Ralph got on his bike and began to ride. Maybe he was too late to help. But he would be there to congratulate her.

Maybe that would mean something. Maybe not. But it was him, doing something.

He started to smile.

Then the moan stopped. Ten thousand breathless screams cut off, replaced by a single living shriek.

It was a woman's scream. Fear, loss.

Pain.

Ralph kept peddling. But he turned the handles a bit, turning the bike in a wide arc so he was facing the opposite way. And he peddled harder now. Faster.

Something had gone wrong.

He had told her. Told her, but she hadn't listened. She hadn't understood.

Some ghosts are stupid – all they want is the evil crap they wanted in life. But some get craftier, more powerful, more twisted. They make plans.

Some of the ghosts turned to look at him now. A few smiled. One winked.

He thought he saw a familiar face in the darkness between two houses. A dress he'd seen often, worn every time the needle came out, every time a new picture pushed under his skin.

Maybe not.

But he peddled faster.

Some ghosts are stupid.

But some get craftier, more powerful.

More twisted.

They make plans.

The scream followed him into the night. She hadn't watched her back. If it was even possible to do that. Some kinds of evil, he thought, just might not be the kind you could protect against. Maybe they were too insidious, too subtle. Maybe they misdirected you until you were in their trap and then it was too late.

He saw the form again. A smile, outstretched arms.

And he pedaled as fast as he could, but he knew that

he couldn't outrun her. Because in the end, she was part of him.

Just like evil was part of everybody.

And when he thought that, he slowed. Just a bit. Maybe that mattered, maybe not.

He felt his bike grow heavy. Felt his legs grow weak.

Felt a cool hand around his stomach.

And heard a voice in his ear.

"Mommy's missed you, Ralphie."

AUTHOR'S NOTE

I remember sitting on a porch a little bit like the one the Douglas family owns, though belonging to a house not nearly so fine. I was a young missionary in South America, and another missionary and I were chatting with a woman who was in her late forties. Her four kids came and went, occasionally stopping to talk with us, to drink some soda pop, to just hang out.

The visit went pretty late into the night, then she said goodnight and we left.

It was ostensibly a social visit, but everyone there knew the real purpose: her husband had threatened to beat her to death. Then the kids.

We were there to protect her.

The woman wasn't of our faith, but we had chatted on numerous occasions. We were friends.

And she trusted us. Enough that she turned to us for help when her husband made this threat. He had beaten her before – badly – but this was new. Another level.

Going to the police was out of the question: in this part of the world, at this particular time, women were still just a small step above chattel. To complain about an *actual* beating would be a ridiculous waste of time in the eyes of the cops, let alone complaining about a prospective one.

My missionary companion and I didn't feel good about the idea of hunting the husband down and going all Charles Bronson on him (well, we felt kind of *good* about the idea, but it didn't seem very missionary-ish, let alone

Christlike), so we decided to just sit with her in the hopes that her husband would stay in the street after getting drunk, rather than coming after the family.

It seemed to work. By three or four a.m. he hadn't shown up.

But when we went to see her the next day she was wearing large sunglasses and limping. It was horrifying, somehow all the more so because it was so cliché. And there was really nothing we could do about it. Short of murdering the guy, he would keep beating his family, and they would take it.

That's what an awful lot of people do. The kids have no option, and a disturbing number of the beaten spouses *feel* like they have no options.

Maybe worst of all, though, is the self-perpetuating nature of this practice: so many children who are beaten also turn into child abusers, and their children continue the chain, on and on *ad infinitum*. It's horrifying, and with that same woman's family I started to see this very principle at work as the son – who got as many stripes as anyone – first turned inward, then lashed out and became harder and harder as a person.

I don't know how they turned out. I hope they are okay. I hope the man got help and turned his life around and has spent all the years since then giving love to his family to make up for pain they suffered.

Failing that, I hope Mom packed up in the middle of the night and ran out with the kids while he was drunk as a skunk, hid in a different part of the country and is now happy and safe under an assumed identity, with the guy unable to leave his home because of radically explosive diarrhea that strikes every six minutes, twenty-four/seven.

(I was a missionary, but I still have problems with forgiving some things, some people.)

At any rate... a lot of this fueled *Twisted*. Not a happy story, because parents hurting children who grow up to hurt their children *can't* be a happy story. But hopefully this one has a point.

Everyone in *Twisted* is doomed, and none of them really did anything wrong. Or, better said, the things they did wrong began with teachings at the knee of people who were supposed to teach them love and care and hugs, but who instead taught them hate and bile and beatings. It was all these people knew, and that brought them to the slippery slope that was their downfall, and the downfall of all those around them.

In real life, I do think people make a choice, take that first step that sends them sliding. You can't point back and say, "But he did it first!" and get instant and automatic absolution. But there's no doubt that a real cycle exists and getting caught in it makes life much scarier, more difficult, and fraught with real danger.

I can't speak to what it's like to abuse a child: I've never done it. I *can* speak to what it's like to have mental health issues that require professional help. It's scary, it's overwhelming, and it makes some people (like me) feel like less of a person sometimes.

But getting that help is better than the alternative.

Much as I hate the idea that I need help to run something as basic and intimate as my own brain, and much as I hate the fact that I have to take medication every day to keep my sanity train from derailing, I vastly prefer it (when I'm thinking rationally) to the idea of hurting myself (and through that action, hurting the ones I love), or completely losing control of my life.

All this to say: if you're reading this and you've lost control and hurt a child, then you've done something appalling and there's no two ways about it. *BUT* there are ways to get help, and ways to get better.

And better is always, well... better.

In this case that's especially so because, unlike just being regular ol' crazy (like me), people who abuse are – again – likely to end up teaching other people that abuse is the only way to live and the only way to allow others to live around them.

That is not true.

There are better ways.

And better ways are just... better.

Michaelbrent Collings
November, 2014

Resources:

U.S. Department of Health and Human Services, Child Welfare Information Gateway section on Child Abuse and Neglect: https://www.childwelfare.gov/can/

The Information Gateway Reporting Child Abuse and Neglect (mandatory reporting and how to report suspected abuse:
https://www.childwelfare.gov/responding/reporting.cfm

The National Child Abuse Prevention Month (tip sheets for parents and caregivers for taking care of children and strengthening families:
https://www.childwelfare.gov/preventing/preventionmonth/tipsheets.cfm

Child Maltreatment: Past, Present, and Future:
https://www.childwelfare.gov/pubs/issue_briefs/cm_prevention.pdf

Long-Term Consequences of Child Abuse and Neglect:
https://www.childwelfare.gov/pubs/factsheets/long_term_consequences.pdf

Preventing Child Abuse and Neglect:
https://www.childwelfare.gov/pubs/factsheets/preventingcan.pdf

Understanding the Effects of Maltreatment on Brain Development:
https://www.childwelfare.gov/pubs/issue_briefs/brain_development/brain_development.pdf

The Centers for Disease Control and Prevention (CDC), Understanding Child Maltreatment:
http://www.cdc.gov/violenceprevention/pdf/cm_factsheet2012-a.pdf

Prevent Child Abuse America:
http://www.preventchildabuse.org/index.shtml

Helpguide.org, Child Abuse and Neglect:
http://www.helpguide.org/articles/abuse/child-abuse-and-neglect.htm

If you would like to be notified of new releases, sales, and other special deals on books by Michaelbrent Collings, please sign up for his mailing list at http://eepurl.com/VHuvX.

And if you liked *this* book, **please leave a review on your favorite book review site**…and tell your friends!

ABOUT THE AUTHOR

Michaelbrent Collings is a full-time screenwriter and novelist. He has written numerous bestselling horror, thriller, sci-fi, and fantasy novels, including *The Colony Saga*, *Strangers*, *Darkbound*, *Apparition*, *The Haunted*, *Hooked: A True Faerie Tale*, and the bestselling YA series *The Billy Saga*.

Follow him through Twitter @mbcollings or on Facebook at facebook.com/MichaelbrentCollings.